CHANGING HISTORY

To Heidi...,
And your infinite
power.

[signature]

CHANGING HISTORY

A Novel

How Kuff

iUniverse, Inc.
New York Lincoln Shanghai

Changing History

iUniverse books may be ordered through booksellers or by contacting:

iUniverse
2021 Pine Lake Road, Suite 100
Lincoln, NE 68512
www.iuniverse.com
1-800-Authors (1-800-288-4677)

Because of the dynamic nature of the Internet, any Web addresses or links contained in this book may have changed since publication and may no longer be valid.

This is a work of fiction. All of the characters, names, incidents, organizations, and dialogue in this novel are either the products of the author's imagination or are used fictitiously.

ISBN: 978-0-595-46444-9 (pbk)
ISBN: 978-0-595-90740-3 (ebk)

Printed in the United States of America

This book is dedicated to the people from the top of the world ... the Tibetans, wherever they may be through time and space.

Acknowledgments

Thanks to my family and friends who supported me during this prolonged effort. Thanks to Dania Sheldon for her excellent editing advice and to Suzanne Hayes and Mike Haley for their enlightening illustrations. And finally, thanks to Abella Blue Martin for her natural exuberance for life.

Prologue

In the dark of night in the sky above, we move slowly and survey the ground beneath us. We glide silently and sense the danger in the patterns of lights below. Avoid the lights. Death resides there. Find the path between the lights.

Every passing gets more difficult. We see small isolated patches of light expand and connect together. Avoid the lights. Find the safe path through the darkness. But the safe path gets smaller with each passing.

In the darkness there is life. With the expanding light our hopes and lives dim by the day. But we persevere. We are strong-willed. We are still many. Yet before the lights we were immense.

Our sanctuaries are dwindling. The machines have no compassion for us. We are the wild and free. We know no artificial boundaries. And we do not kill over imaginary lines on the ground.

Without us they are bound by the walls they build. They do not realize what they lose if we disappear.

One House

On the ground it was bitterly cold and a fierce wind was howling down the mountain. Snow was falling in sheets and quickly blowing into huge drifts. For a brief moment, the wind cleared the air and the total whiteness opened to reveal a group of people attempting to descend the steep slope. They were desperately trying to follow a narrow ribbon of trail that had disappeared under the snow. To their right was a sheer cliff that fell precipitously to a roaring cauldron of whitewater far below.

Three were straining to push bicycles laden with bulky saddlebags and panniers. But the tires continued to collect snow and ice, making it nearly impossible to turn the wheels. Every few minutes, they had to stop and clear the tires. They were being led by four others carrying large backpacks, walking slowly and deliberately, trying to make out the trail and keep from slipping and falling. Snow and ice covered everyone and everything.

The person leading the group yelled, "I think I see something ahead! Yeah, maybe some buildings ... and smoke!"

Someone else in the group called out, "Hallelujah! We're not going to die!"

They neared a small cluster of buildings, and dogs began to bark from behind a short mud wall. A tall, brownish-red-skinned man with long black hair blowing wildly in the wind opened the gate to the compound and stepped outside. As the travelers got close, he excitedly motioned for them to come inside.

✤   ✤   ✤

The travelers eagerly followed the man across an empty courtyard to a low, flat-roofed, earth-colored building. He turned to smile at them as he reached to open a small wooden door. Warm air thick with smoke and incense wafted out as he bent down and disappeared inside. They took off their packs, propped up the bikes against the wall, and one by one leaned over to step through the door into the darkness. They found themselves in a close, low-ceilinged room illuminated only by a few small windows along the east wall. A rusty metal stove in the center of the room glowed red and a large pot of water on the top of the stove was beginning to steam.

Benches with tattered cushions lined the walls. Short narrow tables, stained dark from years of use, stood in front of each bench. Smooth wooden posts bore the weight of ancient beams that supported a ceiling blackened from years of smoky fires. Faded tapestries hung from the posts and several of the beams had been painted with brightly colored frescoes, but the paint was peeling and it was difficult to make out the details.

Once the group had stepped inside, their host looked them over carefully. "Welcome to our teahouse. My name is Sonam. You are safe and can rest here."

He picked up a leather bellows lying next to the stove, placed the narrow end under the firebox and pumped hard several times. Immediately the fire started to roar and he smiled. "We will have hot tea right away." Then bowing graciously, he exited down a dim hallway into the back kitchen.

As the travelers' eyes adjusted to the low light they noticed a man and woman sitting along the far wall, watching the commotion of their entrance. The new arrivals began to strip off their outer layers, shaking snow and ice on the floor around the stove. Coats, hats and gloves were hung up to dry on ropes tied between two of the posts, and shoes and boots were set out around the firebox. People huddled close to the fire, warming their hands and bodies while the wind whipped and shook the walls of the building.

Though they had arrived as a group, the travelers had just met in the confusion of the snowstorm. They began to make introductions.

"What a wild day!" exclaimed a powerful young woman with piercing blue eyes peeking from beneath her black yak fur hat. A long blonde ponytail hung down her back.

"Man. Don't you know it," agreed the tall man with olive-brown skin and dark, soft, intelligent eyes standing next to her.

"Hey, I'm Ellie," she said shaking his hand.

"Good to meet you. I am Cibi." He smiled then turned toward the others. "Hello. Hello. Hello," he repeated and bowed faintly, his neck muscles protruding and the top of his shaved head glistening in the dim light.

"And I am Lana and this is Raz," said a petite young woman with pale skin and shiny black waist-length hair. She nodded toward the man on her left. Her violet eyes twinkled with amusement.

He was in his twenties, of medium height and build, with dark almond-shaped eyes and reddish-brown skin. His spiky red hair and large ruby earring gave him a fierce look, but he smiled and patted Lana's thigh, saying, "Yes, Raz I am, friend and lover of Lana. Good to be here."

Lana tossed her hair back and laughed. Her ears sparkled from top to bottom with silver and glass beads.

A slender woman around thirty with dark brown skin and bright green eyes twirled around and giggled; as she turned, her braids, twisted and woven with black silk and turquoise beads, clicked and clattered. "Hey Lana. Hi everyone. I am Karyn. I am sooo happy to be here breathing with you. For a while there I wasn't sure what would become of us. Peace to you all."

"And peace to you!" laughed Raz.

"Yes, peace to you," sputtered a ragged-looking young man standing next to Karyn. "I am Ray. Peace to you," he repeated to her. He looked around nervously and tried to smile.

Karyn smiled back at him but said nothing.

Ray looked away and shifted his weight from foot to foot. "I don't know where the hell we are but I'm glad I'm here." He attempted another smile. He might be thought dangerous with his wild curly hair, dark furtive eyes and nose ring, but he looked more afraid than hostile.

Cibi extended his hand, "Hey Ray. Good to meet you," and he shook Ray's hand vigorously.

"Greetings everyone. I am Lorraine," a tall, voluptuous woman with curly auburn hair, fair skin and sad pale-green eyes said in a subdued voice. "I was thinking like Karyn and not sure that we would make it. Thank you all for being strong and getting us to this teahouse."

"Hear hear, I would drink to that if I had a drink," laughed Raz and he raised his hand in a mock toast.

As if on cue, Sonam returned and placed a large teapot filled with tea leaves, a bowl of yak butter, a spoon and seven teacups on one of the wooden tables. He carefully picked up the pot of steaming water from the stove and poured it on the leaves. The room filled with the exotic scent of flowers and brewing tea.

Lorraine smiled. "Thank you, Sonam."

He had tied his wild hair back into a thick ponytail that hung down to his waist. The travelers could now see large turquoise pendants hanging from his ears and a long cylindrical agate bead adorned with swirling black and white eye patterns centered on his red coral necklace. He looked very distinguished. "My pleasure. Yes, have some tea with butter. It will warm you up and cheer your spirits. Noodles will be ready soon. When you are tired you can sleep on the benches. There will be no more travel for a while."

He walked over to the far side of the room, and the travelers turned their attention to the dark corner. They could now see that the man and woman in the corner were wearing maroon and saffron colored robes and were sipping tea while watching them with amusement.

Sonam addressed the woman, "Are you feeling better, Ngawang?"

She placed her hands together in front of her chest and bowed her head. "I am fine," she replied. "Thank you for the warm fire and hot tea. You are a generous host. May you always be blessed."

"Thank you, my dear," answered Sonam. "I am glad that I can help you on your arduous journey. I trust our friends here will not bother your meditations."

"Absolutely not," laughed the man. "As is everyone else, we are fortunate to be here. Though the snow falls and the winds blow, we are all warm and safe. Bless you, Mr. Sonam."

Sonam smiled, turned and went back down the hall to the kitchen, where he busied himself with cleaning, and preparing food.

❧   ❧   ❧

With great delight, tea was poured, butter added and bodies collapsed on soft cushions strewn along the benches.

Cibi took a sip of tea, shook his head and chuckled to himself. "I've been riding my bike through Asia for more than a year and have never seen snow and wind that intense. Pretty cool we found each other … and this teahouse." He extended his arm with opened palm and gestured to include the entire room. "What good fortune!"

Lana laughed, "Don't you know it? Raz and I had not seen another bicycle for the past two weeks. Then you appeared like a ghost out of the snow at the top of that pass. You scared us!"

"And you scared me! From nowhere out of the whiteness you two materialized." He grinned, "I thought you were yetis!"

"Bring on the yetis!" laughed Ellie. She paused for a moment and then added rather whimsically, "What I would do to see a yeti … or even a snow leopard!"

"Instead, you got me," snorted Ray. "I'm kind of like wildlife, don't you think?"

"Yeah Ray, you're kind of like wildlife," mumbled Ellie, "except you follow me around and hound me with questions."

"Hey, who led us through the flying snow to these guys, anyway?" retorted Ray.

Ellie looked away and did not answer.

"It is a crazy-ass snowstorm that brought us together," said Karyn, breaking the tension. "I was resting on the knife edge of a ridge, admiring the valleys falling away below me, when the wind gusted so hard it almost blew me off my perch. Dark clouds appeared from nowhere and within minutes the snow was battering me. I started climbing down and between the gusts of wind and snow I thought I saw someone moving up the slope toward me. *Strange* I thought, and continued my descent."

Lorraine smiled, "Yeah, I saw her sitting up on that ridge and was hurrying to greet the only person I had seen in days. Then it started to snow and I couldn't see a thing. When we somehow stumbled upon each other (and I mean *stumbled*) I was so glad that I immediately hugged her like a long lost sister."

"You surprised me," laughed Karyn. "We quickly made our introductions and then hurried off looking for shelter. Soon we found a little cliff overhang but it was not much protection. We were getting pounded by the wind when Ellie and Ray came by."

"So the four of us continued down the mountain and a few minutes later you guys emerged from a sheet of snow with your bikes. Pretty weird," added Ellie.

Lorraine nodded. "I'm just thankful to be here."

"Yeah, if it wasn't for this wind and snow. I mean, it *is* only October," whined Ray.

Ellie cast a quick glance toward Ray. "We can never know how the weather will turn out. There is beauty in all weather."

"Whatever ..." muttered Ray.

Ellie flashed her eyes at him but said nothing. Everyone was quiet for a moment, then Cibi picked up.

"I agree with Ellie. Weather is weather. It may not be best suited for our plans but there is beauty in all weather."

Ellie smiled. "Thanks, Cibi. I guess I just love nature. The Earth is always beautiful to me."

Karyn shook her head in obvious disbelief. "Yeah? How about barren desert?"

"I find beauty in all wilderness … even if empty and desolate," Ellie answered in a flat voice.

Karyn eyed her curiously. "Don't you like being around people?"

"Oh, I've got nothing against people, but I get comfort from the plants and animals of the wild. Nature inspires me." She frowned slightly then added, "To the point of sometimes getting me into a lot of trouble."

"Oh yeah, how's that?" asked Ray.

Ellie winced, "Well, Ray, I guess my parents and their friends were afraid of what might happen to me wandering in the mountains rather than doing the things that they considered important."

Ray growled, "Fuck 'em, Ellie. There is so much bullshit out there. And why the hell should you listen to them, eh?"

Lorraine scowled. "Ray, let the poor girl be."

She continued, "You know, Ellie, I can relate to what you're saying. For a long time I was depressed and angry, which eventually led to leaving my country. Since then I've traveled alone, often scared. But recently while trekking these mountains my spirits have begun to lift."

Ellie brightened, "I yearned to visit Tibet all my life. When I was a little girl I stared at pictures of curvy stone buildings clinging to the slopes of jagged snowy mountains under dreamy blue skies. And I read tales of spiritual seekers who developed extraordinary powers from studying and meditating in the wilderness."

The man in the corner suddenly spoke up. "Hello to you seven souls. I am Lobsang and my friend is Ngawang. We are traveling between monasteries and were halted by the snow like you. This is a wonderful teahouse and in such an exceptional location."

"So good to meet you," beamed Ellie. "This place *is* wonderful. I feel like I am in a dream … almost magical."

Lobsang laughed. "Yes, almost magical. Our country is the roof of the world and only very distinguished things may live here. That is why the land is so sparse. But that makes the small things in life—like sitting by a fire out of the wind and drinking hot tea, or meeting another traveling soul—all the more pleasurable. We are thankful for all blessings, no matter how small. Bless you, Ms. Ellie."

Ngawang smiled at Lobsang and patted him on the head. "Oh Lobsang, always the philosopher. But yes, what he says is true. We Tibetans are thankful for the air we breathe and the flowing water we drink. Life is so short and changes so quickly that we bless and embrace every moment. Like the weather in these mountains, our lives are in constant flux. So in our mountain monasteries, we pare away all but the necessities of life and focus on those things that do not change from time to time … from life to life."

She gracefully turned to face each of the travelers, smiling broadly and acknowledging their gazes. She locked eyes with Ray for an especially long time. Ray smiled nervously and looked away quickly.

"This country is enchanting," Lorraine said wistfully. "I saw people living much like they must have done for a thousand years … tending crops of barley and greens in ancient terraced plots, using snowmelt for irrigation. Sometimes with yaks or ponies."

"Beautiful flowing water. Oh, how I yearn for the old life," sighed Cibi.

"The old life?" repeated Lorraine.

"I used to be a shepherd with a herd of goats. Together we wandered under the sun and stars, following the grasses and streams through the mountain meadows."

Karyn's eyes widened, "To tell the truth, I never thought much about shepherds. But last week I met a man tending yaks. He invited me to share tea with him. Though we had no common language he told me that he lived in the mountains with his yaks and that they provided milk and cheese and wool. His eyes sparkled as he talked. I left feeling like I was walking on air, smiling with the dreamy blue lake and the snow peaks."

"It is a good life," Cibi said with pride.

"It must be very rewarding to see your herd growing," replied Lorraine.

Karyn nodded, "That's it! That shepherd was so calm and focused. He cares for his yaks and they grow fat and have babies. He can stand on the mountain and look at his herd with pride."

Cibi smiled with a faraway look in his eyes.

Karyn scrunched her eyebrows and shook her head. "That is exactly the opposite of my work on a project team. When the project was complete, the supervisor thanked us and took the results. We'd get a pat on the back for our effort but we never got to see our work being used. It was very frustrating."

"What kind of work do you do, Karyn?" asked Lana.

"I was, I guess I am, a mathematician, but I don't work anymore."

"Oh, a smart girl," chided Ray. "What's the matter, get fed up with the bullshit?"

Karyn looked at him blankly.

Then she sighed, "I'm just tired of selling my life to the highest bidder. Maybe I should become a shepherd …" Her voice trailed off.

"No, I completely understand," said Lana, "Raz and I have been trying to find a place to live and work, but it has been a struggle. We try to do good things but we always end up feeling guilty."

"Guilty? About what?" asked Karyn.

"About supporting *bullshit*," Raz paused and looked over at Ray, "stuff with our efforts."

"Yeah, so we keep moving," continued Lana, "traveling by bicycle, trying to live lightly and not contribute to war or poverty."

"Amen to that!" said Cibi.

Lana laughed, "Thank you, Cibi."

Cibi lowered his eyes, "Yeah, I left my homeland and all that I owned under rather bad circumstances. You know, sometimes it is hard to *not* add to the hate and destruction."

"And *amen to that!*" Raz repeated loudly.

Cibi looked at him for a moment then continued, "So now, kind of like you guys, I travel the world by bicycle and try to be self-sufficient. But unlike you, I don't seek a home. If I can't live in my country, in *my* village, I will forever wander."

A dreamy look came over Lana's face. "God, I love to ride my bike and travel under my own power."

"Definitely," agreed Cibi, "I never feel as free or as high as when I am pedaling my bike over a beautiful mountain pass."

Raz stood up in excitement, "Yeah, on those huge climbs I kind of trance out. I focus on the turning of the pedals. It's almost hypnotic; I lose myself in the motion and seem to float into the empty air."

"Hear hear," sang Cibi. "And what is better after the long struggle than standing at the top, gazing at the world below while gasping for breath in the thin crisp air?"

Ngawang laughed. "In our monasteries we breathe the high air and it excites us. We feel like we are walking on a tightrope, balancing our lives on the mountaintop. We laugh and fall and get up again. For life is not an even keel. Even on the coldest of nights when the wind screams down the mountains and blows through the walls, we laugh at the power of the world and our precarious balancing act."

Lobsang patted Ngawang on the head. "And who is being the philosopher now?" he jested. "Our country resonates in higher being. We may not ride bicycles to the peaks but we dance on air as we release our natural desires to hold onto the events around us."

Ngawang continued, "Not that we don't live in the present, but we respect the changing present. By letting go of our everyday attachments we are able to watch the dramas of our lives unfurl and pass by. We do focus with utmost clarity when necessary, but she of powerful mind knows when and how to let go." She turned and smiled at the women.

❈   ❈   ❈

Is it chaos I seek
Or magnified order
Do we have life confined
Or exist without border
In all of the vastness
Of unknowing space
Could it be only us
With this fear in our face
Are we all that knows
Of the comings and goings
And twisting within
And pulling without
Are we all that see
The incredible light
Magnified for eons
Upon its ethereal flight?

❈   ❈   ❈

"Your monasteries intrigue me," said Karyn. "I visited every one along my travels. The monks and nuns were always pleasant and friendly. But their squalid conditions grieved me. I left what offerings I could."

Ngawang answered in a sad voice. "Yes, many monasteries are very poor and in need of repair. Most Tibetans struggle with basic living. Our old government supported our studies and funded our monasteries but the country was invaded and the government overthrown."

Lobsang shook his head hesitantly as if to say he agreed but was not resigned. "So we live very frugally and continue to carry on our ancient traditions as best we can," and he looked down at the floor.

Lorraine nodded in sympathy. "I'm very sorry. The situation is so sad. In the monasteries I could feel the depth of your culture. I am humbled by the will and dedication of the monks and nuns who attempt to continue the traditions."

"Raz and I swore to each other that we could feel history within the walls of the monasteries. We were drawn into the imagery of the ancient artwork and now I feel like I *must* understand its secrets."

"Me as well!" exclaimed Lorraine. "I found huge walls lined with manuscripts and scrolls. *This is immense*, I thought. I wondered what was being studied that was so voluminous, and was told that the manuscripts provide instruction and guidance on all matters of life."

Ngawang grinned, "Yes, that is our history. At heart we study the existence of mind and the relationship of mind to what we do in the world."

Lobsang nodded, "And in our studies we seek awareness and understanding of that which continues. That which continues and exists everywhere in all places at all times. We seek to experience that which is common to and unites all things."

Ngawang smiled broadly, "Yes, we Tibetans believe that conscious mind is but one aspect of a larger mind that connects us all, and we have studied that relationship for over *one thousand years*."

❧   ❧   ❧

So here we gather on this night of storm
All alone but not forlorn
Let us tell about ourselves
Show something of whom we are
There is no reason to hide or fear
It is warm and pleasant and friendly here
So why not entertain the flickering fire
And each portray without a care
What we are that brought us near

What twisted paths we traveled on
To allow us now to gather round
Perhaps there is something we can see and learn
In how life unfolds with every turn.

How stumbling souls
From all around
Have somehow found this same ground
So sit close by and get to know
What has wandered from far and low
What has come to the top of the world
To scream it out and then unfurl
The flags of nations basked in sun
Below us now is everyone
We come together without bound
To utter once this powerful sound
And all to hear and gain renown
And sit outside of all we've found.

❦   ❦   ❦

Sonam returned with steaming bowls of noodles topped with chopped green vegetables and placed them along with spoons on the tables around the room. After many thanks and blessings, he returned to the kitchen.

Everyone began eating at once, and for a time all that was heard were spoons scraping bowls and mouths slurping soup and noodles. They were famished.

After finishing his dinner, Cibi addressed the group, "So somehow we have met and gathered here at this teahouse. Very curious how seven wanderers traveling alone (except of course for Lana and Raz) came together as a group at this time in this place. Don't you think?"

"I think you're making something of nothing. We just happened to bump into each other," insisted Ray.

"According to Ngawang and Lobsang, we have relations and connections, whether we realize them or not," countered Lorraine.

"It's all so complex, who can tell anyway?" wondered Ellie.

Cibi nodded his head, considering. "Well, maybe, maybe not. But I know how we can try to answer that question."

"How's that?" demanded Ray.

"What if each of us reveals a personal tale leading to him or her being here in Tibet? Perhaps we can find a common thread between us."

Lorraine considered. "Sounds interesting … how could it hurt?" she asked.

"It couldn't. And it will help pass the night," added Karyn, eyeing Ray carefully.

Cibi stood up and smiled. "Cool. So who's in?"

Everyone nodded except for Ray.

"What's the matter, Ray? Are you afraid?" taunted Ellie.

"Yeah, and why are you here anyway, Ray?" asked Raz. "You haven't said much about yourself."

"I'm here because I'm here," Ray answered, glaring at Raz.

He thought for a moment then continued, "Look, I have nothing against telling stories … just that I really have nothing to say that would interest you."

"How do you know if you don't tell us?" insisted Karyn.

"OK, OK, I can tell you a fucking story, alright? But I don't think you'll like it."

"We'll see about that," laughed Ellie.

"OK, so we're all going on a journey," declared Raz.

Lana smiled at him, "Actually, seven journeys, Raz."

"Yeah that's right, we're going on seven journeys."

Lorraine nodded, "And who wants to start things off?"

Everyone looked down at the floor except Ellie. She carefully watched each person then stood up and said, "OK, I'm not afraid. Now you'll hear about the lovely girl from the North," and she laughed heartily.

CHAPTER 2

One Life

Are you afraid of the dark
Don't you know that in the darkness dwells all that is fearful
All that we dread
Don't you know that in the darkness lies all that is unknown
All that might harm
In the darkness is all I don't know
All I can't see
In the darkness dwell my most fearful thoughts
My worst enemies
But in the darkness dwells none that I know
None who see me
In the darkness sleeps my total demise
I know all is lies
I know how to survive
I feel no surprise
I take all in stride.

✤   ✤   ✤

The retort of the gunshot echoed through the mountains in the cold morning air. It was the sound of finality. A step forward from which there was no turning back. I believe that if the mountains could, they would have moaned in unison. A deep bond between human and nature had been broken. The sound of that gunshot forever changed my life. In one second, my faith and trust in the goodness of people was forever broken. When my father pulled the trigger my world ripped in two … the half of fun and love and family, and the half of hardness, personal strength and determination.

You may think that I am being overly dramatic about the death of a dog, but to me that dog was all that is free and wild in contrast to *my* life, which was controlled and tame. The killing of that dog forced me out of my crippling fears and vulnerabilities and changed my life.

So in a way I thank my father and pity the dog.

But it wasn't really about the dog. It was about the wildness within me and my bonds with the natural world. My parents worked hard to develop an appreciation of the natural world in their children. They uprooted our lives in the city and moved us deep into the forested mountains. At the time all I saw were restrictions on my life. I was angry with my parents for their idealism at the expense of my sister and me. I wanted out and the death of the dog gave me the strength and determination to make the journey.

Earlier that spring, my sister Lil and I were out working in the garden, picking spinach and pulling weeds around the beets and carrot plants as we had been doing every day for the past two weeks … obviously tiring of the routine.

"I hate this work, Lil. I am so sick and tired of this incessant work."

"I know. Every day the same old same old. Take care of the animals, weed the garden, harvest the garden, gather wood and haul water."

"It is driving me crazy. I can't think, I am always upset and I can't get rid of this nagging feeling that something is going to happen … something really bad. I need to get out of here. I want to see new people. Young people doing and thinking different things."

"Ma says be patient. It will get better."

"Yeah right," I said sarcastically, "when will things get better? And how will they get better? I'm scared of what will become of me. I feel like a caged animal. I don't really care if I make some bad choices … but I want to get out in the world and make *some* choices."

"Well me too, Ellie. Ma and Pa are just trying to protect us from all the bad stuff out there. They want us to be more prepared before going out on our own … you know, like finish high school. Then we can take a long trip on our own."

We walked up the hill back to the house.

Lil put her basket of spinach on the kitchen table. "Here you go Ma … fresh-picked spinach."

"Thank you, Lil."

"And a basket of my sweat and tears," I said as I dropped mine on the table.

Pa flashed, "Ellie, be nice. Everyone must work. You know we love you and only want the best for you."

"I know, Pa. I am just so tired of this same old work. I swear I am going crazy!"

"Calm down, sweetheart."

I whined, "Pa I just need to do some *thing* on my own without everyone telling me what to do. I cannot keep doing this farm work over and over."

Ma tried to be helpful. "Why don't you come to temple with me tomorrow, Ellie? There are so many things that you could do to help."

"You know I don't like your temple, Ma. I don't want to minister to other people and I don't want other people to minister to me. I want to minister to myself."

"Don't say that, dear. Watch your words. You may regret them later," Ma replied with a worried look on her face.

Five weeks later I was sick, very sick. Sick with whooping cough. I was choking on my own phlegm. Coughing until my guts were coming out. Then coughing more.

Damn those kids. Damn their mother. They had come into the school with sadness in their eyes, displaced (or perhaps it was misplaced) from their home, pleading for a room and some friends. The local people are kind-hearted and let them in. We gave them shelter and food and the kids were invited to school. No one noticed the runny noses and coughs at first. We thought that they just had colds. Little did we know.

Within three weeks, everyone started getting sick with nagging, unrelenting coughs. Coughs that worked themselves down into the bones. Then the body attempted to expel the plague by violently coughing out its inner organs.

Eventually, someone went to the doctor and we learned that we all had whooping cough. Even adults who had been vaccinated. By this time, the mother and kids who had joined us had moved on.

My sister, my mother and father were all sick. And of course I was scared. Afraid what each day would bring. Afraid to live. Afraid I might die. Lil took it all right. She slept most of the time but when awake she would joke about silly things and laugh a lot in a kind of nervous laugh.

All night long I could hear coughing and moaning. My body ached from coughing and my mind ached from hearing coughing. I felt smothered and trapped … like I needed to come up for air. I badly wanted to go somewhere and see people, but for the time being I was going nowhere.

One morning after a hard restless night, our neighbor Leon stopped by while we were eating breakfast. Leon lived by himself down the road. People called him a mountain man. He tried to live mostly off the land and rarely ever went to the store. Pa liked to talk with Leon about the woods and animals and government and politics. Pa said Leon was a backwoods philosopher.

Leon walked into the kitchen with a bright smile on his face. "How are you fine people this beautiful morning?" he asked.

"Not too good, we are all sick with the cough," Pa replied.

"I heard you were sick. Sorry to hear about that. Most everyone around here has that cough these days."

"It spreads quickly and does not easily go away, but you have managed to avoid it. How is that Leon?" Pa asked.

"I am not sure. I have been around kids who were sick, but for some reason I have not gotten sick. You can overcome these coughs. Our bodies are strong and know how to heal themselves," Leon assured us.

"That's exactly what we've been thinking," Ma replied.

"I think the big problem is getting the knowledge from our bodies to our heads. Most of the time we are so filled up with thoughts and ideas from other places that we don't listen to what our bodies are trying to tell us," Pa added.

Ma, Pa and Lil were slowly getting better but I could not seem to rid my body of the cough. I was sore in every muscle from heaving so hard. And I was beginning to think that I would never get better. But one day everything changed … the day that my mother found Oak … or maybe it was really the day that Oak found my mother.

Mama … mama … mama! Where are you going? What is happening? I start to run but something grabs my rear leg and as I pull to get free there is a sharp pain and I hear my flesh ripping. I break free and run helter-skelter through the bushes until I no longer hear the chaser and then collapse on the ground.

Come back to me mama! Help me mama.… but all I hear in the distance is the sound of growling, barking and running. I lie silently alone in the grass just like mama showed me. Lie still and wait. Wait quietly and patiently and she will return. At night it is cold and lonely. I am scared and my leg hurts badly.

I do not cry out. I know that mama will return. Another day passes and I still wait quietly. But I am very cold and hungry and scared and still she does not return. She never showed me what to do if she did not come back. I am getting weaker as the day passes. Flies keep biting and chewing my leg. I am too weak to chase them away. Where is mama?

Another night and I am fading. I lie in the grass too scared to move. Too scared to make a noise. I can no longer focus and begin to fall in and out of dreams. Images come and go in my head and run together … garbled and nonsensical. I see mama walking through the grass in the warm sun and then I see dogs running after her, barking and foaming from their mouths. Then I see me and mama lying together snuggled down in the leaves in the cool night air. And then I am back here, lying bleeding in the grass.

I am roused out of my dreams by something nearby. A person is walking over on the edge of the field. She is coming closer and closer. Muh! Muh! I try to call out. Maybe she will help me. She stops and looks toward me. I am confused and do not know what to do. I blink. Lie motionlessly and silently … I remember what mama taught me. But she is coming closer. I think she sees me now!

Ma was out for a healing walk in the sun. She said the sun was like food for the body. Going back through the meadow, she heard a plaintive "Muh, muh" cry from in the grass to her side. She walked directly toward the sound but could see nothing, so she stood quietly and stared at the grass in the direction of the sound. For a moment, she saw a tiny flicker of movement. At first she was not sure what she was seeing but quickly realized it was the blink of the eyes of a baby deer lying in the grass.

"My, my a little baby deer! How are you, little deer? Oh, you are hurt. Poor baaaby. Where is your mama?"

Looking around and seeing nothing, she picked up the little baby, wrapped it in her arms and walked quickly back to the house.

"Hey girls. Look what I found!" she called out as she entered the house.

Lil came running down the steps and squealed, "A little deer! A little baby deer!"

I ran down following her. "Where did you find it Ma?"

"Oh it's sooo pretty. Can we keep it?" Lil pleaded.

"I think he was attacked and got separated from his mama and has been lying in the field for a couple of days. He is sick and might die. Maybe we can nurse him back to health. Let's wrap him up and give him a bottle of warm goat milk."

I put blankets in a small box and set it next to the stove. Ma handed him to me and I gently stroked his side. "How about a soft bed by the woodstove, little one?"

Lil filled a bottle with warm goat milk and slid a rubber nipple onto the top. She pressed the tip to get some milk dripping. The baby smelled the bottle and slowly began to lick the nipple. A moment later he was hungrily sucking warm milk down his throat. His eyes brightened.

"Look at his eyes, Ma. He looks so happy."

Ma and Lil covered the wood box with the last blanket. "Goodnight, little deer." Lil cooed.

"Goodnight, baby deer. I hope you get stronger and come to live with us," I whispered.

❧   ❧   ❧

The baby deer lived through the night and the next day we named him *Oak—Oak of the Forest*. After a few more feedings of goat milk, he was up and running from room to room, jumping over chairs and sofas, delighting Lil and me. My cough was getting better and I was beginning to enjoy myself.

After a few days, we started taking Oak out for short walks. He loved to follow behind like a little lamb. In no time he learned his name and would come running when called. He quickly became the joy of our family.

One night we were sitting around after dinner, discussing our history of experiences with nature and our good fortune in having found the baby deer. I had been pretty quiet. I was definitely enjoying Oak but my bundle of fears was brewing just below the surface.

I turned to Pa, "Sure we've had many interesting experiences in the mountains, but don't you think we would have many others if we lived in the city?"

"Yes, Ellie, you're right," Pa replied patiently. "If we lived in the city we would have other experiences … some good but maybe quite a few bad as well."

"But we wouldn't have had pets from the forest like Oak," Ma was quick to add.

"Yes, but I'm sure there would be lots of other fun things to do," I said stubbornly.

Pa persisted, "Ellie we moved out of the city for you girls to have a healthy place to grow up."

"But why did you bring us *here* Pa? Of all the places that you could go, why did you move far from everything and everyone that you knew?"

"The city was getting choked with sprawl and noise and dirty air. The wooded hills around us were cleared of trees and replaced with houses and streets and shopping malls. It was dangerous to walk around at night and in some places even dangerous for kids to walk to school."

Ma continued, "We wanted you to live and understand the changing of the seasons, the cycles of day and night and sun and rain and the coming and passing of life."

Pa added, "We had doubts whether we should leave our home and families and move to a strange place but then the cicadas came."

"Cicadas?" asked Lil.

"Yes Lil," Ma answered, "cicadas are insects. They live around trees. And while we were considering what to do we had a plague of cicadas."

"A plague like in the old religious stories?" wondered Lil.

"Not exactly," replied Pa, "in the old stories the people were the victims of the swarm of insects. In our case, the cicadas were the victims."

"You were worried about the cicadas? You left the city and brought us here because you were afraid that something would happen to the cicadas?" I asked sarcastically.

"They were periodical cicadas."

"Periodical cicadas?" I repeated.

"Yes. Cicadas swarm like locusts but they depend upon trees. Periodical cicadas spend 13 or 17 years underground as nymphs. Then they emerge and quickly transform into adults. The adults eat a little and mate. The males die and the females lay eggs and die. Though their adult life lasts but a few weeks they have one of the longest life cycles of any insect."

"And what does this have to do with leaving the city?" Lil asked impatiently.

Pa continued, "The cicadas emerged by the millions. They were everywhere. When you walked they flew into your face and hair."

"Sounds awful. So you left the city to get away from them?" I asked.

"No, quite the opposite. We left the city because we realized that the offspring of these insects would be smothered before they became adults."

"Smothered?" I asked in disbelief.

"Yes, when the nymphs in the ground came to emerge again the ground would be paved over and they would smother. And then we thought about you girls," Pa concluded.

Ma added, "We came to the forest to be where the cicadas ... and the owls, bears, wolves, birds and butterflies can all live freely."

❦   ❦   ❦

Late one cold windy night, a lone and battered dog wandered in from the forest. With every movement of his body he whimpered in pain. Patches of fur were missing along his side and back, where open sores oozed pus. His large dull brown eyes were sunk far back in a huge head perched upon his emaciated body. He seemed resigned to his condition and fate. He was looking for a last bed to rest his weary bones and wait for whatever came next.

In the morning, we found him lying on the porch. Lil and I ran outside to see him, but he could hardly get up.

Pa called him an intruder and a spreader of ill. Lil and I felt sorry for the old thing and wanted to keep him. Ma sided with us. So we let him be and gave him a place on the porch to rest.

Now we had two *pets* from the forest living with us. The old dog stayed out of everyone's way and kept his distance. He was not much of a threat to anybody, but still Pa did not like him.

Oak continued to grow bigger and stronger. He began to wander away into the forest for longer periods of time, but would always come running when called. The old dog continued to hang on, though he hardly ate more than few food scraps from the compost pile.

One night at the dinner table, Pa spoke up. "Girls, we have got to get rid of that old dog. He is diseased and very sick. Whatever is wrong with him may spread to the farm dogs. Tomorrow I am going to walk him out in the woods and shoot him."

"No, Pa! Please don't hurt the dog! He cannot help himself," Lil cried.

I kept silent. I knew it was not the right thing to do, though I wasn't sure why. I felt sick.

Pa was adamant. "I am sorry girls. We cannot let him stay here. It will be better for him."

I was not sure whom it would be better for, but certainly not the old dog.

The next morning after breakfast, we were reading books when a single rifle shot rang out. Complete silence followed, though I could feel the blast reverberate through every cell of my body.

I kept thinking about the old dog lying on the ground, looking up at Pa and wondering why he had been betrayed. He had come for peace and quiet and a simple place to lay down his weary bones and die. Instead, in his last breath he found human deceit. After a life of trying to be a good dedicated servant, he got a bullet in the head.

Immediately I thought of Oak and how he had sadly lost his mother, and was now learning to trust and bond with us. The same people who just killed the old dog.

I ran outside and called him over and over but he did not appear. Lil and I walked all the trails calling his name, but we saw and heard nothing.

Oak never returned. We guessed what might have happened. Perhaps a pack of dogs got him. Maybe a bobcat. Maybe he just decided to go out on his own. But I knew. I knew he found out what we were. No chance about it. Sure cause and effect.

❧   ❧   ❧

Our joy with Oak lingered for a while as a flickering reverie then slowly faded from memory as we settled back into our old routines. I hated the people we had become. I was sure that Oak immediately saw our deceit and knew that we had killed the dog. What trust could he have in us after that day?

No, I did not have the dog's blood on my hands but I was still guilty. I had done nothing to prevent his death. I could have stood up to my father. I could have sworn to protect the dog.

I consoled myself that this would never happen again ... that I would become well and strong and deal with the world on my own terms. I would not be a child anymore. But I was scared, scared sick in the pit of my stomach.

Lil asked me, "What are you really scared of, Sis? I mean really, really scared of?"

"I am really scared of what happened to the old dog."

"The old dog? He's dead and gone. How does that scare you?"

"I keep thinking about what he must have thought … you know, when Pa shot him."

"He didn't think anything. He was just an old dog. He never knew what happened."

"Sure he did. And what scares me is that he looked to us for something. I could see it in his eyes. And we killed him."

"*We* did not kill him. Pa killed him."

"But *we* didn't do anything to stop Pa."

"What could we do?"

"We could do *anything*. We did nothing. *We* killed him; he looked to us for comfort and he got death. All his life he wanted care and loving and he got a bullet in the end. Doesn't that scare you? To think about searching your whole life and it all comes down to a bullet?"

"Now you are scaring *me*, Sis. We can't do anything about that old dog, but we can do plenty with our lives. We're not powerless."

"You're right. We're not. But thinking about that makes me scared. I mean, who can really protect us?"

"Ma and Pa protect us."

"Sure. But who can protect them?"

❧   ❧   ❧

One night it was my turn to feed the horses. Lil offered to go out with me, but I told her I wanted to do it on my own.

I walked to the stable and looked up at the hayloft. It was dark and I feared what might be hiding in the shadows. I put the flashlight into my pocket and took a deep breath. I was going to climb up in the dark, get the hay and return without using the light or running away.

I figured, *what is the worst thing that can happen to me?* Maybe *I would be killed.* By what? *By a crazy man waiting in the dark ready to attack me.* I reasoned that I have been up there a thousand times before and no one was ever hiding. Besides, what would make me so special that someone would be waiting for *me?* Anyhow, if I was killed, so be it. But more than likely I would just get a bale of hay and return down the ladder.

So up I went, my heart pounding. I walked across the floor, felt around for a bale, picked one up, carried it back to the ladder and dropped it down. *Whew … not too bad* I thought. I faced my fear, risked my own death at the hands of who knows what and survived. I felt pretty proud of myself as I walked back to the house.

❈   ❈   ❈

One day not long after, I said to Lil, "You know, I have been thinking a lot about fear and all the things that scare me."

"That's great Ellie. Maybe you can do something about it."

"Yes. I figure most of the fear is about things that I do not or cannot know … like what might happen next or what happens when I die. I'm realizing that if I give in to the fear, I feel all tied up and sort of crippled. So I'm thinking that maybe I should take some risks and face what scares me. Anyhow, what is the worst that can happen?"

"I don't know. Probably nothing."

"The very worst I figure is that I could die. But that seems unlikely. So why be afraid to get hay in the dark?" I laughed.

"That's funny, Sis. You *have* been pretty wound up lately."

"You know, that old dog had no fear in his eyes."

"That's true. He was accepting and thankful for anything given to him."

"Humble, I would say. Humble in himself regardless of the terrible condition that he was in. So he is my hero."

❀   ❀   ❀

Cast away doubt
Cast away ambition
Lie with open arms
Await the blowing wind
Forget just who you are
What shape you're in
Whether you know or don't
Whether you care or not
Let mountains come and go
And flow and flow and flow.

❀   ❀   ❀

As the summer wore on I spent more and more time alone in the forest. I loved to disappear into the woods and sit listening to the animals and feeling the moods of the woods. Sometimes I walked for hours, only to spend an hour or two in a beautiful glade by a lake or waterfall. Occasionally I did not return until after dark. My mother and father were not very happy about my time alone in the forest, but as long as I talked politely and kept up my work there was not much they could say to me.

One night at the end of the summer, around our usual bedtime, I got up from the sofa and went to get my hat and jacket. "I am going out for a walk," I stated.

"You are going where?" my mother asked.

"Just out for a walk, Ma. Is that OK?"

Pa called out from the bedroom, "Ellie this is no time for you to go walking out in the mountains by yourself. You should get ready for bed like your sister."

I stopped, hesitated for a moment then blurted out, "No, Pa. I am going out. Walking in the forest comforts me," and I scooted out and quickly shut the door behind me.

❈   ❈   ❈

The night air was thick and moist, the temperature cool enough to condense my breath. The moon was low on the horizon. Hardly any wind and the forest was silent. I looked back at the warm glow of the lights from the house and turned again toward the darkness. With one more glance back, I started walking briskly into the unknown.

I soon turned off the road, making my way silently into the woods one step at a time. And one slow listen. One slow step and one slow listen. Step by step. Listen by listen. Only the occasional rustle of leaves and the moon, owls and small scurrying animals.

At a high point I looked back up the valley.

The moon at the head of the river. The river flows down to the sea. The sea supports all the land and the land supports you and me.

I kept repeating to myself over and over …

From the sky to the water to the land to me. From the sky to the water to the land to me … Walking step by step through the dark. The starry-eyed girl in the starry-eyed night.

I walked further and further into the woods. I followed old paths that I had explored in the daylight. As the moon began to set, the forest got darker.

I stopped in a glade above a small lake. The moon dropped over the horizon. In the clearing, starlight illuminated the shapes of bushes and trees. I sat motionless for a long time, immersed in the sounds and movements of the forest, seeking to lose myself and find the heart of the forest.

I wandered further without knowing where I was going. I was determined to find mystery somewhere in the darkness, far away from the orderly and known, far from the categorized rules and customs of my society. And I was not afraid.

❉   ❉   ❉

My parents were very upset when I returned at sunrise. They had worried about me all night. So at the pleading of my mother, I went into town to meet with Mr. Shipley, one of the leaders of my mother's temple.

"Hello Mr. Shipley. My mother thought it would be a good idea to talk with you."

"Good. I am glad that you came. Your mother tells me that you have taken to wandering out in the forest for long periods of time, even at night, and sometimes not returning until morning."

"I got back late last night. She was very upset. I told her I was sorry."

"You must be careful in the forest, Ellie. There are many ways to fall in with bad things. Don't forget about your God."

"I don't know about God, Mr. Shipley. I love Nature. When I walk in the woods it makes me feel like I am part of something bigger than myself."

"You *are* part of something big. You are one of God's children. There is always a place for you and a big family that welcomes you. You do believe in God, don't you, Ellie?"

"To tell you the truth, I am not really sure what I believe in. I do believe in the power of Nature. I do believe that we have spirits and that there are other spirits besides us."

"You must be careful, dear. Don't worship false gods. The devil works in many ways. He is always trying to catch new souls. There is only one true way and that is God's way."

"If God is real, then Nature is part of God. Nature is what gives me comfort. I will worship God through Nature."

"Remember that our lives here are only temporal, Ellie. The things of this world may be nice but they are trappings. Don't focus too much on those things or you will miss God."

"If God is all-powerful, then God must have created this world. If it is God's creation, then it must be good, right?" I jested.

"In a limited way, yes. But the world is not God. This world is only the steppingstone to God's Kingdom. It is what we do in this world that will lead us to the real Kingdom."

"I am looking for the real. And I find it in Nature. I don't see any evil here."

❦   ❦   ❦

Slipping into the shadows, I blend with the night ... with the forest creatures, the wind, the moon, the grasses and trees. I glide silently through the shade of hemlocks, listening and breathing and losing myself. I step deeper and deeper into the foreignness of the wild.

I tremble from the unknowingness ... from my smallness and weakness. I tremble for the shadowy things around me. I tremble for the dark itself and for my inner self ... seeking its links to place and time.

I strain to touch the spirits of the earth. I struggle to free myself from my own images and ideas. I struggle to feel and to be aroused by the sensations of place. I fear this as strongly as I want it.

Let the mind leap. Shut down one sense and open another. Feel the presence. Sense what is there before it happens.

❦   ❦   ❦

My parents were losing me. The protective shell that they worked to build around me was cracking. My mother insisted that I return to her temple to visit with Mr. Shipley and Ms. Marcone.

They were waiting for me in Mr. Shipley's office.

"Hello Ellie. Come in. You know Ms. Marcone, don't you?"

"Yes. Hello Ms. Marcone."

"Hi Ellie. Good to see you. Your mother has told me much about you."

"I hope not too many bad things."

"Not at all. But she is concerned about your lack of faith and about all the time you spend alone out in the forest … even at night."

"Like I told Mr. Shipley, Nature inspires me. And I walk because I like to be out in Nature. I am not hurting anyone or doing anything wrong."

"No, you are not doing anything wrong. I think your mother is concerned (and we are as well) because you may be missing the *real* God and getting involved with something that only appears to be like God." Ms. Marcone was choosing her words carefully.

I was not going to budge. "I think that all living creatures are important and that God does not necessarily look like us or think like us. Maybe God is more animal-like. How do you know?"

Ms. Marcone continued, "Do you believe in Satan, Ellie?"

"I guess I do. Though I am not sure what that means. I really try not to think about it."

"Perhaps you should. Do you ever think about Satan while walking in the forest at night?"

"You mean worry about meeting Satan?"

"Yes. Satan can take many forms. Are you concerned that one night you may find something that wants to prey upon you?"

I was getting irritated and tried to keep a calm voice. "Ms. Marcone, I am not worried about an animal preying upon me. The animals are usually more scared of me than I am of them. And I am not worried about meeting Satan. I just like to be in the forest. It comforts me."

"OK, Ellie, we did not mean to make you upset," Mr. Shipley said, "but I think you may be missing the path to God by focusing on nature and the wild.

"God created the world and he is our benefactor. People have been given dominion over the plants and animals. We should not look to the plants and animals to bring us to God." He paused and looked at me sternly: "You must be careful here."

❈   ❈   ❈

The talk of God and Satan was depressing me. I figured we are all of the natural world. We are born to mothers who mated with fathers. Our flesh and blood are arrangements of carbon, hydrogen, oxygen, nitrogen and other trace elements interacting with the world around ... just like the animals.

We are definitely different from the whale and dolphin, but are we in some way superior to them ... or to the fox and beaver? Is there a God for us, but not for the animals?

We are thinking beings. We question our living and our dying. But how about the highly intelligent whales and dolphins? Do they think about their end? They have large brains, communicate with each other in complex ways and form social groups.

Other animals have not built cities or airplanes. But they also have not poisoned oceans, removed mountains and forests or changed the climate of the planet. Nor do they build deadly weapons or create global wars.

So what makes us better than them? Because we can track and kill them according to our whims? Is it our religion and belief in God? Are we better because we have names for things and they do not?

And how do we know that whales and dolphins do not think about *creation*? Or have names for *God* or *ocean* or *island*? And even if they do not, does our naming or our beliefs make us better than them? Are words and naming our greatest accomplishment?

There are many animals more advanced than we are. How about the migratory birds flying 3000 miles twice a year and returning to their same nests? Or the communications of dolphins using two sets of vocal cords? Do they carry on two conversations at one time or do they have complex names that can only be voiced as combinations of two or more simultaneous sounds?

I don't know about any of this. I do know that what humans *call* things affects how we interact and feel. The naming we do sets the bounds of our awareness.

❧   ❧   ❧

One day while working in the garden, I saw Leon walking along the dirt road.

I called out to him. "Hey Leon! How's it going?"

He walked over to the edge of the garden. "Fine, Ellie. And you?"

"Oh, OK I guess."

"What's up?"

I dropped my hoe and walked toward him. "Oh, I don't know. I keep fighting with my mother and father."

"I'm sorry about that. Anything you feel like talking about?"

"I am just so confused about what I am supposed to do and believe. They tell me at my mother's temple that I am going to get into trouble if I spend so much time in the forest."

"The world is a beautiful place Ellie. There is nothing wrong with learning about the natural world."

"They seem to think there is. And my parents also."

"Well, I am not going to talk with you about the temple, because I might say something not nice, and I don't want to get your father upset. But I will argue to my dying day that there is nothing bad or evil about the forest. I live out here because I love the forest. There are many things in the wild that might not suit our tastes, but the forest is the work of God."

"Do you believe in Satan? Are you afraid of the devil?" I asked.

"No, I am not afraid. I *have* seen him before. He was scary but you have nothing to fear."

"What was he like?"

"He was dressed like us. From his outward appearance, he could have been anyone."

"How did you know that he was the devil?"

"His eyes were cold. There was no feeling in him. I was never more scared in my life."

"So you do believe in Satan?"

"If you mean that which lives in hate, torture and vindictiveness and seeks to spread it, then yes. If you are referring to the guardian of hell in the hereafter, then no."

"So the devil you saw was not the guardian of hell?"

"No, he was a person like us but a person who was totally obsessed with a fixed inner vision without regard for the effects and consequences of following that vision."

"What do you mean *was*?"

"He is dead now."

"So he did not have everlasting existence?"

"No, he died just like you or me. But I guess in a way he can live on."

"How so?"

"Well, in his obsession with hate and violence he drew others into the blood-bath. They carry on his interests and notions."

"Wow! People carrying on our ideas and energy after we die. I never thought about it like that."

"Yeah, and unfortunately Ellie, since fighting and killing are so much a part of what we do, this continually affects everyone."

"That sucks." This was getting more complicated. I had begun talking with Leon to try to clear my mind but now I was even more confused. "So do you think there are other kinds of devils?"

"Other than hate, torture and violence? No."

"Do you believe in life hereafter?"

"If you are referring to a place in the sky where the good and righteous go and exist as ethereal manifestations of their current selves, then no. I think that when we die we kind of dissolve … bit by bit, we just slip away."

"That's scary. You mean we just slowly melt away?"

"Yeah. We all must pass."

"Well that's really scary. I mean, it makes me feel so alone and—and … meaningless. Like, what's the purpose of my life if all things eventually pass away?"

Leon looked up the hill toward the house. "Look, Ellie, I don't mean to scare you. Maybe it is not such a good idea for us to discuss this."

"Oh please, Leon. I need this. I have been getting hounded by the people from my mother's temple."

"Exactly, and that is what your parents want. So I don't want to fan the fire."

"We are not doing anything wrong. There is no law against talking!"

"That's true, but there are laws about corrupting underage girls!"

"Oh God. Not this again. I am almost an adult. I can think for myself and make decisions for myself, even if I do live with my parents. Don't treat me like a little child who cannot hear the truth."

"I'm sorry. But you understand my position, don't you?"

"Yes. But don't disrespect me either."

"OK, Ellie. I will talk about what I think, but I will not suggest that you do anything. Fair enough?"

"Fair enough," I replied.

"OK. Yes, it is very disturbing for me (or most anyone) to glance, even slightly glance, at the idea of the inhuman meaninglessness of existence. To think about a view of nature and the universe and time that does not favor us disturbs people greatly. Considering a universe that works in ways and processes that do not acknowledge the continual existence of humans, or mammals even, or the Earth is definitely scary.

"Why do you think that religion is so popular? Religion goes hand in hand with the awareness of our slippery unknown end. Religion and tradition give humans a sense of human-favored existence. It is our desperate hope to bring meaningfulness into an unknown and fearful situation. We strive to make sense of our growing consciousness of the everyday nature of unrelenting change that is our existence."

We were silent for a while. I was trying to understand what Leon was saying. "I guess all religions offer a vision that is most beneficial for followers of the religion, a plan by which to live their lives. That is what Mr. Shipley was trying to give to me. I guess that is really why we have religion, isn't it?"

"Yes, each religion attempts to describe the inscrutable unknown and our relations and obligations with it. And each offers guidance, assistance and support for its followers."

"Attempting the inscrutable! How funny. But seriously, don't you believe that there is anything at all for us when we pass away … or dissolve as you put it … or is that our total end?"

"Well, did you believe my story about the devil?"

"Did you really meet a man like that or were you just making it up?"

"No, I really did meet a man exactly as I told you."

"Then do you really believe that what we do carries on after we die?" I asked.

"Well sure. It seems just natural to me that we pass on to others and they pass on to us all kinds of stuff … physical, emotional, social, psychological, philosophical and spiritual."

"Ah, in that case we are all connected and when someone dies it is like a leaf dying on a big tree. That makes me feel better somehow. Thanks, Leon."

❄   ❄   ❄

I continued to escape into the forest, seeing and learning more than I had ever imagined. I slipped into the night like a whisper. Black as nothing. Shrouded from all. I did not know what to do. I did not want to know what to do. I sought something other. I struggled to escape from every learned idea so that I might find something raw and untouched.

I looked outside for a sign, for some verification. Something separate from what was within me. I burned to escape the naming ... to flee from the responsibility and burden of connecting the dots and completing the structure.

Was it a good structure?

I did not know. I only knew that it was the shared and agreed-upon structure of my parents, their temple, school and community. Oh, how I ached to connect with something deep, earthy and primal. So out in the wild black night I wandered.

And what did I find?

I found myself. I found the darkest corners of my fear. And in my gut I came to know a reality thick with image and emotion ... stronger and more forceful than any other part of my life. So then what is real? Is this world of ours real or is there truth in the darkness of the night?

I have to believe both. Surely we can agree on common names and meanings, and that agreement is very powerful and allows us to do many amazing things. But surely also the world of sliding in the deep darkness, of animals crouching and stalking, of natural portentousness, bites as strongly to the bone.

❄   ❄   ❄

Oh I wish I had the power and strength
To choke out this darkness that covers my soul
That lights my night wanderings through to the core
That drags me to places I've not been before.

But all is for naught
It is just fated to be
A dark night's wander
Alone in the trees
I pull and I plug these holes in my soul
The fabric of life upon which I hold.

You see I'm nothing at all
And then something yet
With power to disturb and bump bare
Those thoughts that are holy, hallowed and clear
For in the clearness I find vigor and might
But it all sort of dies by the side of the night.
In the night you know nothing
It is all dark and clean
Whatever can happen
Whatever that means
Without light to guide we move by our senses
We tune into movements, rustlings and shrills
We cling to the pictures held deep in our minds
That really exist and hold sway over times
All what's inside is all that has been
We are never without our humble origins.

In the mix and the mash
Of consciousness and naught
We dwell in the past, present and future of thought
We are what we are in the thickest of ways
We try to escape each one of our days
We struggle to conquer the beast that we are
But it always survives and delivers the scar
So what is a girl lost in heaven to do
Should she pick up the pieces and move right on through
Should she disassemble the deck

And remove what is right
And display what is only
Known in the night
Should she open the shutters
To the bright light of day
Examine her failings
And mend her old ways
Should she search the new paths
Or travel the old
Should she wander afar
Or come in from the cold?

❧   ❧   ❧

Ellie finished her story and the room grew quiet. She looked pained and kept her eyes fixed on the floor. Still no one spoke. She fidgeted for a while and then continued, "So eventually I left my home and family. I could not fit into the place they had made for me. And looking for some answers, I followed my childhood dreams and made my way to this land."

Lorraine slid over on the bench next to her and slipped her arm over Ellie's shoulder. "It's very difficult to leave all that you know and love. You are a strong and determined girl, Ellie. You have much to be proud of."

Ellie sighed. "I just couldn't fit into the place that my parents had made for me. I had to make a choice and I followed my heart and instincts … instincts that I did not even know I had."

Lorraine looked at her with compassion. "Ellie, I think that people have a lot of capabilities that aren't commonly recognized. You had to struggle because you found something real and meaningful that the people around you could not see and did not accept."

"I couldn't reject what felt so true to me."

"That is so important, Ellie," said Lana. "Freedom is not easy. With it comes a lot of responsibility. It is often much easier to follow the trodden path and not think or act on your own."

Ray perked up at Lana's last words. "You've got to act on your own Ellie. It is all you have. That's what keeps me going. Don't worry about the order and institutions of society. They're all bullshit."

Raz shook his head, "Yeah, Ray, but though we try, we can't actually act on our own. Remember what Leon told Ellie about the devil man living on through others?"

"That the things you do carry on into the future?"

"Yes, so you have responsibility for what happens in the future."

Ray bristled. "Hey, you can't pin responsibility for the future on me! I spend my life outside of society. I'm not even legally in this country. I follow my own path and I don't abide by bullshit laws. And I will not be defined or confined."

"High aspirations," said Cibi. "So what brought you to *this* place?"

"I walked into Tibet through the mountains and slipped around the Chinese border crossing. I have no passport. I follow no country. I am here to be at the top of the world. I am here to be above everything below."

"You are a rebel," said Karyn. "I want to hear more."

Ray shook his head in disbelief. "You sure you want to hear this?"

"Definitely," answered Karyn, "*I* would like to feel so free."

"Well, alright then," said Ray with a puzzled look, "I'll tell you a tale of my sick and confused life." He stood up and walked back and forth across the room several times, mumbling to himself. Then he took a deep breath and fell back onto the bench, sighing loudly. A moment later, he sat up straight, smiled to himself, cleared his throat and began his tale.

CHAPTER 3

One and Only

Lying in bed looking up at the ceiling, I feel small and alone. I try to organize the patterns and count the lines. Careful observation is my defense against being controlled. *They* want something from me. I am not sure what, but I know that I must not let them know that I am aware of them or of their interests and expectations. I keep cool and show nothing.

My gaze rivets upon a dust ball lodged in the ceiling corner. Sweat bristles on my forehead as I shiver with insignificance. I cannot rouse myself from the vision of a miniscule dust ball in a vast immeasurable universe. Everything seems so distant and unapproachable. All effort worthless.

Is this me? Is this my place? I try to push these thoughts out of my head, but the feeling will not go away. Somehow, something so small makes me feel utterly helpless, as if I matter not a speck in the scheme of things.

🍁   🍁   🍁

Crack of dawn and we've been up so long
Since another day and we are still out to play
Watching the traffic go round
Business suits and working vans
Everyone up chasing the sun

Chasing the sun to some work somewhere for someone
Radios on and coffee close by
Sleep in their eyes and nothing in their minds
It's a procession
It's a waltz
Everyone now jump on the bus
The new day is dawning
There's work to be done
Everyone, everywhere is moving to the beat
The sound of the dollar rings through the streets.

Just two young guys watching with grins
The workday begins and we sit and stare
Frightening ourselves with the numb-like confusion
Making us realize our ultimate delusion
Everyone looking just straight ahead
We sit on the sidelines and maintain the trance
We cannot understand this humanly flow
We'll not be caught in this social net
We'll maintain our freedom and independence of mind
If this is our kind we'll give them no time.

✻   ✻   ✻

It was 6 a.m. and my buddy Sal and I were sitting by the side of the road, watching the city wake up. The streets were slowly filling with cars and trucks. It had been a long night for us. From Sal's, out to eat, to a party, to the girls' place, back out to eat again, and then walking the streets, talking about the bullshit lives that we live.

"Just look at them, Ray. Kind of a circus, don't you think?"

"I know, Sal. They're all in their own world, just staring straight ahead. And they don't look very happy."

"Would you? How would you feel if you stopped at this same intersection every day, whether you wanted to or not?"

"Kind of old, I guess," I mused.

"Well, welcome to adulthood, man. Got to get a job and go to work. Got to live on a schedule."

"Like when we're in school," I blurted out.

Sal grimaced. "Man, don't mention that now."

"Sorry, Sal. All I'm saying is that it's easy for us to sit here in our seat of judgment, with clothes on our backs and our bellies full, and laugh at the world going by."

"Yeah well, I don't need all this shit. I can live on my own and I don't have to end up at this traffic light every fucking morning. I'm gonna get out of here."

"I'm with you. Got to do something to avoid this. But where exactly is *out of here?*"

He shook his head, "I don't know, man. Let's just drop out."

"Drop out? You mean like *tune in, turn on and drop out?*"

He laughed. "Yeah, something like that. Just don't follow this shit. Do something different."

"Oh man, but everyone and everything is pushing us to be part of this," I waved my arm toward the cars at the traffic light.

Sal frowned. "We just don't have much time, Ray. Our days are numbered, so we've got to do it right."

"I don't get what you mean."

"Well, suppose you live 80 years."

"Oh, you mean 80 years is not such a long time? Hey, I'll be happy to live half that long," I laughed nervously.

"Well, maybe we'll only see 40 but imagine if we reach 80 years. At 365.25 days in a year that will be 29,220 days. And if you do live for only 40 years you'll see only 14,610 days."

"Doesn't seem like too much when you put it that way."

"No. Not really. But our time for creativity, fun and enjoyment is even less."

"Sure. We have lots of things to do."

"Exactly. So let's consider the time that we have for doing our own thing."

I laughed. "Now you've got me curious."

"OK. Got to have a job, right?"

"Yeah, it appears that way."

"OK, so if you keep a 40-hour per week job for 40 years then 2000 hours per year times 40 years means about 80,000 total hours of your life is spent working."

I considered for a moment, "That's a scary lot of time. And our time is even more limited, since we also need to figure hours spent sleeping, eating, cleaning and grooming ... which are all necessary but not exactly creative pursuits."

"For sure. What do you say about 9 hours a day?"

"Sounds about right. Nine hours of each day of our lives."

"So 9 hours times 29,220 days of our 80-year life makes another 262,980 hours, if my mental math is correct."

"Good work, Sal. And I was also thinking about time spent commuting or preparing for work."

"That's right. Let's figure we spend an hour a day for 250 workdays a year over 40 years. That's another 10,000 hours."

"Right. And sick or injured days?"

"What do you say Ray, maybe 4 days a year?"

"Probably more down days than that, but that's close enough. That adds another 320 days over 80 years."

"Right, so 320 days of our 80-year lifespan is spent being sick."

I thought for a moment, "Yeah, but we've already counted 9 hours of those days as time spent sleeping and grooming. So the sick and injured time should be counted as 320 days times 15 hours per day or 4,800 more hours."

"Excellent, Ray. Now if we add up all the hours spent on necessary stuff we get 80,000 + 262,980 + 10,000 + 4,800 = 357,780 hours over eighty years. And dividing that by 24 hours per day comes out to around 14,908 days of an 80-year life spent on non-creative activities. And subtracting 14,908 from our 80-year lifespan of 29,220 days we are left with 14,312 days for ourselves."

"So if I live to be 80, which I probably won't see, I have only around 14,000 days to do stuff that I want and then my life is gone."

"Liberally speaking. It really could be much less. You could be sick more, or work more, or not live that many years."

"Then each day is precious. I can count to 14,000 in about three hours."

"It's a flash and then you're gone. So what are dudes like us supposed to do with our time?"

"Man, I don't know. Thinking about it scares me."

"Imagine spending 40 years of your life working at a job that you don't enjoy. Sitting at this traffic light every fucking morning. Doing shit for other people who you don't respect. Finally getting sick and lying on your bed, dying."

"Sounds like crap."

"Yeah. And imagine thinking back over your days on this planet and all you see is 40 years of working and trying to get away from working. I bet you would be thinking *what the fuck was that all about … shouldn't I have done something better?*"

"That's bullshit!" I yelled.

"Yes it is, Ray. As I said, our days are numbered and so our time is precious."

"Now I guess I see your point."

"And you know Ray, even when we have personal creative time it isn't always enjoyable. We all have ups and downs. So it's all about attitude."

"Attitude, huh?"

"Yup. Attitude and resiliency. Don't fixate on a specific course. Take what life gives you and let it roll. You can't stop the tide of events but you sure can choose to not let them overwhelm you."

"I like that," I replied. "Focus on the present, stay loose and change as the moment requires."

"Now you've got it, Ray. Take each day as it comes and roll with it."

"You know those times when I have tried really hard to obtain something, it usually ends up slipping away anyway."

"I know what you mean. Don't fight too hard against the current. And don't try to dock yourself, since there's no solid point to hold onto."

"All you can do is smile, smile, smile."

I had to laugh at this. Here were Sal and I, migrants from the night, sitting at sunrise, watching the world go by. And all we could do was smile.

*   *   *

How many days do we get to play
How many days to make our own way
How many days until time comes undone
How many days to lie in the Sun?

How many days will I wonder away
Of no more days and no more play
I figure them this

That if you survive for a full 80 years
You'll live just 29,220.

Twenty-nine thousand days in a row
Is your complete existence for all that we know
Each ten years amount to only 3652.5
Three thousand six hundred and a little bit more
In one decade is all that you'll see
It seems so precious these few days to me
I can count that high in a few minutes' time
Whew I am here and then I know not.

Sure those days are numbered so few
And what I will say is nothing new
But the message is hard because all the stuff
That surrounds you each day and requires your must
But within the moments that make up the day
Is your entire existence in this form in this way.

❧　　　　❧　　　　❧

We were in world history class. Our teacher, Ms. Albert, was talking about the latest region currently plagued by violence. She was trying to engage us in a discussion of the history and politics surrounding the countries.

"I read in the news that there was more violence overnight. And this morning, all sides pledged to renew diplomacy talks. What do you think will come out of these new talks amid the renewed fighting and violence? Anyone?"

I kept thinking of the uselessness of the discussion. For one thing, *we* were not going to do anything about it and anyhow, for as long as anyone could remember there were always wars, if not there then somewhere else. A horribly rhythmic pattern throughout history ... the history that we had been discussing in class.

I raised my hand.

"Yes, Rayfield. What do you think about the chances of peace in the region?"

"Excuse me, Ms. Albert. I just don't know what is to become of us."

"What do you mean … *become of us*? As a result of current politics? This year? What exactly are you talking about?"

"I mean, it seems like we keep repeating the same mistakes. I question whether we'll ever figure out these problems. Will we survive?" I asked.

Lester in the back row yelled out, "Hey Ray, eventually we won't survive, eventually we'll all be gone," and began to laugh.

I turned around toward him, "I don't mean us individually …"

He called back, "No, neither do I. I mean in the large scale of the universe, we're just the blink of an eye … We, or something like us, have walked this earth for a million or so years. In the scale of billions of years, we'll be dust."

"Now, now, Lester. Let's not get all doomsday here. Rayfield has a valid question." Ms. Albert was trying to keep our discussion focused on world events.

But I savored every moment of class when we steered instruction from the boring official curriculum to one of our free-ranging, open-ended discussions. I kept up with Lester. "I guess you're right. I mean, the Sun will eventually burn up, right Ms. Albert?"

Alan, an overly studious science guy, piped up. "Exactly. The comfortable solar radiation levels that we currently have on earth are time-stamped. They have only existed and will only exist for a limited time. Our technology will only take us so far in counteracting those changes."

Lester continued, "Sure, in our lifespan that seems incredibly long. But in universal time that is trivial … so to me, the question of whether we will survive or not is moot. OF COURSE WE WON'T SURVIVE. In universal time we are doomed … Sorry to say so, Ms. Albert."

She was feeling a bit out of control. "Lester, as we've been discussing in class, there have been changes throughout human history, and changes will surely continue. But it makes no sense to speculate about events beyond our comprehension."

Lester would not budge. "I agree, Ms. Albert, that all history is change. I'm just saying that perpetuity is a long time. And if we have any chance for long-term existence, we'd better learn to travel to other worlds and adapt to changing universal conditions."

We could all feel Lester pushing Ms. Albert. This was fun.

Kali, a smart girl who always sat in the front row, jumped in. "Space travel. That's what we need. Don't you want to travel in space, Ms. Albert?"

Ms. Albert ignored Kali and tried again to address the class. "OK everyone. Let's focus. We are here to discuss world history. Can we get back to point?"

But she was fighting a losing battle. I, for one, was not giving up.

"Sorry, Ms. Albert, but this seems very important to me. We were discussing possible outcomes for the current fighting. Our study of world history makes me think that we keep repeating the same cycles of violence with different groups in different places."

"Yes, that's unfortunate, Rayfield. We seem to keep making the same mistakes. But I wouldn't write us off. We are getting better."

"We are?" I asked skeptically. "Seems like we just move from war to war, which makes me wonder what we'll leave to history. What do you think future generations will find of our remains, Ms. Albert? You must admit that Lester does have a point about us being doomed."

Ms. Albert was looking for an answer. "I imagine that our ceramics, hard rock structures as well as hardened metals would last the longest … though I'm not a materials scientist. Assuming that someone came along in the future at a time after our civilization was gone, they would find those types of remnants. Does that answer your question, Rayfield?"

"Actually, Ms. Albert, our electromagnetic wave disturbances will last longer than our building materials," Alan quickly pointed out.

Lester liked this idea. "Yeah, our television and radio shows are being beamed out into space. The electromagnetic waves from our broadcasts are traveling outward from us at the speed of light in an expanding bubble. Intelligent life in the universe will be receiving *The Simpsons* and *I Love Lucy* shows mixed in with our music and news as encoded radio waves. Right now, the shows from the 1950s are about 60 light years from earth. In one billion earth years they will be 1 billion light years from Earth. So our legacy continues."

"Great. Now we're polluting the entire universe with our entertainment crap, not just *our* planet," Kali said sarcastically. The entire class broke into laughter.

"That's right," added Alan, "a cosmic bubble of radio waves is expanding outward from earth as we speak. Only certain frequencies of radio waves can escape our atmosphere. Broadcast radio and television waves are among them. Our radio and TV shows are traveling outward at 100 light years each century. It takes about 4.3 years to reach the nearest star. So if someone near Proxima Centauri is tuning in they can catch *The Simpsons* about 4 years after we watch it here."

Well, that was it. No way Ms. Albert could bring the focus back to world history today. The class had come undone. We were thrilled.

❈   ❈   ❈

In school the bell rings and we jump from our seats
We move very fast to the next daily meet
When the bell rings at noon we stand to the beat
And hurry our butts to the cafeteria to eat
We know we have 45 minutes to be done
We wolf down our food and run out to the sun
Anytime in the air away from the walls
Is the time that we love most of all
Most of all.

❈   ❈   ❈

I had no interest in any of my classes in school. Though I definitely wanted to expand my knowledge, there was no room in my classes for general discussion. We managed to frequently disrupt the planned curriculum lessons in Ms. Albert's classes and spend time talking about things of interest. But in other classes we were not so fortunate. The hours dragged on as we discussed names and dates and places.

It seemed that the purpose of school was not necessarily to gain great knowledge. Instead, it appeared as if we were in school primarily to be socialized … to learn exactly what was necessary to become good workers. Precisely what Sal and I had vowed never to happen.

I knew that I had to get out but I was just not sure how or where to go. Actually, I was not even sure what *to get out* meant. All I knew was that I did not want to fit into the society into which I was being pushed.

My counselor said I needed to study hard and get good grades, and the world would open to me. Yeah, real open. Open to be another dummy in the car on the way to work in the morning.

Oh what the hell does it mean to be an adult? What do I need to do to *grow up*? Why was I faced with all these choices? All I wanted was to hang out with my friends and not be part of all the shit. I needed to escape somehow, somewhere. But to where and from what? I thought there must be more to life than pulling the drudge. Living life like the next box of people down the street.

❦   ❦   ❦

They say I'm good with the facts and the figures
It's all so much bullshit
It means nothing to me
To them it's like the biggest mystery
I just want to live outside of these walls
There's too much control in everything I do
I want to be free and express my creativity
I want to escape the pressures you bear
I want to know something that I can hold dear
Something from someone that sticks in my ear
Not just the facts the numbers and years.

✤   ✤   ✤

As my interest waned, my grades continued to slide. My parents were increasingly pressuring me to change my life and stop hanging out with my friends. They kept repeating that my future lay in school and were threatening to send me away to a military-like boarding school.

The more they argued with me, the more I rejected their ideas. I withdrew and spent most of my time alone or with friends. I avoided my family, and when I was with my friends we increasingly laughed about the aimless brittle lives of our parents.

I eventually stopped going to school. My parents found out that I had been skipping out and, not knowing what else to do, sent me to a psychologist. I told the psychologist my thoughts about the world of hypnotized people. He listened carefully. He was intelligent, acted like he understood my ideas and appeared to empathize with me. But the next thing I heard from my parents was that the psychologist was recommending confinement and therapy. I started making plans for my departure.

✤   ✤   ✤

Sal insisted that mental illness was a social phenomenon. He said mental illness was based upon a normal bell curve of population behavior. He maintained that anyone who strayed too far from the center of the curve was considered out of the ordinary. If you strayed far enough from the mean you were considered insane.

"Yeah Ray, think of past geniuses like Da Vinci or Galileo or Einstein. As their ideas wandered far from the norm they struggled to communicate with the people around them, and if they'd failed they could have been considered insane."

Sal was the most intelligent person I knew and I could not help thinking that he was talking about himself. Some kids at school called him crazy and some teachers were afraid of him. He was strange, but I liked that about him.

"Yeah, but they weren't," I replied, wanting to defend my best friend.

"That's not exactly true, Ray. Galileo was under house arrest for heresy. Da Vinci had his personal problems. And how about Socrates? Remember he was put to death for offering new ideas to young people."

I was starting to understand what Sal was saying, and I added, "Imagine all the people in the past who were geniuses in their time but were branded insane and imprisoned or killed or ostracized because they were far from the norm of their society."

"Yeah I know. It's scary to think you can be considered crazy simply because people don't have the tools to place what you say in context."

"Yeah," I said, "and pretty sad. It makes me wonder about my experience with the psychologist."

"I think the key is to maintain an understanding of the general ideas and accepted norms of the people around you. Perhaps if at the time you had realized the psychologist's frame of reference you might have had more success by speaking directly to his internal questioning."

"I think you're right. I pushed him to see my perspective without considering how he might understand my words."

"Yeah, the two of us love to explore and venture away from accepted ways of doing things. If we disregard or forget our roots we'll lose track of the concerns and ideas of everyone else. Though everything may appear to make sense to us, we will not understand the thoughts or actions of people who judge us because they don't understand us. So it is absolutely important to always consider the accepted notions and ideas of society."

"Even if we think they are bullshit?" I asked.

"*Especially* if we think they are bullshit. Society's nature is to protect itself. If the ideas and practices of its members move too far away from the core thinking and actions, the group cohesion breaks down. When that happens, the institutions and customs that define society's existence begin to lose force and meaning. So, for society to survive it must pull its citizens to the center and develop methods to maintain the status quo.

"There will always be elements that work to change the general picture, but for the group to survive the changes must be slow enough for a large percentage of the population to follow along."

"Sounds reasonable," I said.

"Now, it is necessary for some changes in the group … to prevent stagnation, inward implosion and to adapt to changing conditions. But from the perspective of maintaining group cohesion, changes must also come slowly without much force."

"Ah, but if I follow you, *we* represent radical change. That is why we are dangerous. That is why my psychologist wants to lock me up and modify my thinking and actions."

"Exactly, Ray. We represent a threat to the social foundations that he and our parents rely upon. We are so-called *enemies of the state*."

✻   ✻   ✻

It is pitch dark and I am alone and scared. I feel separated and withdrawn from everyone and everything I know. I have no refuge. I have no support.

I am afraid to be alive for fear that I will die. I am transient and impermanent. Nothing can help me. Nothing can save me. This is the world and here I am … nothing but a little speck inside a great, unforgiving, unknowing void.

And then there are the *others*. All around me are the *others*. Everything I do is watched by them. But I must never let them know that I know that they are there.

So I keep to myself, knowing that every minute I am being judged. I don't know for what reason. I am not sure what the consequences will be. But everything I do is under scrutiny. As far as I can tell, everyone I see and know are part of this great watch and judgment, as well as countless others whom I know nothing about at all.

But why me? What is the importance of me? Why *me* as the subject? I wonder to myself and never mention any of this to another soul.

❧   ❧   ❧

What we are lacking is what we are most
What we hold strongest is just but a ghost
What seems so solid
Disintegrates to dust
All that is special
Becomes nothing but rust
So what can I hold that keeps me right here
That allows me to live
And push back the fear?

❧   ❧   ❧

Sometime in the middle of the night I realized that I was home alone. I could not sleep and I could not remember exactly how I got there. Between bouts of screaming and ranting, it occurred to me that at the party I had been given something really strong that was messing with my mind and keeping me up. My head felt like it was bursting apart with thoughts that I could not silence or put aside. And before I knew it, I got lost again within them.

Where the fuck am I? What the fuck am I supposed to do here? Why do I keep thinking this shit? What the hell is going on?

It's all so fucking fake! I mean, off they go to school or work, pursue their meaningless bullshit, and then smile and abide by the rules and customs. They know it is bullshit. They just don't want to admit it to themselves. Thinking that would destroy too much of what they have assembled (or what has been assembled for them) of their world. Just smile and go about it. Laugh and chuckle over the situation without really admitting to or affirming what is going on.

I am going fucking crazy here! I can't seem to stay within my skull. My head is bursting with bits and pieces of useless information and I REJECT IT ALL! All I want to do is just exist and function, but I guess not really, since I see. I see. I SEE!!!!

And I can't stop seeing. I can't stop thinking. I am perplexed and confused and don't know anything. What that hell am I doing? What the hell was I thinking? Who the fuck am I? What the fuck am I supposed to do?

No, I have no fucking God. Sure I've been to church. Sure I've heard the rap. Sure I've listened. But no fucking way! Just look around you. Is it pretty? Is it nice?

What I see is death, destruction, hate and armor. Oh, yeah with a lot of pretty, pretty smiles. What does God have to do with this? Where is the Almighty Lord? Bullshit I say! Bullshit.

From where I sit, where there are people there is shit. Where there is nature there is beauty. When people overrun nature you get shit. Simple as that. Too many people, too much shit.

So what the fuck am I supposed to do? Sit around and laugh about it? Feel superior because I can see it and laugh about it?

Yeah right. Then I just look at myself and you know what I see? Shit! Fucking shit! So me fucking too! Shit. All of it shit! And what the fuck am I supposed to do? Why the fuck am I here?

Oh "Art" you say. I am here for Art. What the fuck is that? I am here to create items that display or invoke responses in people about the shit situation in which we live? Is that Art? Should I spend my time trying to manifest my vision of the shit situation to others?

Hmm ... Sounds amusing. Sounds time-consuming. Sounds compelling. Or not. Do I want to inflict my shit vision on the world or should I just remove myself and my shit? Where are we going? What is the future to me? Where is value to which I can attach beyond myself?

It must be God, then. I must be missing the point. I can climb from the shit with a vision of God. With a vision of God I can climb from the shit. Imagine that. Climbing from the shit. Shit climbing above and beyond the shit creature that I am, out of the shitpile into the sacred beyond. Imagine that.

Perhaps I can climb from the shit and produce Art about the process of climbing from the shit, or perhaps about experiences of being out of the shit. Then the people in the shit will be better able to see the path out of the shit and become shit emancipated. And we can all live and believe in the world of our God ... without the shit.

Wait, but what the fuck is all the shit in our world here for? Oh, to teach us to climb. A clever plan by God to teach us to reach out and climb. Cool. I like to climb, but how about all those poor souls who don't get to climb, who get run over by the shit? Just foot soldiers, I guess, just pawns to be disposed of while teaching us to climb.

So we are the better people, obviously. I mean, if the pawns are lost by the wayside then what the fuck? They are dispensable. Thus, we are more valuable. So then not all people are created equally since, some have just got to go. Right?

I mean, as long as I climb and cling to the right stuff then I am cool and those peons are … well, just peons. Amazing fucking world! Here we are talking about freedom and equality, and really it's all about privilege. Yeah, it all comes down to who you know.

What the fuck? Yeah right, like I'm going to climb the shit-stained staircase out of this hellhole. No thank you! I'll hang onto that which I can see and feel, touch and taste. To hell with your manmade shit. To hell with it!

Fuck the people. Love the world. Fuck the vampires. Love the girls. To hell with the blood-sucking schools and jobs. What the hell does that all amount to if you live in a world of shit?

Touch. Taste. Be fucking real. That is what is important. That is what I must do. Thank you. Thank you. Thank you. Morning is almost here.

Soon enough, I was gone. I scraped together what money I could, packed a small backpack and left in the middle of the night.

I was anxious and nervous as I walked and thumbed my way for the next day and a half through city and country. The road ended in a resort town by the ocean. I thanked my last ride, got out of the car and ran to the beach. Feeling triumphant, I threw my pack in the sand, fell into the surf and immersed myself in the waves. I had been struggling to keep myself upbeat but finally overwhelmed by my senses and emotions, I started to shiver and shake … releasing weeks of built-up tension. And I began to cry.

Emerging from my self-pity, I realized that what I really needed was a girl … a beautiful young girl with a sparkle in her eyes and an alluring *come to me* bounce in her hips. Up on the boardwalk were plenty of girls, hanging out, walking with friends, looking for something to do. So I dried myself off, stashed my pack under the pier and headed up to the boardwalk.

❦   ❦   ❦

"How are you doing?" I asked two pretty girls sitting on a bench, one of them petite with short blonde hair and the other taller with long black hair.

"Pretty good," they answered.

"Yeah, me too," I replied. "I just got here and I'm looking for something to do."

The blonde-haired girl looked me over and gave me a smile. "Well, we were just going to walk down the boardwalk and check out what's happening. You want to come along?"

"Sure," I answered. "Sounds like fun. I'm Ray. What're your names?"

"Fay," answered the girl with the long hair.

"And I'm Dina … but you can call me Dee."

"Cool. Glad to meet you."

They got up and we started walking. We joked for a while about where we lived and about the crazy scene at the beach. They were vacationing for a few days, and were looking for some fun and a break from school. We ambled and talked and I casually put my arm around Dina's shoulders. To my delight, she moved into the embrace and pressed her hip against mine.

We kept walking and talking and joking about school, parents and resort-town life. After a while, the girls saw some friends and we walked over to say hello. They were going to see a band and asked us to join them.

Dina looked at me and said, "No thanks. We'll catch up with you later. Ray and I are going for a stroll." I nodded.

❦   ❦   ❦

Dina put her arm around my waist. We walked down streets, laughing and talking. She held me tight. When we stopped by a canal to watch some seagulls, she leaned over and kissed me lightly on the lips.

I kissed her back in earnest and she responded passionately. I breathed deeply, savoring her sweet smell and gently stroked her back and hips. She kissed me again, this time opening my mouth with her tongue, teasing my tongue to follow into her mouth. She was beautiful and willing and open … as much as I could dream or hope for.

She whispered in my ear. "Hey Ray, you want to come up to my hotel room?"

"Sure, I'd love to," I answered, my heart racing.

We entered her room hand in hand. She closed the door and turned to me again with a long, wet kiss. Dina, my blonde-haired flowering beauty, was ready and waiting for me. I could hardly contain myself. She wanted my embrace and my passion. I wanted to bury myself within her, to taste her and immerse myself in her essence.

She walked across the room to the bed, turned around with her hands on her hips and flashed a big, seductive smile. Her wide-open eyes were saying *I am an animal. I want to play. Come to me now.*

At that time I knew nothing of the crazy events that made up my life. I knew nothing of fucked-up politics. I knew nothing of war and hate. I knew nothing of parents and school. All I knew, all I wanted to know in the entire world, was this sweet goddess of the feminine … this beautiful girl whom I was so intensely enjoying. I sought her most intimate self and bathed myself in her abandon as we writhed and moaned in our passion.

Yes, I am flesh and she is flesh. But together we traveled beyond the flesh of our bodies. We lost ourselves completely in the present. We knew nothing other than our immediate coupling. We abandoned ourselves to our animal desires … and those desires exploded into our psyches as feelings and thoughts flashed back and forth between us.

ur ordinary selves. We were fucking God. We were God fucking. She gave me her most intimate self and I filled her with mine. For that time, for that moment, we were not the lonely ones. We tasted the power and became the life force of the world.

❋   ❋   ❋

Male and female
Female and male
Differences and similarities
I know what I want and that's what you've got
It's sleek and sexy and exudes what you are
It's so animal and arousing
It takes my breath away.

You've got what I need and it's all hot and sweaty
You know what I want and you tease me to get it
When we're coming like light in the night in the storm
All I once knew is completely forlorn
At that time in my life
There's nothing else there
At that time in my life
I know not a care
At that time in my life
When just you and me
Know one another as deeply as can be
I dissolve all remembrance
I lose track of time
And all that I know is utterly sublime.

❋   ❋   ❋

Dee and I stuck together after that. We went everywhere as a couple. When Dee's friends were getting ready to head back home, she told them that she was staying with me. We were not sure what we were going to do. We were in love and did not want to part. Dee had enough problems at home and had no desire to return. We had little money, no place to stay and no plans. We just wanted our time together to never end. Fuck the rest of the world.

So for the next couple of days, we spent our afternoons lying in the sun, our evenings strolling through the crowds on the boardwalk, and our nights in bliss hidden somewhere in the dunes, away from the rest of the world. Life was good, but not bound to stay that way.

One night, while lying in my angel's arms in the sand, I woke up in a sweat and trembling with fear. I remembered the dream as my consciousness began to return.

> *I was swimming in the ocean and the current was very strong. The waves kept increasing and I had to fight harder and harder to keep away from the coral reef below. As the waves swelled they lifted me up high toward shore, then without warning dropped me down to within inches of the razor-sharp coral.*
>
> *I kept struggling to swim back toward the channel in the reef but several times I was thrown around in the turbulence and scraped against the coral. Blood started to mix with the water around my legs and arms. Sensing imminent danger, I swam like a madman toward the deep channel. After a long struggle, gulping water and gasping for air, I finally made it to the channel and let the waves wash me through back into the tranquil waters behind the reef. I started to relax from the effort and turned to look back at the channel. I could see a shark racing towards me. I tried to run the final few meters to shore but it caught up with me just before I could get out of the water. To save myself, I struggled to wake up.*

The next night while we were sleeping in the dunes I woke up to the sound of a vehicle driving toward us. As I opened my eyes, I could see searchlights moving in our direction.

"Hey Dee! Wake up. We have visitors."

"What the hell is going on, Ray?"

"Get up! There's a machine coming at us!"

"What? What the hell?"

"Dee! That's what I'm saying. Get up quickly!"

The searchlight focused on us and a voice boomed out over a speaker, "Hey you two. Stay right where you are. This is the police!"

"The fucking cops. They're going to take us away," I moaned.

"Alright you two. It's illegal to sleep on the beach. Put your hands on your heads and walk toward me!"

Dee exclaimed, "Fuck I hate the cops. Always here at just the wrong time. What fucking luck."

"Don't worry, Dee. I love you babe."

"I love you too, Ray."

"Put your hands on the roof of the car. Spread your legs. That's right. Damn, you two are just kids. What are you doing out here?"

I answered, "We're just trying to get some rest. We didn't realize that we were breaking the law. We mean no harm."

"I bet you don't. Let me see some ID."

"I don't have any."

"Neither do I," echoed Dee.

"Oh, a couple of runaways, huh?"

"No! We're not runaways!" we both yelled emphatically.

"How old are you, son?"

"Eighteen."

"And you, honey?"

"I'm also eighteen," Dee replied.

"Yeah right, and I'm 21," he laughed. "OK you two. Hands out. I really hate to do this but …" he cuffed us, "into the car!"

We sat quietly in the back seat of the jeep as he drove off the beach and down the street. He stopped by the side door of the police station. As we pulled up, another officer came out.

"Ok buddy. You get out here. Your girlfriend is going with me down to Central."

He grabbed me, took me inside and locked me in a small dirty cell in the back of the police station. The bed was covered in vomit and the floor stunk of urine.

I yelled out, "Hey you call this a fucking jail? You guys are pussies. You think you can keep me here? Fuck you! Throw *me* in this cell full of puke."

My tirade and the following tirades through the night just brought laughs from the other room. In the morning when they came to transfer me to another jail, they couldn't open the cell. I had jammed the lock trying to pick it open during the night. It took another hour and a half to clear the lock and get me out. They were not happy when I left.

🍁   🍁   🍁

I want to exist alive and alone
I remove myself from society and go out as one
I wander around in this park of my mind
I'm thinking and thinking and trying to find time
But no matter wherever I rant and I roam
I am still sitting alone on this god-fucking throne

This throne where I sit is different from none
It just allows me to see the light of the sun.

I know I am more than something alone
I know that I exist without any damn throne
I know that I am mad and yelling about
All those things mundane that we can't do without.

❦   ❦   ❦

From single cell to cellblock. I was now in a large room with a dozen other inmates. Some were serving time for petty drugs, some for stealing cars, others for robbery and violent crimes. I fit right in. The one thing I had going for me was my ability to talk. And talk we did … about all kinds of subversive activities. Seems that the jail was filled with subversives—like me, arrested for vagrancy.

One day I was talking with Ryan, a cellmate who was locked up for destruction of government property. Ryan had been in and out of jail for the past five years, mostly on charges of disorderly conduct and insubordination. I was finding out that Ryan was a rebel against every and all forms of authority. He was not sorry or apologetic about any of the crimes of which he was accused.

I asked him, "Do you blame anyone for your place in this jail?"

"Hey, you know I realize that I have brought this all on myself … and I'm proud of it. I blame no one except myself."

I laughed. "Well, my fucking parents told the judge that I was incorrigible and they refused to get me out of jail, so these stupid police are keeping me here until they figure out what to do with me. All for fucking sleeping on the beach without ID. Bullshit!"

He continued, "I knew each step of the way that I was slipping outside the laws of society. I grinned in the thrill of being there and relished the sheer denunciation of the bullshit. To consciously act in such a way as to defy those whom you view as ignorant, hypocritical, self-appreciating buffoons is a great act of freedom. You should try it sometime."

"Yeah, I kind of do already. There is just so much bullshit."

"More power to you, Ray. More power to you."

"Thanks, man. I appreciate that," I said.

"And to express an idea and perform an action that directly annoys and aggrieves those idiots is an even greater delight. To freely act in defiance of useless rule-mongers excites the body and liberates the soul."

"Ryan, that is just what I need ... to excite my body and liberate my soul, standing up to the fucking useless rule-mongers."

"Right on, Ray. Breaking the bonds of civilized training brought me to a new understanding of what it really means to be human. We are more than that which is contained within the bounds of our culture. Breaking outside the rules of our society makes us truly human.

"Our culture wants to keep order and sustain itself. People existing too far beyond the bounds are detrimental to its very existence. So our society attempts to purge the outer fringes, but the bounds vary considerably among cultures."

I mused, "So in other cultures, maybe we might not be sitting in jail right now?"

"Exactly."

❦   ❦   ❦

Eventually I was moved out of the jail to a state-run facility for problem boys. I was placed into a single locked room with one other resident. Sam had gotten in trouble for leaving home and stealing cars. He was a funny guy full of jokes, with no respect for authority.

During the day we had school, psychological testing and group training. I figured that since we had failed high school socialization, we were now undergoing remedial training. Here you either advanced or you were labeled dead-end with no chance of release. I figured that with our joking and bad attitude there was no chance for Sam or me to successfully complete the training.

Every appointment I had with the staff psychologist or psychiatrist seemed to end badly. One day, a particularly difficult session ended up in an argument about statistics and normal behavior.

"So, Rayfield, I hear that you have been having problems with your group therapy and religious studies."

"Yes. I guess I have."

"Can you tell me about your difficulties?"

"Sure. Those people are trying to push me to be someone that I don't want to be."

"Really. In what way is this happening, Rayfield?"

"First of all, I don't believe or practice any of the religions that they discuss."

"Well, what is your religion?"

"Presently, I don't have a religion. God has never helped out my friends or me and it seems that the world is filled with violence and hate. So of what purpose is God?"

"It is very difficult to see the works of God. That doesn't mean that God does not exist."

"Well for me the issue is irrelevant. I pay attention to things I can experience and if I cannot see the work of God, I pay him/her/it no mind."

"Rayfield, you're here because of your disregard for authority. You did not listen to your parents, your school or your religion. We are very concerned about you and the values you are developing in your life. We're here to help you."

"I have experienced school, home life and religion, and none hold a place for me."

"We are trying to help you become a productive member of society. Society is governed by rules and traditions. You seem to be rejecting them all. And my past experience with similar residents shows me that unless you begin to play by the rules and improve your social behavior, you are heading on a path to criminality. This is strongly supported by statistics developed from intensive follow-up studies."

"I don't care about your statistics. They are just predictors and don't define anything. All your statistics are based upon "*normal*" behavior in our society. And I reject much of the behavior of our society. I don't want to be normal."

"You may think what you want, but our research indicates that criminal life will be the outcome."

"You mean most of the time?"

"Yes, our research indicates that when a resident fails our behavioral benchmarks for family relationships, education and religion, then about nine times out of ten they end up in prison as an adult. This is not my opinion. This is fact."

"I don't care about your facts. I'll break the statistical rules and show that you're wrong."

"Rayfield, you are not helping your case for an early release. We need to see progress in your activities."

"Sorry. I do what I can."

"Ok. How about group therapy? I have reports that you're always trying to disrupt the group and move the discussion away from therapy."

"Yeah, it's pretty boring, so I try to talk about things that are interesting."

"You mean interesting to you?"

"Yes."

He looked me squarely in the eyes and said in a stern voice, "Group therapy is for the *group*. You are being disrespectful and belligerent when you work against your therapist. You are not being fair to the other residents who need and want the therapy."

"It's bullshit. You're trying to make some percentage of the group follow your ideas of accepted behavior. How about the others who don't fit in? I won't oblige to become one of your statistics. I am an independent person."

He looked at me over his glasses even more sternly. "If that suits you. But you're just digging yourself a hole. All avenues out of this facility require you to participate and to develop more positive attitudes about society. We are trying to make you a home within normal society so that you don't spend your life in confinement," and he turned away.

"I am *not* going to be bound by your statistics. I don't care if they say I have a 60% chance of succeeding or a 75% probability of committing a crime. It's all just prediction. I am *not* bound by the fact that most people fail at the things that I want to do. I have the ability to do many things differently than what you predict based on patterns in the past. I will break out of those patterns. I will not be defined by them."

"Rayfield, predictive statistics are developed via analyses of collected data. They attempt to give probabilities to future events or trends. They are not definitive."

"I have studied statistics and I know what they're about. I don't trust statistics or statisticians. There are many ways you can view data. Statisticians play with numbers and groupings to get results that they want to see. They choose the view that yields the desired conclusion and only report statistics that support their theories."

"I think you're being cynical. I also think that your views are not very broad. You seem to be using statistics as a motivation for your errant social behavior."

"Statistics are not a motivator for me. My only motivation is to not become stuck by your predictions. Anything is possible."

"Rayfield, you are taking a personal approach to this. There are many good and valid uses for statistics. They work very well as predictors for general populations. Scientists use them all the time in research and studies."

"Well, that may be so for studying general trends. But you are building cages when you use them to tell people how to live. Statistically, the strongest tendency is toward the middle of the group. If people use statistical trends to shape their decisions they will generally only allow and accept behaviors that support the middle ground. This tends to limit extreme behavior and maintain the status quo." I paused and looked over to him. He looked incredulous. I continued anyway.

"And besides, when you tell me that I have a 70% or whatever chance of becoming a certain person, that does not consider me, my interests or my background … only general trends. That's bullshit. Maybe I'm more suited to be otherwise. I *can* and *will be* different in my reactions to situations, different from what you've observed and predicted."

As I was finishing my anti-statistics rant to the psychiatrist, I realized the depth of the hole that I was digging. If he didn't think me anti-social before, I was sure that he now did. So I figured at this point it really didn't matter how absurd this sounded to him anyway.

He responded as if he was answering the question I was thinking. "And I do believe that the reason you are in this facility is because of your extreme behavior. So if I were you, I would be thinking about how to get into the middle of the spectrum of accepted behavior. Your constant striving to be different is preventing you from moving forward."

I couldn't contain myself. "But extreme behaviors are what move us to do new and different things and to expand beyond our capabilities. If we don't expand, we stagnate." I thought perhaps he might see things my way.

"That's all for now, Rayfield. I do want to see progress in your group therapy. And I want you to consider what type of future you want to live. It's your choice. You definitely are smart enough to make the right choices to get yourself out of this mess."

I said goodbye and shut the door. As I was walking down the corridor, I kept thinking how it was necessary to break the statistical boundaries in order to keep growing and moving. I vowed to myself to be something beyond what was predicted for me. I believe in free will. I will not be defined. I will be an unpredictable abhorrence.

✢   ✢   ✢

Sam and I continued to plan our escape. Sam wanted out as badly as me. He had a girlfriend that he was missing and some buddies ready to move with him across the country.

Every day we were allowed outside with supervision in an exercise area for about 30 minutes. The L-shaped field was surrounded by an 8-foot-high chain link fence topped with three tight strands of barbed wire angled towards the inside. At the far end of the field, the fence turned and ran directly back to the building. It attached to the wall just around the building corner, creating a very small area that was not visible from the main exercise field.

One day out in the exercise area, a skirmish between two residents got everyone's attention. We took our chance and quickly slipped around the building corner. I wedged myself between the brick wall and the fence and, leaning back against the wall, wiggled my body and walked my feet up the fence. I pushed hard against the wall and continued working my feet higher until they were on the top of the barbed wire. Forcing my back against the wall, I pushed hard one more time and lifted my lower body up onto the barbed wire. Once on top I rolled over, pushed away and dropped to the ground.

On the other side I turned back to Sam. "Let's go! Hurry up. You can do it."

Sam followed my example, rolled over the barbed wire and dropped to the ground. "We did it, Ray. Let's get the hell out of here!"

Over the fence and into our freedom. Hearts pounding, we walked and ran through the streets, always looking over our shoulders for the police. About an hour later in a busy commercial district, we quickly blended with the crowd. A phone call later and we were cruising the streets in my buddy's car.

✤   ✤   ✤

Know what now will ever bring
Is fated for human wondering
Know what fate does cleverly hold

Just seek the present and be bold
Just one bite is way too much
You can never have what you can't touch
You can never be what isn't done
You can never see the unlighted Sun
I can never feel the pain
Of restricted access in my brain
I can never sense what's not
Part of all of what I've got
I can never tell what's true
So all I do is release you.

❧   ❧   ❧

While telling his tale, Ray got increasingly excited … pacing the floor, gesturing with his arms, raising his voice for emphasis. By the time he finished he was moving rapidly around the room, yelling and waving his arms in the air.

Now that he had finished, he walked over and collapsed backward onto his bench. After a moment he leaned forward, hung his head between his legs, and began shaking it back and forth as if to deny what he had said.

Karyn watched him closely. "Are you alright Ray? I know that was hard."

"I'm fine. Fine. I'm just thinking. Give me a minute. Really, I'm OK."

Everyone was quiet.

"Hey Ray, it's alright," said Raz. "I've been through a lot of shit myself. It's nobody's business what you do with your life. Don't let them get you down."

"Of course not," echoed Lana, "and it shows that you're strong when you refuse to fall in line. It's nothing to feel bad about."

Ray looked up at Lana. There were tears running down his cheeks. "I've just been trying to get away from them all pulling and pushing on me. I don't know what I want but I don't want to be what *they* want me to be."

"Ray," Lorraine called sharply, and she looked at him until they locked eyes, then continued in a soothing voice, "we're all searching. We're all looking for something to make us whole. Same for me and same for you." She nodded and smiled gently.

Ray shook his head, "I just feel like I've got to keep moving. Like I've got to keep from crystallizing into something … into anything at all. I refuse to make the same mistakes over and over again."

"I respect you, Ray," offered Karyn.

"You respect *me*?" he asked in disbelief.

"Yes, Ray. I respect your determination to not be caught by the bullshit around you … something that I'm not always so good at."

"It's a tough battle, Ray," said Cibi. "Always watch for opportunities and don't become predictable. Don't let people define you as the one who always tries to not be defined."

Lorraine nodded. "We're all lost souls just trying to find our home. You're like everyone else Ray, as much as you fight against that fact."

Lana offered, "You know, Raz and I tried like hell to get away from who we were and what people wanted from us."

Raz added, "But we couldn't."

Ray looked up. "You couldn't? Why not?"

"Because we realized that we weren't free," answered Lana.

"What do mean you *weren't free*?" asked Cibi.

"Eventually we realized that we couldn't avoid our history. We're not born free. We come into this world with the weight of the past."

"Fuck history!" snapped Ray. "I won't be defined. I won't be confined."

Lana looked sternly at Ray. "Try as you might, you can't deny it, Ray. It will always catch up with you. Your family, your home, the land you come from, all have circumstances and history. And you inherit those circumstances and that history when you are born."

"Let me tell you a story, Ray," said Raz.

CHAPTER 4

As One

As the light of day emerges
The hardness of what's been and known
Begins to crumble beneath me
I strive to hold the rising day
But I find myself asking
What life before
What life again
A puzzling piece
A speck of dust
A dazzling burnout
On this planet of rust?

As we tumble from high and rise again
We grasp at our own reflection
In the works that we create
We know our own insignificance
Yet are blinded by our light
We look without and we look within
But all we find is Mind
And Mind is what we Matter.

❦   ❦   ❦

Lana and I were young lovers with a passion for travel. We had been on the road for six months since leaving our home and jobs. We departed our world of tradition and comfort, and took to wandering without any clear idea where we were going. We just wanted to get away from the daily routines that were pulling us into the complacent ways of our friends and families. We had seen too many of our friends, wise with ambitions and ideals, pulled by social, economic and familial obligations into the same small-town values and habits that they had previously so vehemently rejected.

We traveled without specific destinations or schedules. We traveled with little money. All our belongings were in our backpacks: some clothes, a few personal items, sleeping bags, a tent, a small stove, cooking gear, and usually enough food and water for several days. We were able to go anywhere and everywhere we wanted, and we traveled to the city, the mountains, the desert and the ocean. Every morning we woke up feeling vibrant and free.

Occasionally we would stop and work for a day or two to get more cash and supplies. We had few fears and no restrictions. We were as alive as the wind. But as the wind can change at any time, we held no expectations. Without fixed plans we adapted easily.

Using our thumbs as flags, we often traveled by the grace of others driving in our chosen direction. Each day brought new people, places and ideas. Sometimes, if we liked the people we met, we traveled or stayed with them for a while. Then when the notion struck, we departed and went in our own direction. We were ambassadors of life exchanging ideas, hopes, revelations and sometimes fears with people along the way.

But as freedom goes, you get the good with the bad. We had little control of whom we met, where we went and where we stayed. Sometimes we found ourselves in scary situations with people on edge … bothered by unknown problems and occasionally over-spilling with pent-up anger.

Though vulnerable, we tried to always be respectful of other people's positions and places. Who were we to judge without knowing histories and circumstances? We tried to relate about basic human issues with everyone we met ... sometimes for our own defense.

Most people treated us well and we strived to see things from each person's point of view. We talked about things of mutual interest and tried not to confront people, their ideas or sensibilities.

As we followed our course of unknown travels, destinations and circumstances, we felt like we were standing unfettered in the karmic wind. Is there retribution for our past actions? If you take advantage of people and situations, do the effects of those actions re-enter your life? Does this possibly extend through multiple incarnations? Even though we may think we are unattached and free, are we affected by the repercussions from past events?

True or not, we were without a windbreak. No deflections. No secure environment to protect us. We stood by the side of the road, not knowing who would stop or what baggage they might carry. Whatever life brought, we tried to accept and make the best of it. And we really enjoyed letting the winds of karma swirl around us.

And so came the Leather Man.

❈   ❈   ❈

We were thumbing a ride through the desert on a hot and dusty day. It had been hours, with sparse traffic and no car slowing down or stopping. The heat was getting oppressive and there was no shade to be found. As we looked down the long open road into the distance, the mirage suddenly opened and a car appeared ... moving in our direction.

"Hey Lana. Check it out. There's a car coming!"

"Yeah I see it. Look cool and relaxed. No one wants to pick up a couple of hot and bothered, stressed-out migrants," she quipped.

Sure enough, within a minute or so we could see a late-model luxury sedan slowly moving toward us. We stood at attention along the side of the road, stuck our thumbs in the air and tried to put on big smiles. The car slowed as it approached and we could see the driver checking us out. He passed us then pulled over and stopped a short distance away.

"Yeah, man," I yelled, "let's get the fuck out of here."

We grabbed our packs and ran toward the car. I walked up to the passenger window. The driver lowered the window and I could see a good-looking, tall, muscular man at the wheel. He was unshaven and alone.

"Where you guys headed?" he asked.

Lana answered, "Out of this desert heat into the mountains."

"Yeah, it is kind of hot out there. Throw your bags in the trunk and hop on in."

Lana sat in the front seat and I got in the rear. He looked closely at Lana as she sat down, and then turned around to look at me.

"Cool, thanks for the ride, man," Lana chirped.

"No problem," he answered and then was silent.

"Hey, well, good to meet you. My name is Lana and my friend is Raz."

He gave no response, so Lana continued, "What's your name?"

He turned to look at her. "Does it really matter?"

"I guess not," Lana answered, a bit sheepishly.

He started up, driving kind of slowly at first, but then he soon began to pick up the pace. Within a few minutes we were screaming down the road at high speed. I looked around the car more carefully. The entire inside of the car was brown leather. There was a leather teddy bear on the back seat next to me. I also noticed that Leather Man (as we took to calling him) was wearing leather boots, pants, shirt, hat and gloves. And next to him in the door pouch was a big hunting knife in a leather sheath.

His gloves had Velcro straps and as he was driving he repeatedly opened and closed the straps. I was beginning to feel a bit uncomfortable, so I tried to make conversation.

"You been here before?"

He looked at me sternly in the rear-view mirror. "I have not stepped foot on this hallowed ground, but I know it well."

I was not sure how to answer, and my unease in his company was growing.

Lana, sensing the discomfort, picked up, "We're also just passing through."

"We are all just passing through, dear. This land does not belong to us."

"Of course not," I answered, and once again we fell into silence.

We drove for a couple of hours, and then he slowed down and began to turn off onto a small dirt road.

"Hey where are we going?" I asked in alarm.

"I am stopping for a little rest." He pulled over to the side of the dirt road, stopped the car, turned it off, put the keys in his pocket and got out. "Are you two going to stay in the car? This is a good place to stretch your bones."

Lana and I looked at each other nervously and slowly got out of the car.

Leather Man once again eyed us up and down. "So, who are you people and what brings you around here?"

Lana slowly answered in a low voice, "We're just traveling … and have been on the road for 6 months. Just trying to learn about people and living."

"Good plan. Have you learned anything?"

"What do you mean?" asked Lana.

He raised his voice. "Have you learned about who you really are and how you are a part of all this?" waving his arm to include the desert around us and the distant mountains.

She hesitated and looked toward the mountains. "Well, we're trying to figure out what to do with our lives. We didn't want to stay in our hometown, so we're out taking a look around."

He softened a bit. "To figure things out you have to know yourself. You are the observer in your world and all things that you see are colored by your preconceived notions, wants and needs. It is hard to see that which is around you clearly without knowing about you, the seer."

"I think I understand you," Lana answered in a faint voice.

Then he turned to me. "To be clear, I am not some kind of psychological or physiological expert. I am simply a living person and all people share a basic nature. I can talk to you about that basic nature because it is within me. I need only look in an unbiased way toward myself ... as a human."

"But if what you see is colored by what you already think, how can you take an unbiased look at your ... at *our* basic nature?" I was a little afraid to voice my opinion but his words strongly drew my interest.

He fixed his powerful gaze on me. "You must remove the observer in yourself and become the action of observing. By removing the observer, you can approach the nature of the moment. However, if you try too hard to accomplish this, your own effort can be an obstacle to your goal. It requires fine balancing to not get in the way of experiencing the un-self moment."

This puzzled me and apparently Lana as well. She asked, "We are looking for knowledge and what you are saying sounds reasonable, but how do you propose for me to *remove the observer* when I am looking at something ... so that I can look without bias?"

"There are many ways. I like to engage in an activity so fully that I lose my sense of self during the intense concentration. At those times, my internal self-oriented thoughts are turned off and my awareness is fully in the present moment."

"Like what kind of activity?" asked Lana, a bit puzzled.

"Anything that requires total self-absorption to the point that nothing stands between you and the world ... when you are so actively engaged in what you are doing that you are not thinking about anything else. Not that you are unconscious, but rather *very* aware of what you are doing and what is going on in relation to what you are doing. It could be sharpening your knife or skinning a deer or sitting in meditation or chopping wood. The activity does not matter. What matters is your total absorption in the activity."

Lana nodded and the puzzled look on her face faded a little. "Aaah … I think I follow you. Most of the time we are thinking and reacting to the world around us, and our thoughts and ideas distract us from seeing what is really there. Right?"

Leather Man smiled. "Exactly. When you are not in a critical frame of mind you can be totally absorbed. This is precisely when you experience yourself in the world without your discerning awareness."

"And during those times we can see our basic nature?" I asked.

"During those times you are experiencing a window into our basic nature. You must explore that on your own. I am just saying that the opportunity is there."

"So what do *you* think is our basic nature?" asked Lana.

"Well, to understand that you must know and appreciate your past."

"My past?" echoed Lana.

"Yes. You do not exist in a vacuum. Your ability to stand here is dependent on many things prior to this moment."

I ventured, "You mean like us hitching a ride with you?"

"Sure, that for one. Also, your mother caring for you as a baby. Your father meeting your mother. Your family coming to this country. The efforts of your country to control and populate the land. And though you may not want to think about it, the destruction of the native people who lived here before this land was conquered and colonized."

Lana was incredulous. "What? Native people? Dependent on them? I'm not a native!"

"They got a bad deal. It is only by lying, cheating, killing and stealing that this country was colonized. The natives did not willingly give it up. This was their home for thousands of years before it was stolen from them," insisted Leather Man.

"Wait a minute," I said, "don't you think that the colonizers were fated to take the land since they were the more highly developed civilization? Don't you believe in the march of progress?"

"No, I do not believe that this destruction occurred because of fate or natural progression. I think these lands were stolen simply because of their value. The thieves may have believed that they were acting in the name of their God and that the natives were less human or more savage. This may have provided them and their allies some justification for the killing, slavery and torture they inflicted. But I see no divine providence. They took what they wanted because they were arrogant and had better weapons."

I disagreed, and said, "But the colonizers had more developed technology than the natives. Isn't that proof of their superiority?"

Leather Man was getting excited. "Hell no! Just because you have more highly developed weapons than I do doesn't mean you are necessarily better or more advanced. In fact, you may be less advanced if you need to resort to highly technical devices to assert yourself. Perhaps the natives never had those weapons because they had no need for them. Perhaps they had developed ways of living that did not require advanced technology."

"So you're saying that this history is part of us now?" I asked.

Leather Man nodded. "Well think about it. We are standing on stolen lands. Living in houses on stolen lands. Drinking water and growing crops from stolen lands ... and we have hardly acknowledged the results of our deeds. We have condemned the natives to tiny isolated reservations with little natural resources for sustenance. We have forced our culture upon them and made them abandon their traditional ways."

Lana ventured, "But our culture has so many problems and threats that it makes me wonder what is our supposed superiority. Look how we're changing these lands into industrial wastelands, denuded forests and contaminated waters."

"Exactly. The natives did exist favorably with the natural world. There was a balance of Earth and humans that our modern society cannot seem to comprehend," Leather Man said sadly.

I asked, "So do you think that technology draws us into bad relationships with the natural world?"

"Advanced technology can surely separate its users from nature. Think of the difference between driving a car across this land versus traveling on foot or horseback. Traveling by car makes you an observer and isolates you from the natural world, rather than bringing you closer."

"Alright," said Lana, "but I can't believe that we need to abandon all our technology to become closer with the natural world. I think the problem lies in accepting all technology simply because it exists, rather than selecting what is best for people and the world."

"Agreed," he answered, "but there is a type of arrogance inherent in technological societies that makes it hard for entities outside of the sphere of technology to be heard or understood. The natural world becomes secondary to society's desire for domination and comfort."

Lana asked, "So do we owe something to the native people? Should we feel responsible for what has been done?"

I answered defensively, "Well *we* personally did not do anything."

Leather Man looked at me sternly. "Maybe not. But we do exist upon their blood and bones."

He paused for us to consider his words, and then continued. "If they had not been forcefully evicted from their lands we would not be standing here and we would not be living in such comfort. We can ignore our debt as our ancestors have done, or we can take responsibility for the actions of the past and seek to provide redress for the descendents of those suffering from the deeds of our ancestors."

"OK, I can agree that we may have some responsibility, but we are not guilty," I stammered.

"You are guilty as long as you do not stand up to your responsibility. You cannot change the actions of your ancestors but you can work to change the results of those actions. And if you do not then you are guilty."

"Great, that makes me feel wonderful," moaned Lana. "And how about the slaves that were used to build the country? Are we also responsible for the actions of the slave traders and slave owners?"

In a weary and saddened tone he continued, "Once again, we would not be living in the same style and manner had part of our society and culture not been built on the backs of slaves. So, for the same reasons we are responsible for those horrific deeds. And if you do not accept your responsibility as a beneficiary of that horror and act upon it, then once again you are guilty."

"Boy, we sure are not born into this world free and unencumbered, are we?" asked Lana to no one in particular.

"No, we are born into a milieu with given conditions and with actions and reactions to which we are compelled to respond. Have you two ever heard of karma?"

I answered, "Yes, as I understand it some believe that we are not totally free … that the results of our actions follow us, and eventually we must face those consequences and deal with the actions that have contributed to our present condition. Karma is thought to be the weight of our deeds affecting our current lives."

"Yes," said Lana, "and some also believe that karma stays with you from life to life as you are reincarnated, time and again."

"Good. That is a strong concept and a good starting point for you to understand the responsibility that we carry with us for the slavery and killings of the past. It is our karma, and for us to move beyond that karmic relationship we must first accept it and then perform actions to mitigate the events of the past."

With that, Leather Man smiled briefly and walked back toward his car. He opened the trunk, removed our bags and placed them on the ground. He turned to us one last time. "I am leaving," he said. "I am leaving you on these reservation lands. Here you will learn."

Without looking back, he got in his car and drove down the dirt road to the empty highway. We stood in silence and watched the car move off slowly into the distance as the sun set behind us.

❦   ❦   ❦

Is it yours to give away
Talk to my mother
Talk to my father
Talk to my grandparents
They are all around
When you speak to me
You speak to them.

Don't tell me that nothing you've done
Has ever occurred before
You build up your wisdom by stepping on graves
But the memories are lasting
Their impact lives on
Though you cannot dream them
And no one can speak them
Every stake that you drive
And the earth as you strive
To hold and to plunder
To make spoils for all
Is a stake in the heart
And your doom to your fall.

OK laugh at the nonsense
Brush it aside
But you will only walk as far
As the weight that surrounds allows you to go
If the weight is not noticed and the burden not told
You'll still carry the baggage
You'll carry for all
And you will come down
As the buildings do fall
You will see clearly that nothing you do

Can outshine history's unmaking
Of balance and form
That exists quite apart and alive from your norm.

So consider that all that you do and perform
Is balanced by all that you did to conform
Is balanced by all that was given to you
Is balanced by all that was taken away
Is balanced by all the bloodshed and hate.

Step to your maker
Dance your great dance
At some point you will realize
Just how deep is your trance
Just how long you have strung out
The punishment time
How you have sidestepped the boundaries
And outpaced the scorn
But some day you will die
And some day they will say
That all that he did was undone in a day.

❧   ❧   ❧

One night after a long day of travel, Raz and I found ourselves on the outskirts of a small city, looking for a place to spend the night. We could find no trees, ravines, parks or other sheltered places to make our bed in privacy. As we wandered in the darkness we noticed some buildings out on the edge of development. There were no lights on the streets or in the buildings so it looked like we might find a safe place to camp.

We walked along deserted streets of empty buildings and broken glass. In the darkness we could hear rats scuttling away as we approached. On the far side of an empty expanse of rusting train tracks we spotted a solitary, crumbling, two-story brick building. Every window was busted out, part of the roof was falling in, and on one side there was a huge hole in the first-floor wall.

When we arrived at the building Raz announced, "Well, I guess this is home for the night. Just walk in through this hole in the wall."

The inside floor was a mass of broken bricks, glass and wood.

"Anybody home? Anyone here?" I called out.

No answer. Just more rustling sounds somewhere above on the second floor.

"Probably just rats," I mused.

"Yeah, rats. Let's go upstairs and see if there's someplace a bit more comfortable," suggested Raz.

The stairs were covered with bits of plaster and other debris. I took out my flashlight and walked upstairs.

Looking around, I yelled to Raz, "Hey it's much nicer up here. At least there are four walls and a bunch of rooms. Check out this one back in the corner."

Raz followed me into the room. "Yeah, babe. This is pretty cool. An old mattress. A desk. A ratty sofa. I could get comfortable in a place like this."

❧   ❧   ❧

In the morning I was awakened by a cacophony of pigeons. Apparently, the birds liked the roof and attic of this old building as much as we did. Most likely the pigeons had been the source of the rustling sounds we'd heard above our heads during the night. I was glad that it had not been rats.

Raz woke up as I zipped away my sleeping bag. He quickly got up and stuffed his bag and blanket into his pack. We grabbed our backpacks and walked outside into the chilly morning air. Across the railroad tracks, we could see the hustle and bustle of town. In the opposite direction there was a trail leading away from the tracks into the desert. It disappeared into a hidden ravine where smoke was rising.

We followed the trail down the ravine among scrubby bushes and trash scattered on the ground. We rounded a bend in the trail and suddenly we were standing in the middle of a well-used campsite. An older-looking man with thick bushy gray hair, a woman in her thirties with ruddy cheeks and short brown hair, a muscular-looking man with a full beard and shaved head, and a thin young man with a long ponytail were sitting around drinking coffee. A pot of water was hanging over a small fire, boiling away.

"Hey, how's it going?" I said in greeting.

"Fine. What are you two up to?" asked the woman.

"Oh, we spent the night in that old building by the train tracks."

"The old palace," muttered the older man.

"Yeah. It wasn't too bad. But there were a lot of pigeons," Raz replied.

"That's why we call it the Pigeon Palace," laughed the young man. This got a good laugh from the others as well.

"You guys want some coffee?" asked the older man.

We both answered, "Please!"

"You got cups?"

Raz and I each pulled a cup out of our packs and he filled them both with hot steaming coffee.

We took seats on the rocks surrounding the fire pit.

They introduced themselves as Hank, the older man, Phyllis, Ergo, the man with the shaved head, and Beal with the ponytail.

"You guys doing OK today?" asked Raz.

Ergo answered, "A little stiff this morning. I slept under the bridge and got woken up by a bunch of coyotes."

I perked up. "Coyotes? I love coyotes. They're misfits … very cool."

"Yeah, I heard something and woke up, and there was a circle of them around me."

"No shit," said Raz.

"Yeah. I tried to pet one of them but they ran away."

"I don't think they like people touching them," I said.

"No doubt," answered Phyllis. "So what brings the two of you to our camp this morning?"

"We're traveling," I answered, "been on the road for seven months. We were looking for a place to crash last night and found the palace."

"Cool. Been anywhere interesting?"

"Most everywhere is interesting," answered Raz.

"Boring or interesting, I guess," mused Beal.

"It's how you look at it," responded Raz.

Ergo slowly got up to pour himself another cup of coffee. He moved hesitantly as if to avoid hurting himself. "Ooh ... the pain. My damn back is killing me."

"You need to get some help with that," Phyllis said a bit wearily.

"I've told him that he can make his back better. He's stiff like a board because he doesn't take care of himself," insisted Hank.

"I know. I know. Go toward the pain. You keep telling me," Ergo replied in a slightly mocking voice.

"Exactly. Don't shy away from it. Keep pushing and stretching in the direction of the pain and it will recede. Find the limits and exceed them by just a little. You will never get better if you don't actively work on making yourself better. The best exercise for your aching back is walking."

"But it hurts so damn much!"

"It takes effort and pain to heal. Our bodies are constructed to stand upright and when walking, we strengthen and teach all our muscles their natural motion."

"As they say, *No pain, no gain,*" chuckled Phyllis.

"You keep telling me this about my pain. But why should I listen to you? What makes you the expert, anyway?" growled Ergo.

Hank shrugged. "Hey, do what you will. Millions of years of knowledge about survival live within us. My advice comes from using that knowledge to heal myself. I listen closely to my body not only in times of enjoyment but also when suffering in pain. I rarely take any drugs to mask the feelings of my body … even aspirin."

I looked carefully at this man. His eyes were bright. His skin had a healthy *out-in-the-sun* look to it. He moved easily around the campfire. I said, "I like your ideas about pain. I've found that accomplishing difficult things generally requires some pain. It seems that many people are afraid of pain and do all sorts of things to avoid it."

He turned to me and smiled. "Yes, pain can be good. It teaches us our limits … and if we are strong we can encourage ourselves to surpass those limits."

He was piquing my interest and I wanted to know more about him. "You look healthy and agile. If you don't mind me asking, how old are you?"

"I am a full deck."

"What?" I was a bit perplexed.

"Fifty-two cards in a deck."

"Oh yeah. I never thought of it like that."

"Four suits of 13. Four 13-year cycles. Thirteen is a powerful number."

"It is?"

"Think about it. Thirteen years old … big changes in your life. Then 26 … right there in your prime. Then 39, gaining the age and experience and reflecting back. Then 52, and you are again pondering the seasons of life … and WHAM … you got knocked for a loop."

"You seem to be enjoying your time," I joked.

"What's a man to do?"

"I don't know. I continually ponder that question myself."

"Good girl. Just keep in mind that your time is limited, so make good choices. And as you get older, time goes faster so the choices become even more important."

"Time goes faster as you get older?" I asked skeptically. This seemed like a pretty far-fetched idea to me.

"For sure. Think of a one-year-old baby. When living her life from one to two, she is living her entire life over again. For her, every day is a rather large fraction of her total life experience. A four-year-old is living one quarter of her life over again from ages four to five. A 20-year-old lives 1/20 of her life over again during her next year. And by the time you are 52 like me, a year represents 1/52 of my life … not very much."

"I see what you're saying. But a year is 365 and a quarter days … the same for everybody," I maintained.

"Ahh. But have you ever spent an hour waiting for something and it felt like three hours? Or been so occupied with enjoying something for one hour that it felt like five minutes?"

"Sure … depending upon what I am doing," I answered.

"Exactly. Time is relative to what you are doing. When you are experiencing your entire life over again in one year, that is a very rich experience compared to your history, so it seems to take a long time. On the other hand, after you have been through 52 years and have that long history, a year seems to go by pretty damn quickly. So with all other things being equal, the years get faster as you age."

"Being equal? What do you mean?" I asked.

"Well, each moment can be intense or more relaxed. So within your year of experiences, different events can seem to take a long or a short amount of time. That provides for lumpy experiences of time."

As we were speaking, a group of men and women who looked to be in their twenties walked up and joined us around the fire. They had been camping farther down the ravine and appeared to be friends with the four already at the camp. Beal introduced us as residents of the Pigeon Palace, which brought a laugh to everyone. He poured fresh coffee all around.

As a way of introduction, Hank added, "Hey, talk about relative time, Tony here just got back from a two-year stint in prison. He can tell you about the relative nature of time."

"You been expounding your time theories to these young people?" laughed Tony.

"Of course, Tony. You know me."

"Yeah, well, do what you can to stay out of jail, people. Time stretches forever when you're in a cell. And unfortunately, it's way too easy to find yourself there. It's scary how many people are put away for victimless crimes."

"Man, that sucks. When you need cops you can't find them, and when you don't want them they're knocking down your door," someone said woefully.

Tony continued, explaining to Raz and I. "Yeah, I wasn't hurting anyone. I had just gotten to town and a policeman thought I looked suspicious. He stopped me, asked me a bunch of questions and called me a vagrant. Then he searched me and found a small amount of drugs. I had them only to help myself along, but I was declared a menace to society and locked up for two years."

Raz felt compelled to express his thoughts. "If you live the straight and narrow you won't see much of them. But if you stray a little and break the laws you lose your rights."

Tony turned to him, "Ok. So I am a citizen with rights who violates the law and becomes a criminal without rights?"

"Exactly," answered Raz.

"And how about my punishment and loss of rights? Should it be meted out according to the severity of the laws that I break?"

"Definitely. How else could it be done?" answered Raz.

"And should the loss of my rights be adjusted if I break an unpopular law? Should I lose my rights and be punished by the system if that law is viewed by most citizens as unfair and unjust?"

Someone spoke in jest, "Happens all the time. Get used to it, Tony. Why are you so damn special?"

Tony ignored him. "And what if I have been imprisoned for years for a crime without a victim, but which violated a few sentences in a legal book, and then the law is declared unjust and repealed? Is someone responsible for those years gone from my life?"

"Hey, that's the way it goes, Tony. Nothing is perfect. At least the law eventually changed and maybe you gained from what you learned in prison," jested Ergo.

"Yeah, well, I learned how to live in extremely close quarters with many angry and violent men. Oh, and I also learned how to be a better criminal."

"Doesn't sound like that helped society," I blurted out.

"Yeah, isn't government supposed to make our lives better? Why should it have anything to do with what goes on inside our homes behind closed doors?" asked Hank, grinning.

"Yeah. Yeah. I like it. Government out of the bedroom!" exclaimed a young woman.

Some of the group started to chant, "Government out of the bedroom! Government out of the bedroom!"

In a loud voice Beal proclaimed, "Hear hear. Remove victimless crimes! Should the government act as a moral agent? Should the government tell us what is right and wrong?"

"Hell no! They should support our personal lives, not take them away," someone shouted.

"Yeah. Why the hell should the government regulate what we do in private with sex, or drugs or parties when everyone consents and no one gets hurt?" asked Hank indignantly.

"Imagine the money that would be saved by changing those laws," mused Phyllis.

"And people would be happier because they would not be fearful about doing things they naturally desire," added Beal.

Ergo was not convinced. "But how about all the drugged out people doing their work? And kids getting hooked on drugs? Sounds like a real fucking nightmare."

Tony answered quickly, "Hey wait. Being legal for consenting adults at home does not imply legal for people at work. And who said anything about kids?"

"Once you let the cat out of the bag, you can't control where she goes. You know as well as I do that if drugs are available they'll get to the workplace and schools," Ergo insisted.

One of the young women disagreed. "Wait a minute, Ergo. That's the way it is now. The laws do not work."

"Exactly. Right now there is a huge crime network very adept at distributing drugs. Despite the efforts of the police, drugs are available most everywhere," said Tony adamantly.

Hank laughed. "The fact of the matter is that people just want to use drugs. From time to time we all want something that removes us from our ordinary lives."

"It's true," I said, "within most native societies, extra-ordinary experiences—many involving drugs—are supported and often revered."

"Yeah. It's a natural fact. People just want to be stoned!" a young man exclaimed, at which point several of the young crowd started singing, "They'll stone ya when you're driving in your car … they'll stone ya when you're playin' your guitar!" accompanied by a big laugh.

Hank continued, "So the problems we have are *not* with the drugs themselves. Our problems are with habitual use and addiction … in the overwhelming of a life with drugs. Drugs do their dirty work when they become the prime interest at the expense of other activities."

Phyllis mused, "Maybe if we help people pursue multiple interests they will not become obsessed with just one."

"Perfect, Phyllis," replied Hank, "education and opportunity. If people have access to knowledge, tools and opportunities they will likely prosper rather than languish in obsession."

Raz spoke up, "There is a hell of a lot of money being made in the production, distribution and sale of drugs."

"And a hell of a lot of crime as well—extending from the big distributors and manufacturers down to the heavy users, who do almost anything to obtain money for drugs," said Ergo.

"Yeah, Ergo," added Hank, "and if drugs were legal their costs could be controlled. Isn't it better to provide legal drugs at low cost and eliminate the drug-related crime, criminals and jail cells? Sure it would be better if people did not obsess on drugs, but some inevitably will. It's a natural cost to society for not being perfect. We should accept this cost and work to minimize it."

"But how about those who believe that drugs are wrong and immoral and fight hard to keep them away from their children?" insisted Ergo.

"Like she said, drugs are everywhere. Our laws do not work. Our kids need real alternatives for their future to prevent them from obsessing on drugs. Think of the educational and occupational opportunities we could create by redirecting funds from drug-related enforcement, prosecution and incarceration," answered Hank.

Ergo was still not convinced. "Don't you think that by legalizing drugs we send the message that it's OK to use them? And won't that contribute to more drug use?"

Again, Hank had a quick answer. "We *are* an addicted society. Whether it is drinking beer, smoking tobacco, watching TV, driving cars, popping pills, having sex, eating, going to church, making war or reading the fucking paper, people are obsessed. We are striving for something out of the ordinary. Sure you can do any of these things without being addicted, and that is my point. You can be addicted to just about anything. In many ways it doesn't matter what you're strung out on, just that you're strung out."

Phyllis shook her head in disagreement. "Yeah, but drugs are harmful and many of these other activities are not."

"Ok. Like what is not?" asked Hank.

"Eating. It's necessary."

"Well how about if someone obsesses on food and must eat all the time? Whenever there is any pause in the action of the day, this person eats and eventually gains 200 kilos."

"Ok. Bad choice," she answered. "How about reading the paper?"

"Imagine if someone was so obsessed with reading the paper that he had to have it first thing in the morning or he could not start the day properly … and he had to read the entire paper to not miss any words?"

She acquiesced, "Sure anything is harmful in the extreme. But going to church?"

Hank patiently described another scenario. "Well, now imagine someone who needed to have everything in their life defined and answered by religious texts. Does it not harm their development to be so obsessed with doctrine and correct practice that they can't act freely or spontaneously?"

❧   ❧   ❧

You have no business in my private life
You have no business within my four walls
You have only lies from which you espouse
That you're protecting me from my own big bad self
But as I see it I have only me
I have only my life in its entirety

There is no place in my home for your spies
It's none of your business with whom I do lie
It's none of your business about what I partake
It's none of your business about that which I speak.

It's only my business if I want to die
It's only my business to express what is I
The worst that can happen to all that are free
Is for someone to force us to be otherly
I have only life
Of this I am sure
I don't give a shit about your afterworld more
I see what I do
And think what I think
As long as my actions do not conflict
With the health and well being of all that's around
You have no business upon my grounds.

But every lone day that someone is pulled
From within their four walls and brought to the hold
That someone is forced to give up what is free
Because of your petty morality
That keeps us indentured or even as slaves
To the high holy ground that you so do crave
From the thin frail pages of some old dusty book
You lie and you steal like too common a crook
But someone you force to bend and to fold
Will one day rise up and release your sick hold.

❋   ❋   ❋

Time stopped and started for us unexpectedly from that day on. Sometimes we were grounded and focused, and other times just wandering along with no sense of direction. We were in fact reeling from our encounters but did not realize it at the time.

At one point we landed in a small mountain community. We liked the people, and they liked us and encouraged us to stay for a while. They said we could squat in an old cabin down a dead-end track bordering a large forested wilderness. We were feeling very tired from continual travel and decided to give it a rest.

For a few weeks Raz and I lived an idyllic life. We spent our time out in the forest, walking among ancient trees, looking at wildflowers, listening to the songs of a myriad of birds, glimpsing wild animals … all the while seeing no cars and hearing no motors. We began to develop daily rhythms with the sun and the moon, walking and reading, sitting and thinking. We spent many evenings visiting with neighbors and discussing life in the mountains.

One evening while visiting Bruce and Maggie, we were startled by the rumble of large trucks on the dusty road in front of their house. The trucks were hauling bulldozers and log skidders. Bruce jumped up to get a good look. "They're coming, Maggie. They'll probably be bulldozing roads tomorrow morning. We have got to get the word out."

"What's up?" I asked Bruce.

"Most of the forest around here has been heavily logged, but the big wilderness south of here is untouched. There are no roads into that forest and it's very rough terrain. The timber companies have been pressuring the land managers to sell the timber. We've been organizing people to protest the logging. Apparently the forest managers have heard enough and have given the OK to begin bulldozing logging roads."

Maggie continued, "We've been meeting with forest managers and politicians, and thousands of people have sent in protest letters. We've got the support of scientists and the general public, but the timber interests are in bed with business owners and politicians." She sighed heavily.

Bruce shook his head in frustration, "Yeah, the biologists warn us about possible extinction for more than two dozen plant and animal species that live in this forest. And the forest hydrologist predicts that the bulldozing and logging will cause the hillsides to wash out, clouding the rivers with sediment and killing the fish."

"And the forest managers ignore this," Maggie said sharply.

"What do the local people around here think about this?" asked Raz.

Maggie sighed, "Cutting trees and milling wood have been pretty much the only industries, so most everyone welcomes more logging."

Bruce grimaced, "Yeah, and we're thought to be the bad guys trying to put people out of work and take away their jobs."

"Can't mess with a man's livelihood," muttered Raz.

Maggie continued, "Forest uses are changing. More and more people are coming from outside this area to recreate in our old forest. They're using the trails for hiking, backpacking and mountain biking, and the rivers for fishing, canoeing and kayaking. They spend their money in the local stores and shops, but still a lot of people don't like the outsiders. I think they're afraid of change."

"But won't the logging drive away the tourists?" wondered Raz.

"Definitely," answered Maggie. "The forest will be reduced to scrub, and the water quality and flow of the streams and rivers will decline. We've gotten a lot of support from recreational groups."

Well goodbye to our days of wine and roses, I thought. I looked at Raz. He smiled. "So what can we do to help?" I asked, a bit reluctantly.

Maggie looked at Bruce. "We'll have a meeting tonight to work out a strategy. Why don't you guys go there with us? I'll start making some phone calls."

❦   ❦   ❦

That night about 60 people gathered at a campsite by the river. We naturally formed a circle around a big fire pit. Conversations were buzzing about what to do to stop the logging operations.

"We need to form a human chain to block the bulldozers from moving into the forest," someone suggested.

A skeptic countered, "They'll just remove us and continue."

A professional woman still dressed in her business clothes presented a strategy. "We have to get the media out there so that people can see what's happening. Our message needs to be clear and we need to show urgency. The only way we will succeed is by gaining a lot of public support to pressure the forest managers and politicians."

Someone asked, "Won't the politicians help us?"

An elderly man wearing a shirt and tie answered, "Not without a lot of pressure. They all have strong alliances with the timber industry."

A scruffy middle-aged man was in doubt. "It seems like a losing battle. How can we poor volunteers combat a big industry that has budgets in the millions?"

"Through our determination and actions. Our planet home is at stake!" shouted Kaelin, a fiery young man with long black braids who was shaking with emotion.

Bruce agreed. "Actions are what provoke results. Directly expressing our ideas and beliefs with our bodies and our lives gives us power beyond words."

Stephen, a wild-looking man with wiry gray hair who lived near Bruce and Maggie, added, "Our power resides in pure, unadulterated bottom-up action. Top-down action is fascism. Bottom-up action is social change."

"And if we can get support from others for our actions, our power grows," added the professional woman.

A middle-aged woman holding a baby mused, "Maybe at some point we can get people to vote only for candidates willing to defend the forest."

"You think that the voting process is free and fair?" asked a young man.

"Sure. We vote and the person with the most votes wins. Simple," she answered.

"But aren't people's decisions influenced by TV, radio, newspapers, advertisements and endorsements?" he asked.

"Sure."

"And isn't all that media partial to the economic and political powers that support or control them?"

"I guess so. But it sounds like you're preaching futility." She was getting frustrated.

"Exactly. Futile. The whole voting process. The whole political process. And the politicians!" yelled the young man.

Someone in the crowd shouted out, "Well what do you expect a person to do? Voting is the key to freedom and democracy."

Kaelin could not restrain himself. "Voting is a panacea. It gives us the impression or perception that we can get what we want when we are really just getting screwed over."

"What voting really accomplishes," growled Stephen "is to keep us *believing* that we participate in an open democratic process and that our resulting government is free and fair."

He continued, "Voting was a radical freedom from direct rule by the elite and powerful. But it has unfortunately become largely ineffectual in our economically and politically controlled world."

Bruce clarified, "Voting works best in small groups where people meet face to face to discuss and decide common issues. However, it fails for large groups with open markets where money equates to power."

Estaur, a young woman trying to participate while keeping her three small children occupied, added, "We vote, and maybe we can change the politicians and perhaps also the façade of the power structure. But the rich and powerful are forever behind the scenes, pulling the strings. The politicians decide how the rewards will be divvied. Then they devise plans to tell us just the right information to get support, and give us just the right perks to keep us complacent. Same old story, over and over."

"Thanks, Estaur," said Stephen, "and those looking for power consult psychologists, social scientists and market analysts. They are dressed by wardrobe consultants, taught to stand and speak by actors, fed ideas by political strategists and financial powerhouses, and given words to say by speechwriters. They adjust the image and message, poll for sample statistics—to find out what people think—and repeat. Over and over. All the while disseminating confusion, lies and misinformation about opponents. So when you vote, exactly what are you voting for?"

"So you're saying that voting is futile?" asked a bewildered young man.

"Look, voting is OK," answered Stephen. "If the election is close and the differences in the end results are great, go vote. Just don't expect too much and *always* be careful of politicians."

"Not all the politicians are bought and sold," the young man insisted.

Maggie answered, "There are dedicated politicians who work against imposed power for the interests of the people who elected them. But power attracts, so politicians naturally move toward it."

Stephen elaborated. "Politicians are seeking to insert their ideas and opinions into the activities of society. They think their ideas are superior or better suited, or they want to feel and exercise the power associated with such a position. And to survive in the cutthroat world of asserting power and influence, they must play the games of power and influence.

"And the more they play and the more connected they get, the more they have to play. And the more pressure is put upon them to play. And the more they become indebted."

"So you think we should just cast off the political process—kind of in an *ignore it and it won't bother us* sort of way?" asked the young man incredulously.

"No, we need to change it. I think we should do away with politicians. Politics are part of human society and there will always be action around the process of deciding upon and creating our social and economic structures," answered Stephen.

"How can you do away with politicians when we have politics?" someone in the crowd asked.

I found this discussion rather troubling but kind of ironically funny at the same time and jokingly offered, "Suppose we disallow any person wanting to be a politician from entering politics? People who enjoy wielding power should be suspect."

To my surprise, Kaelin picked up on this. "Yeah, I like that! We could get our politicians from the ranks of people who don't want to be politicians … like a military-style draft," and he laughed deeply.

"Sure," agreed Stephen, "like a jury duty subpoena. Randomly select candidates from the public and conscript them into service. Test them to see if they have great political ambitions. And if they do, disqualify them from service," and he began to laugh along with Kaelin.

"And who would decide the agenda?" asked the professional woman, not sure whether to jest or speak in earnest.

Someone in the crowd yelled out, "We all do. We vote on an agenda and the conscripted politicians do *our* bidding." Laughter erupted all through the crowd.

"Hey, sounds like a great world! Conscript people who do not want power into power, make them perform the jobs *we* want and then send them out to pasture. What a turnaround!" beamed a round-faced, round-bodied, balding man laughing and drinking a beer.

"Yeah, and we can vote with our taxes," pronounced Stephen in a more serious tone.

"Our taxes?" Bruce asked, a bit perplexed.

"When we pay taxes we indicate how *our* tax money should be spent. We specify the percentage of our payment going to each budget category."

Someone yelled, "Fuck the military!"

"And fuck the timber industry!"

A young man asked, "How about people like me who don't pay taxes? Do we have a voice?"

Stephen answered, "Everyone could vote on a common agenda and part of the tax money could go to a general fund to support the common agenda."

Raz leaned over, put his arm around my shoulder and whispered, "You should be a politician. I think you're a natural," and he winked and chuckled.

I glanced sideways at him and shook my head in amused disbelief.

"And …" added Bruce in a commanding voice, pausing for a moment, "*we* can influence the agenda by the things that we do … especially if we use the media to get our message out to the world. So it all comes back to our actions … which means that at 6 a.m. we are prepared with our first line of defense. Does anyone have another option?"

"Let's stop them with our bodies!" a few people shouted.

"We can chain ourselves together along the canyon entrance where it narrows between the rocks," Kaelin proposed.

People in the crowd began to volunteer.

Bruce looked over the crowd and nodded with satisfaction. "Good. We agree on a course of action. We must plan carefully. We'll have another meeting in an hour to discuss tactics."

By 6 a.m. there were fourteen of us sitting cross-legged with locked arms across a narrow canyon entrance heading south into the forest. A line of bright orange flagging indicated the course of the proposed logging road from the hillside above us down into the canyon below. We were chained together with cables and locks entwined around each of our midsections and anchored to trees and rocks on either side of us. It would be very difficult to remove the bonds without harming at least one person. And the large rocks on either side made it impossible to run machinery around our human chain.

Raz and I agreed to join Maggie and Bruce in the blockade. We wanted to be part of something that really mattered. Being part of a group, bound as one, brought us together with people dedicated to a purpose ... a purpose higher than personal gain. Something we were seeking.

At 6:30 the loggers arrived and were quite surprised by the 100 or so people milling around their trucks and equipment. They noticed our group chained together on the slope below and called the police. Shortly after, six police cars arrived with dogs and riot gear. A few minutes later, reporters and cameras were also on the scene. It was beginning to look and feel like a circus.

People kept running back and forth from the parking area down to our blockade, bringing reports about who was arriving and what was being said. We were getting nervous and we locked our arms tightly.

"Have no fear. We have the power," proclaimed Lars.

Lars was a seasoned activist who had been previously arrested several times for civil disobedience. He had become the de facto leader of our group. I felt safe with him.

"The police won't hurt us. The media are here. They will try to work this out through diplomacy first. The dogs and clubs are here only to scare us. Keep focused and show no fear," he insisted.

The Chief of Police, Officer Amdad, came walking down the hill. He stopped a few meters away, looked at us and the chains and locks, and began shaking his head. "Bruce, what have we gotten into here? Looks like you're headed for trouble. Isn't there a better way to do this?"

Bruce answered, "We've tried, Officer Amdad, but no one has listened. We're not here to hurt anyone. But we will not move and allow the loggers to bulldoze into the forest."

"You realize you'll be arrested for this ... and you won't win this fight. Things will be a lot easier for you if you dismantle this blockade before the federal officers arrive."

"We're not moving," Lars stated flatly.

Officer Amdad looked at him, shrugged and turned around to walk away.

A few minutes later, we heard a bulldozer start its engine.

Lars spoke in a sure, even voice, "They are going to run a bulldozer down the hill toward us. Remember they won't run over us. Everyone is watching. This is just more scare tactics. Focus on each other and our task at hand, and try not to pay attention to the bulldozer. Stay calm."

The dozer moved down the hill with its engine roaring, snapping small trees and pushing them out of the way like toothpicks. Sand and dust and exhaust filled the air as its treads ripped at the forest floor and its blade scalped the earth.

As it got closer we could smell the diesel fuel and feel the heat of the engine on our faces. The dirt and dust thickened and obscured our view and we could see nothing but the huge machine bearing down on us. The ground began to shake. Trees snapped and fell.

Lars yelled above the noise, "Focus! Focus on our strength! Don't think about the machine. We can stop it. Don't fear!"

Though we could no longer see around us we heard people shouting. I tried to focus and squeezed tightly on the arms of my neighbors. The blade came within a meter of our feet then backed up. It dug into the ground and started moving forward again. I thought we were going to die as the loose dirt pushed forward and began to cover our feet and legs. But suddenly it stopped. We could hear yelling and then the motor turned off.

Lars congratulated us. "Very good. We won round one. Great patience everyone."

Our friends and supporters came and circled around us. Everyone was jubilant. Reporters were asking questions and the cameras were recording everything.

Someone came running down the hill yelling, "They're leaving! They're leaving! The loggers are leaving."

Sure enough, the loggers got in their vehicles and drove off, along with most of the police. Only one patrol car and two officers stayed behind. The bulldozer was still sitting right in front of us, as if to remind us that they would soon return.

We congratulated each other on our courage and determination. The chains locking us were removed and we all let out a sigh of relief.

Lars warned us, "Now remember, this is just round one. The challenge will get harder and the stakes higher as we move forward. We have plenty to celebrate but we need to stay alert and prepared for their next move."

Someone setup a makeshift table, and an assortment of food and beverages were laid out. Everyone was hungry, and with our bellies full we laid back to relax in the sunshine.

In the afternoon, eight federal officers dressed in camouflage arrived in black SUVs. At first they stayed and talked with the local police in the parking area. After about an hour they spread out and circled around us, surveying the situation but always keeping their distance.

We eyed them suspiciously but they never came close and never said a single word to us. As dusk fell we were pretty relaxed, sitting laughing and chatting around a large fire at our makeshift camp.

Raz pulled out his tobacco pouch and began to roll a cigarette. "Anybody want a smoke?" he asked.

A young couple, Bo and Don, both nodded and Raz handed them the tobacco tin and rolling papers.

Lars smiled and declined, "No thanks, Raz. I used to smoke but gave it up."

"Good idea," answered Raz. "Wish I could do the same."

"It's all about focus and concentration," Lars replied.

"We all need focus," I said. "By the way, great job keeping us focused this morning, Lars."

"No problem. You all did great. So much can be accomplished when we concentrate on the task at hand. That's how I quit smoking cigarettes."

"Really. I'd like to do that," said Raz. He looked over to me with a smirk then continued, "I've tried a few times but never succeeded. Any suggestions?"

Lars thought for a moment. "It's all up to you, Raz. You need to decide what is important and focus on making it happen."

Bo asked, "How did that help you quit the sticks, Lars?"

"One day, I just up and quit. I'd never really thought much about it and was not especially concerned about my health. But I was very interested in getting the most out of life."

This sounded a little like Leather Man and got my curiosity going. "What do you mean *getting the most out of life*?" I had been hounding Raz to give up the habit.

"Well, at the time that I quit smoking I kept thinking about enriching my life experience. I was so excited about life that I wanted to be as immersed in and aware of my experience as possible.

"And I started thinking about my smoking habit. God I loved it. I loved the taste and smell, the inhale and the exhale. I loved to smoke first thing in the morning, after every meal and before bed. And all through the day I would smoke to take a break and relax."

Raz nodded, "Exactly. I love 'em like that."

Lars continued, "But my desire to experience life at its fullest was pushing on me. I realized I was using my sense of touch to hold the cigarette, eye-hand coordination during smoking and my sense of taste when inhaling. I also realized that I used smoking to distract myself from the happenings at hand by my involvement in the smoking experience. I realized that I did not focus on my activities as fully as possible. In fact, I decided that was precisely what I enjoyed most about it ... giving myself a break from what was going on around me."

"I know what you mean," concurred Don.

Lars continued. "And this bothered me greatly. After a particularly long argument with myself I opted for focus and concentration, and quit smoking. I was striving to be independent in my thinking and actions, and I realized that while procuring and consuming cigarettes I was being manipulated. That message was so strong that I've never gone back."

"Whew! I wish it was that easy for me," Don exclaimed.

"It's not easy, but the first step is not too hard. Declare allegiance to yourself and promise to seek the most from life. All else will naturally follow."

"I see that," replied Don. "I just always have to deal with so much shit that having a smoke has become a major enjoyment."

"It was for me as well. But if you do decide that you want the fullest experience, your convictions will bring you through. I made this decision on the Ides of March in my eighteenth year and have never looked back."

I asked rhetorically, "What do we have if not our lives and the consciousness of our lives?"

"Exactly," said Lars, "our greatest gift and our greatest power is our consciousness. When we reduce our awareness we lessen our potential."

"I think of consciousness as my sense of myself," I replied.

"Yes," agreed Lars, "consciousness is an awareness of your actions and the actions around you."

"Do you think that makes us different from other animals?"

"Well," answered Lars, "we do a lot of thinking. This becomes apparent if you watch someone try to solve a dilemma like *what should I do when a friend is in trouble but refuses help*? They think about the consequences of speaking out, of not speaking, of responsibility as a friend, possible consequences of action and inaction, et cetera."

Bo had been listening intently and asked, "But don't other animals also think in similar ways?"

"Surely," replied Lars. "Watch your cat. When she wants to go outside, what does she do?"

"She meows and stands at the door."

"Good, and when she wants to eat?"

"She climbs up on her table by the food dish and sits there, and sometimes meows."

"Exactly. So she is thinking about what she is doing. She watches the actions around her and when she sees you she walks to the door and meows."

"OK, OK. But don't you think our consciousness is higher than hers?" Maggie asked.

Lars pondered. "Hmm … *higher*, now that is a tough concept. What do you mean by higher? She knows what she wants and produces a behavior that realizes her ambition. That seems to be pretty much what we do."

Raz countered, "Yeah, but I do things for concepts, not just for immediate results."

"Concepts?"

"Yeah, like I'll go to the store and buy some flowers to give to my sweetie Lana … just to be nice to her."

"To make her feel good?"

"Well yeah."

"Don't you think Bo's cat does the same?"

"Noooo."

"How about when she goes outside, catches a mouse and brings it back to her kittens?"

Raz answered, "That's just instinct. Her instinct is to reproduce and make more cats like her."

"And you don't think she is aware of what she is doing? Don't you think she thinks *get some food for the kittens* and then goes out to find something? I mean, not in those words, since she does not have our words, but in concepts."

"Well, she definitely acts without wordy thoughts but I suppose she knows what she is doing when she leaves the house to find the mouse."

"So would you not say that she is *conscious* of her behavior?" insisted Lars.

"I guess so. But she doesn't have the idea of *feel good* like I have about Lana."

"Perhaps not. Perhaps her notion is to *help out and provide* and not specifically *feel good*. But nonetheless, she knows what she is doing. She acts upon that knowledge and produces results."

"I have the idea that I want to make my sweetie's day a bit better, and want her to enjoy her life and appreciate me. I act with long-term goals in mind," insisted Raz.

"And I would argue," maintained Lars, "that so does the mama cat. She may go out and hunt for two hours before catching something and bringing it back to the kittens. Maybe her frame of reference is not as long as yours, but she definitely acts in ways to provide results at a later time."

Bo was not convinced. "OK. But how about right and wrong and all that?"

"Ahh, that's different," answered Lars. "Now you're not referring to consciousness but conscience-ness … considering right and wrong."

"Yes," said Bo, "I have a sense of right and wrong and I think about the balance, and act according to what I think is best."

"Sure. Your actions are guided by your value system. And I would maintain that the cat acts precisely the same."

"What?" Don, Bo, Maggie, Raz and I asked incredulously.

"The cat may not have an abstract system of right and wrong, but to her she knows what is best and not best. And I believe our sense of right and wrong evolves from that exact notion.

"To the cat, *best* and *not best* are directly related to comfort and survival. And I maintain that our sense of right and wrong has developed out of our history of learning to protect ourselves, along with our efforts to change society into what we imagine is best for our comfort and survival."

"And I guess that makes mama cat a conscious being," Bo said half-heartedly.

Lars concurred, "I don't know how else you explain her behavior."

I asked, "So people and cats … and I suppose monkeys and apes?"

"Yeah. And dogs and horses and bears and frogs," answered Lars with a laugh.

"Frogs? You really think that frogs are conscious?" I asked skeptically.

"Well, they are alive and they do things to stay alive. They sense their environment and direct their behavior accordingly … like moving from a dry area to a wet area and from a non-insect area to one with a profusion of insects. They call for a mate and couple together. They may not feed their young, nor be filled with awe and wonder (but who knows), but they observe and interact within their world. They know about themselves at a very deep and basic level, and direct their actions toward satisfying their needs."

Don added, "In my meditation class we've been learning how to lose the pitter-patter of thought and experience the world directly. This is taught as a path to higher consciousness."

"Very nice," said Lars.

"And now you've got me thinking that by meditating I am moving in the direction of the frog with its lack of preconceptions, direct experience and direct action."

Raz smiled. "I like that … frogs at the pinnacle of consciousness. Pretty ironic."

"Kind of blows your sense of special place in the order of things, doesn't it?" laughed Bo.

Lars continued, "And I will take this even further by maintaining that these trees around us are conscious."

This was too much for me. "What?" I asked, "that's too far out. Trees are fixed. They grow in place. They don't make decisions. They have no awareness. Trees are simply fiber matter."

"Ok. I know this is a big jump but I think that trees know a lot more than we imagine. Do you think that these trees," and Lars waved his arm around him, "know that we are here right now?" He smiled slyly.

Bruce shook his head. "Whew. That's a big one."

Don ventured, "Since our chains are around this one," and he pointed to the large cedar tree on our right, "I would imagine it knows something is up. Trees respond to cuts in their bark, so it must feel our chains."

Lars nodded. "We must be careful not to confuse our notions of the words *know* and *feel* with what the tree experiences. For the tree, these words refer to *awareness* and *response*, not our symbolic word concepts."

"Right. The tree responds to tears in its outer skin. Not in anything like words. Obviously, more dramatically to stronger stimuli, but nonetheless in some way the cedar tree feels our chains," said Don thoughtfully.

"Maybe it knows we are trying to rescue it," joked Maggie.

Lars continued, "Trees take a longer time to respond to stimuli than people. To understand them you have to imagine their situation.

"If you stand between a small tree and the sun, the tree will slowly stretch out and grow around or up and over you. This may take several days or weeks, or possibly months or years. The tree senses you and responds accordingly to continue its life and growth. But if you were to stand in front of the tree for a short time it would hardly notice or respond to your existence … similar to you not noticing a very small insect quickly fly by."

"And the tree certainly knows when the sun is shining, since it's getting a charged energy drink delivered throughout from the photosynthesizing leaves," added Don.

"Ok. Here's another big one. Do you think this cedar tree senses community?" asked Lars.

"Hmm … do trees know that they are part of a forest?" Bruce mused.

Bo was quick to answer, "Now that you have me thinking like this, I would have to say 'certainly'. Trees are connected underground by fine roots that may merge from tree to tree. There are also mycorrhizal fungi growing in and around the roots, creating a living web underground."

"And you can imagine that when a tree is cut down, its roots go into shock. The natural exchange of fluids within the tree is ruptured. Internal pressure drops and the stump *bleeds* excess fluids. When this happens, the trees around it sense the change within the connected root systems and the information is passed on. When many trees are cut down, something like shock waves must travel through the root system. So the forest feels the bleeding of the trees," Lars said with great sadness.

🍁   🍁   🍁

Ancient forest
Here and gone
While we turn
And run
And run
Inside your branches
Along with your mane
You render us familiar
In a dance in the rain.

🍁   🍁   🍁

That evening, news about the confrontation in the woods spread quickly. Groups of loggers and their supporters gathered in the town square. People were yelling about the *goddamn tree huggers* ... about Bruce and Maggie and the outside agitators. We were being blamed for all the ills of the community, and the word was that we would continue our fight until all logging was stopped and all the mills were closed. People were shouting for the removal of all foreigners, by *any* means. Had it not been for our standoff with the federal police, there would have been a mob of angry people descending on our camp-site. We slept soundly in blissful ignorance.

The next morning we became the object of fiery sermons at local churches.

"God looks down on us and sees all the things that we do. The Kingdom awaits those who live the righteous life. As we pass our time here on Earth we are constantly judged on our efforts toward that righteous life. This world in which we live is a proving ground to test our purpose and faith. We are here solely so that we may have the opportunity to rise up and gain redemption.

The reward for our righteousness is everlasting life. On Earth we are faced with a continual struggle of Good versus Evil. To walk the path of redemption we must refuse Evil! At all times we must keep our eyes on His Kingdom. When we pursue the objects of this world too closely, we lose sight of the True Kingdom.

We have been given dominion over Earth and our task is to shape this world to point toward Heaven. God forced Satan to flee His Kingdom and now Satan takes refuge among us. We must not become enraptured with the objects of this world! This is Satan's playground. God and the Devil are fighting a great battle for our souls. We have the choice to either look up and walk toward redemption or fall down into earthly trappings. When we focus our efforts on the protection and care of this earthly world, we lose sight of the path to Heaven.

Matter is hollow. Scientists tell us that at the very heart of matter is the atom, and within the atom is empty space. And within that empty space are bits of energy that exist and do not exist simultaneously. It is surely a thing of wonder to learn that within our material world is vast emptiness. This shows us that true life is not within matter. Only by faith and worship of the Holy One can we find real substance. Satan works to make the objects of this world appear substantial. But this is an illusion.

Teaching our children to love the earthly world and scorn the works of man plays directly into the hands of the Devil. We are born into sin and must lift ourselves from sin to become the spirit of God. This is our challenge! When we cling tightly to the objects of this world, we release our hands from the Kingdom of God. This is the test that awaits us—and with God's blessing we shall overcome! Hallelujah!"

That afternoon we were told about the angry crowds and sermons and were discussing what had caused us to become the object of such hatred in the community.

Lana and I were distressed. We had come here for rest and refuge. When we got involved with the protest we thought we were doing good by helping protect the forest.

Lana was defiant. "I love nature. Some of my best experiences have been in the wild. So am I somehow evil for my love of the natural world?"

"Of course not!" boomed Bruce. "There is no evil here. Our Earth is beautiful and fills me with wonder. In the natural world I feel as if I am part of a greater being.

"So I dance with the devil because I am grounded in the world. I dance with the devil for the love of the dance and the love of the devil. I do not want to kill or hurt anyone or anything. I want to *be* and celebrate *being*. I am here briefly and too soon gone, and I want to dance along the way. I love this world and swear to do what I can to protect its awesome beauty!"

For the time being we were at a standoff. We were not sure why, but the federal police kept their distance and the loggers stayed away. We continued our protest camp as news continued to arrive about angry crowds and demonstrations back in town. Insults and threats were hurled at anyone thought to be supporting our efforts. An angry crowd surrounded the courthouse and demanded that the sheriff arrest all of us. Bruce and Maggie were being touted as the ringleaders, and people were yelling all kinds of threats toward them and their friends.

Everyone at the camp was on edge. Lana and I discussed our options and reaffirmed our commitment to the blockade.

As day two began to fade into twilight, Jenny, a neighbor of Bruce and Maggie, came running down the hill to our camp. She was panting and breathing heavily with a terribly fearful look in her eyes. We were all immediately alarmed.

She ran up to Maggie. "I've got really bad news," she blurted out.

Bruce ran over in alarm. "What's going on, Jenny?"

"They've burned your house! I heard a bunch of trucks speeding by on the road from the direction of your house. I ran down to see what was going on. The dogs were barking like crazy and the house was burning out of control. There was nothing I could do. I ran and called the fire department but by the time they showed up the blaze had already leveled the house. I am so sorry."

"Fuck ... Fuck! Fuck! Fuck! Fuck!" yelled Bruce. "Those motherfuckers!"

Maggie started crying. "Everything we own is in that house! Ten years of our lives were in that house! Why? Why has this happened?" she pleaded to the sky above.

Bruce hugged her and we all gathered round. We were shattered. The strength and determination that we had been feeling moments before had evaporated. I felt alone and powerless.

"Maggie and I have to leave now. We need to go back home," Bruce said, shaking his bowed head.

He hugged Maggie and they started walking back up the hill. Jenny followed. I looked at Lana and could see tears in her eyes. During our weeks in the community we had grown very close to Bruce and Maggie. Without speaking, we both started running up the hill after them.

We stood in a line, feeling the heat of the fire and watching the flames consume the remainder of Bruce's and Maggie's possessions. The house had collapsed but there was still a large pile of burning rubble.

"Maggie, I feel so bad for you. All your belongings. Everything you collected. Only the memories of all those things can stay with you. Oh damn them! Damn those fucking ignorant people!" cried Jenny.

Maggie shook her head as if to deny what was happening. "All gone. Gone forever. I guess they never wanted us to be here." She sighed and Bruce held her tightly.

"Though we lived here for ten years we didn't really fit in. We were always considered *outsiders*," lamented Bruce.

"You know, I'm sick and tired of being told that I haven't been around long enough to be *local*. Though I've lived here almost 20 years and my children were born and raised here, yet it doesn't feel like home!" growled Stephen.

"Yeah. What bullshit!" screamed Bruce, shaking his fist in the air.

I was thinking of Leather Man when Lana spoke, "We're all just passing through this land. This ground does not come free. It's given to us over the tragedies and bloodshed of others. We must acknowledge and pay homage to those before us. You are not alone."

Maggie sobbed, "But this," and she pointed toward the flames, "is *our* tragedy," and she cried even harder.

Lana looked gently at Maggie, "I know this is so difficult, but now you are free, Maggie. You have no encumbrances. You have no weight. This is your clean start. Though it will always be part of your history, you can change and make this a blessing."

"What do you think, Maggie?" asked Bruce, holding her tightly. "Can this be an opportunity for us? An opportunity to renew and rebuild our lives?"

Maggie wiped her nose and eyes. "I always talked about getting away, of leaving and changing so many things. But not by fire. I never imagined anything like this," and she began to sob again.

Jenny started to sing softly …

Freedom sings in the licking flames
Memories rise up to heaven

Collect and collect and organize
But the order dissipates
Except what's held deep within.

We stood quietly and listened to Jenny sing the verse several times.

Finally Bruce spoke. "I hear you Jenny. And I believe that we do hold everything within. I believe that everything that we ever do, everything that happens to us, becomes part of us and never leaves. So in a way I cannot be sad. Maggie and I are fortunate for all the good things that have happened here. Every single memory resides with us and makes us what we are."

I nodded, "Yes, the things that we do and the choices that we make are always with us."

"As well as choices that are made for us," added Lana.

"Yes," I said again, "we bear responsibility for the choices that are made for us as well."

"*The choices made for us?* What do you mean by that?" asked Bruce.

"When someone does something from which we benefit, those benefits become part of us and we share responsibility for that action. And being responsible, if the action is bad and we accept it, then we are guilty … guilty by association." The last three words came slowly. They were new to me and as I spoke, I puzzled over them.

"Guilty by association? Give me a break! We are victims. We aren't responsible for actions other than our own," said Maggie defiantly.

Lana tried to help. "Look at me, Maggie. I admit it. I am guilty. We have worked to protect this forest near your homes and that is good. But logging this forest is just one instance of many terrible actions performed in our names by our government. Raz is not saying that we are guilty for those actions, but if we sit by idly and do nothing we *are* guilty for our failure to act."

"Well, what do you expect Bruce and me to do?" Maggie asked with exasperation.

I answered, "Maggie, I am not trying to burden you. You are victims and I am so sorry for you. This is an opportunity for you to exercise your freedom. But please remember your responsibilities when you make and accept choices."

With that, I walked over to Lana, kissed and hugged her. "Now we must leave. Goodbye to everyone. We love you, Bruce and Maggie. Thanks so much for all you have done for us. I know that you will recover and rebuild your lives. You are fine and rare people ... people of integrity and determination. We will always love you and never forget what has happened. We may never see each other again, but our lives are bound together. Always and forever."

Lana wiped tears away and spoke in a shaky voice. "God bless you and all that you do. Be strong and keep your voices clear. You are beautiful people. Lights in the night. I love you all. Peace."

And we walked off into the darkness. We soon left the heat of the fire, but the light of the flames glowed on the trees as we slowly pulled ourselves back up the mountain to our cabin.

That night, Lana and I coupled like we never had before. Our passion consumed us and we forgot about everything in the world but our immediate moment. We fucked like we were sucking the marrow of life ... as strong and alive as we had ever been. We exchanged not a word but melded as One. We were part of the expanding universe. We were the tree of life extending through all people and all things through all time.

You turn me on
You make me wet
You make me wild
I am yours tonight
Don't worry about nothing
I am here with you

Whatever happens out there is far from us
When we are together all is fine
All the crap totally out of mind.

And you for me and me for you
Let's come together and after we're through
Let's come again and again and again
Let's come for today and tomorrow and when.

Just touch me here with your war-torn hands
Kiss my breasts and hold me close
Bring all your strength to pass onto me
I am your vessel
I can take your might
Fuck me today, tonight until daylight.

Yes I'll kiss your breasts
I'll mix them with wine
I will savor their texture their shape and their tilt
There is nothing more beautiful that I've ever felt
I will lick your sweet navel and wander below
I can feel your treasures in all of their glow.

Oh baby you know that I am always yours
You can come when you want to I'm open for you
My sweet honey pot is all glistening with dew.

Oh baby oh baby how wonderful you are
I can feel you forever
I am part of you now
I swell with my pride and you beckon me in
I think I could stay until the end of all men
When I'm so deep within you and you grasp at me there
I forget who I am and that here we lie bare.

Oh yes oh yes you do it to me
When you're rocking my world it's all fantasy
I am totally yours and I open below
I want you to take me, to shake me, to rape me
I want you to tatter this vestige of heavenly soul
To draw from within to totally unfold
This creature I am that makes such a scene
Writhing and shaking and losing demean
To be what I am as an animal ought
To call out in violence but never be caught.

I escape who I am when I enter you
You lose what you are and together we two
Exit this world and all of its strife
To go out in the dark and make love with the night.

I escape who I am when you take me away
You make me scream out and I open my legs
All that I know dissolves into passion
I am one with the night
I am dark from my dreams
I have lost all my loneliness and am brought to my knees.

Raz and Lana had been sitting next to each other, alternating the telling of their story. When one paused, without a word or even a nod the other would immediately continue the tale. When Raz finished speaking, Lana reached over and stroked his forehead. He turned toward her and they hugged tightly for a long time … entwined as one in the long thick tresses of Lana's hair.

Lorraine had been listening intently through the entire story, sitting and rocking gently back and forth with her eyes closed. She looked up. "You two are a beautiful couple. You complement and support each other like yin and yang. I am so happy for you."

Lana smiled, "Thank you, Lorraine. We *do* love and depend upon each other."

"Without Lana, I'm not sure where I'd be," added Raz.

"You guys really try to deal with a lot of shit," said Ray.

"Indeed we do, Ray. We feel obligated to do something," answered Raz.

Ray nodded. "I know it's pretty fucked up. I figure I can do something by making myself extreme, something far away from the fucked up norm."

"That's a good start, Ray," answered Raz, "but Lana and I felt like we could not ignore or flee the atrocities carried out by our government ..."

"In *our* names," Lana inserted emphatically.

Raz continued, "Yes *in our names* as citizens. We felt like we could not sit by idly, using goods and services from the government while passively accepting its actions."

Lana continued, "So we had to choose to act in a way that we thought was responsible—"

"—which we figured would either land us in prison for a very long time," Raz paused for a moment and then lowered his voice, "or get us killed."

Those last words seemed to echo around the room.

Cibi sat up straight on his bench. He began to speak but hesitated, then in a voice shaking with emotion he said, "My country has been ripped apart by violence. I was forced into the middle of it and compelled to do something. But I felt like I was swimming upstream against a massive current. I felt like I was fighting history." A pained looked came over his face. "And now I'm guilty," and he lowered his eyes.

Lana nodded in sympathy, "Perhaps we all are, Cibi," she said. "Raz and I left our country and continued to travel, looking for some place to live responsibly without guilt. But wherever we went, we kept seeing the same problems.

"To keep our independence and avoid contributing to global crises, we swore off petrochemicals and took to cycling. The lure of the Himalayas and the promise of Tibet kept us moving."

Karyn shook her head. "I tried to do the right thing for my government. I listened to what they told me about being on the side of good versus bad and I helped them go after the bad guys."

"But the sides weren't as clear as they let on, were they?" prompted Cibi.

"No, they weren't. They paid me well and I was able to buy all kinds of nice things. But I felt like I was being used and that my life was slipping away."

Karyn chuckled to herself and tossed her head back. She stared straight ahead with a look of great concentration, then nodded her head and began to speak.

CHAPTER 5

One Mind

Mathematics is the study of relationships and patterns of relationships among entities. Mathematics is within all that exists and all that happens, since everything consists of entities with relationships and patterns of relationships. The entities may be counting numbers, light waves, nuclear particles, social behaviors, bacterial populations ...

♣ ♣ ♣

It was 6:00 a.m. and the alarm was ringing. I kept thinking, "Get up Karyn! You stupid girl." Yes, I was being summoned to awaken and get ready for work. Last night was another bout of losing myself in the bottle. Thank God for fermentation and distillation! And thank the devil for this wracking headache. My life used to be so carefree and easy. I never realized how simple was the life of a student.

I was employed out of graduate school by a large company, using my mathematical skills to help make products for the military. My current project was creating tracking systems for personal missiles and bombs ... smart weapons to be used against individual targets. My trackers locate and target a single person 300 kilometers away. But I never witnessed their actions. The bombs were developed somewhere far from my office and deployed against enemies on the other side of the planet. I never saw a single bomb or missile explosion.

No, I worked in a clean, roomy, air-conditioned office adorned with serene pictures of mountains and seashore. There was no mention of blood or pain or killing. We were professionals doing work assigned to us, developing products to be used fighting and killing enemies around the world ... whoever and wherever they might be. I was told that I was a patriotic citizen and a great asset to my country.

Only two years previous I was a graduate student at the university, filled with pure idealism and a love for humanity. I believed that I could right the world's problems through hard work and dedication. But during my short working life those feelings quietly slipped away. At work, I increasingly felt that the products of my labor were taken from me and used in ways I would never know. I justified what I was doing by continually reminding myself that my efforts helped make the world a better and safer place. But I wondered *better and safer for whom?*

I started each day in the shower washing away the residue of the previous night. The drinking and the parties and the men meant nothing to me ... just a means of pushing away the smell and taste of my troubling work. I am still amazed at how quickly the sense of personal power and hopeful exuberance can fade from your life.

I took the bus to work as usual. But as I got off and turned to walk down the street to the front entrance, I was confronted by a crowd of several hundred protestors waving signs and yelling at people on their way into the building. I had no choice but to walk through them to reach the entrance.

Someone shouted at me, "*You* are killing women and children with your weapons of destruction! Stop the violence!" I turned to see a girl about 16 years old waving a sign that read, *Take responsibility for your actions. Stop the WAR.* She gave me a ferocious look as if I was her worst enemy. I tried to smile but she looked away and shouted louder. People all around were yelling at me as I continued to push my way forward.

I wanted to say something in my defense but could find no words. I felt ashamed to be walking down the street and cowardly to not respond. A young man stepped in front of me to block my progress. Trying to maintain composure I politely asked, "Could you please move out of the way? I need to get to work."

"Get to work? Is that where you're going?" he retorted.

"Yes. I am trying and if you would please step aside I could do that," I fired back.

"Going to make more bombs for the war machine. You call that work?"

"Hey, I'm just trying to make a living," I snapped.

"Whatever. It's a sad state of affairs if you can't make a living without adding to the violence."

"Look. I am sorry. I'm not trying to hurt anyone. I'm doing what I can for my country. Now could you please step aside?"

The young man refused to move and several other people came to stand by his side. He continued, "What is an intelligent, good-looking woman like you doing making weapons that will maim and kill innocent people? You're a fool if you think that you're somehow helping. You are a pawn of the war machine."

I couldn't answer. What could I say to convince him that I was a lover of humanity? If I walked into that building I would be his enemy … and maybe for good reason, I thought.

I stepped into the street to get around him. He yelled after me, "You are guilty! If you work here you are a supporter of the killing," but I shut him off as I stepped through the front door.

❧   ❧   ❧

I took the elevator up to the ninth floor and walked to my office. Shirley, my officemate, was waiting for me with a big smile on her face. "Quite the reception this morning, huh?"

"Whew," I replied, "they wouldn't let me get into the building."

"I imagine the police will be here shortly and break up the crowd."

"At least they're peaceful. Just exercising their right of free speech."

"Well, maybe. But they have the wrong target. We're working to prevent war, not make war. They think since we help build weapons *we* are the bad guys. But you know as well as I that we're making better weapons that will kill fewer innocent people and maybe even prevent further wars."

"So they tell us."

"You're not letting their silly protesting get into your head, are you?"

"I don't know. Do you ever think that maybe our weapons just further the hate and destruction?"

"Hey, we're the good guys and our bombs and missiles go after the bad guys."

"Do we really know that? And how do we know how many innocent people are also killed?"

"Nothing is perfect. We live in a complex world. It would be great if we could stop wars but we can't. So we help make them cleaner and more winnable," insisted Shirley.

"When you were studying mathematics at the university, did you imagine using your knowledge to make weapons?" I asked.

"Do you remember about six years ago when the university was granted some millions in corporate funding for applied mathematics and intelligent systems?"

"Yes, that was when I was starting my graduate work," I replied.

"Well, that funding was used to increase instruction in systems modeling, probability theory and self-actuated networking. I jumped into those classes hoping to eventually get hired using those skills."

"Which qualified you for building weapons systems."

"I guess it did."

"Well there's something wrong with that."

"How so?" she asked.

"At one time I really respected higher education. I believed that the university was part of a rich history dedicated to acquiring and promoting general knowledge and understanding of the world."

"Ahh … and it bothers you that it's not really about knowledge for the sake of knowledge?"

"Yes! Though I now realize what a stupid idealist I was. Universities are run like businesses, with expenses and budgets. And to maintain their budgets they must satisfy requirements from their funding sources. Large corporate interests that provide a lot of money change the direction and nature of the curriculum offered. Research is not pursued because it's interesting. Research is pursued because it's supported by donors."

Shirley smiled, "Research is expensive. The donors know what skills they will need for their businesses. So they support instruction in disciplines that further their corporate goals. Is that a problem?"

"Yes. That bothers me. Universities were originally established for the pure pursuit of knowledge, guided by scholarly interests and ideals. Now our universities are driven by corporate-type bottom-line money decisions with a lot of focus on military applications. When any new knowledge or technology has possible military use it's made secret and research is conducted as quickly as possible to figure out how to use it against our enemies."

"Yes, before other people use it against us."

"Exactly," I said, "develop the bomb before the enemy does so we can use it against them before they use it against us."

"That's important! You don't want us to be attacked by the weapons we develop, do you?"

"But doesn't this have to stop somewhere? Is it just paranoia breeding more paranoia? Is it really best that the university becomes a resource center for the military?"

"I know what you mean. Really cool stuff always goes first to the military. Then after they've milked its cutting edge properties, it returns to the public."

"Exactly. And *that* is what is really bothering me," I said thoughtfully.

All through the day, people in the office joked about the demonstrators. The police moved them away from the front entrance but they remained along the sidewalk all down the block. People viewed them as misinformed and misguided. We were surely not the enemy, since we were doing absolutely necessary work for the benefit of our country.

I was not able to concentrate that day and spent my time wondering what would happen if *our* work was halted. I figured that even if we refused to develop weapons systems, others would soon fill our places and resume our activities. I felt unsure and very unorganized.

When I left the building in the evening the sidewalk was still bustling with demonstrators. I started walking toward the bus stop when the young man from the morning saw me. He walked over and asked, "Have a good day building bombs?"

I should have been angry at his callous approach to my ethical dilemma but how could he know my thoughts? In the morning I had been taken by surprise, but this time I was prepared and not at a loss for words. I looked at him closely. He was lean yet strong-looking with a thick head of curly brown hair. He had a short scrubby beard and wore loose-fitting jeans, a t-shirt and some old sneakers.

"Well, actually not such a good day at work," I replied.

"Oh no. Feeling a little bothered by all the commotion out here?"

"I guess a little," I smiled weakly.

"Well then I suppose we are doing our job ... to get you thinking about the death and destruction that you perpetuate."

"You know these people are not your enemies."

"Oh yeah. How so?"

"They are just doing their jobs ... trying to help our country."

"Then they and *you* are deluded. You are pawns and slaves to the corporate military machine. You don't even know how brainwashed you really are."

"Because we don't think like you?"

"No, because you don't think!"

I was getting angry. Here was this flippant kid telling me, a professional mathematician, what I knew and didn't know and thought or didn't think. I struggled to hold back my anger and calmly answered, "You have a lot of gall to talk that way about people you don't even know."

"Well then I guess I have a lot of gall. But the story is the same. Sold your talents to the highest bidder ... believing all the crap about how your work is so necessary and important to your country. I just can't believe that a woman like you, seemingly so intelligent, believes such bullshit."

"Look, I would like to discuss this further with you but I need to be getting home."

"Yeah right. Go home and lie in bed and believe all the bullshit and lies that you've been told so that you feel better about building killing machines. You're just like everyone else ... too arrogant and self-assured to even question what you're doing. Pathetic."

"And you the same. What makes you any better with your pert little answers to our problems? Maybe you don't see the big picture."

He laughed, "At least I have an answer and am not wading in the muck like you."

"Maybe your answers are simplistic emotional responses and you're so guarded that you don't really want to look at the big picture."

"Touché. You *do* know how to fight!"

I laughed. This man was beginning to intrigue me.

"No, really you do seem like a nice woman … but I wonder what you're doing here. Want to talk about it sometime … away from this crowd?" His eyes twinkled.

My heart raced. He was cute and definitely bold and beginning to interest me. "Sure, why not?"

"Cool. How about this evening? We'll have coffee and talk philosophy?"

We met later that evening in a small neighborhood café. When I arrived he was sitting at a table in the back.

"Hey, how's it going?" I asked.

"Fine. I wasn't sure if you were coming. I thought maybe you agreed to meet because you were feeling intimidated by all the demonstrators."

"No. Not at all."

"Great. Anyway, my name is Goff."

"Good to meet you, Goff. My name is Karyn."

I sat down at the table and ordered a coffee. "So did you have a successful day today?"

"Actually, it was a great day. We had a lot of energetic new people joining the demonstration."

"Ah. I guess that gives you more power to work over the employees."

"Now be nice. We're just trying to bring attention to what is really happening behind those closed doors … to let people know that their money and time are going to support a war effort that benefits only the rich and powerful."

"Fair enough. Not that I necessarily agree with you, but I do believe in free speech and the free exchange of ideas. It never hurts to gain more knowledge … whether you agree with the facts or not."

"Very enlightened. How surprising. I don't expect that from the typical military contractor."

"Well *I'm* not your typical military contractor."

"I can see that."

"So what do you do … I mean besides disrupting people's workplaces?"

"Hmm, I'm not sure how to answer that."

"You know … what do you do to support yourself?"

"OK," he laughed. "I'm a trouble maker."

"Full time, huh?"

"Yeah. I am here to disrupt the status quo."

"No status. No quo," I laughed.

"Exactly. And what do you do … I mean specifically for the bomb makers?"

"Well actually, we don't make missiles or bombs. We develop and design their components. I'm a mathematician."

"Nice clean work. Never have to get your hands dirty. I knew you were smart, but why is a girl like you doing *this* work?"

"Look, to tell the truth I don't really want to do this work. I was always interested in pure mathematics … studying general systems and relationships."

"Ah, but this is where the money is, huh?"

"Exactly. The mathematics that we do involves finding optimum solutions for situations with specific and varying conditions to produce desired results. It's all about cost and result probabilities. In the process we may develop new mathematical ideas and methods, but they're the byproducts of the drive for results."

"And results are how the bills get paid."

"Yes. My interest in math really began when I learned that mathematics was a universal language that could be used to communicate with any intelligent being. It has been proven that a mathematical system developed by intelligent beings elsewhere in the universe would be equivalent to ours. They may not use the same names or number base for counting but it would work like ours."

"Yeah, well they may not have ten fingers."

"Exactly. There is nothing sacrosanct about counting by tens. They could count by twenties like the Mayans or twos like computers. But at any rate, they'll have operations like addition, subtraction, multiplication and division that will act like and produce the same results as our math."

"Cool. The language is not important, nor the number system, but the concepts and operations will be similar, if I understand you."

"Yes, and intelligent alien creatures will factor numbers and discover prime numbers, just like us."

"Sorry for my ignorance, but my math is a bit rusty. What exactly are prime numbers?"

"Primes are numbers with no other factors except for 1 and themselves, like 3, 5, 7, 11, 13 and on and on."

"Oh yeah, now I remember. And there is no biggest prime number, right?"

"Right, as far as we know. And primes are universal, so if we sent out a series of prime numbers represented by a sequence of clicking sounds and an intelligent being heard them, he/she would be able to respond with the next prime number."

"Pretty cool."

I smiled, "Yeah, I think so."

"But are you mathematicians always correct? Do you sometimes get it wrong and follow an incorrect path?"

"Well yes ... sort of. There are major problems in mathematics that have been studied and solutions attempted for hundreds of years. In the process there is a lot of work done that leads nowhere. So in that way, there is always math being done that is not correct ... but eventually we figure it out."

"But after years and years of studying something as correct, do mathematicians ever go back and say *Uh oh. We screwed up. This is all wrong. We need to do it a different way*?"

"No, not really. I mean, sometimes there is more to a problem than first appears. It may be thousands of years later when this is discovered. Like the Greek mathematician Euclid's assumption that parallel lines never meet."

"That's what I learned in school and it seemed correct to me. But you're saying that this is wrong?"

"No. Not exactly wrong. The Euclidean postulate is correct if the space in which the lines exist is flat. But in curved space parallel lines may meet or even diverge. We didn't know about or consider curved space until recently."

"This is interesting. I never thought about mathematics like this. In math class it was always *work this problem in this way to get the right result*. Never a discussion about what it all meant."

"I find it fascinating to view mathematics from the system level. But math is also dependent upon small pieces of basic logic that bind together the entities and relationships. This logic has been disassembled into innately apparent postulates upon which we all agree. And the entire logic structure of mathematics has been derived from these basic building blocks."

"Ok. So you're saying that mathematics is correct if you follow the basic logic rules. But can you prove that these basic logic rules are right?"

"Good question. How do we know that the logic rules are correct?"

"Yes. Do you just accept them on faith? Are they so basic that no one can argue against them?"

"Well actually, there has been a lot of thought about exactly that question. In fact, Kurt Godel, an outstanding Czech mathematician, proved in 1931 that you couldn't use the internal rules of a system to prove that the system is correct. He said that it's impossible to prove that the logic of mathematics is correct *using* the logic of mathematics!"

"Impossible? So isn't it all kind of futile then? I mean, why keep working when you'll never know if your results are right?"

"Oh, but like I said, it is correct within the rules of its logic. *And* it is continually verified in the real world. For example, two mathematicians in the late 17th century, Sir Isaac Newton and Gottfried Leibniz, co-invented calculus. Newton then used the calculus to accurately predict changes in the movement of objects from the effects of gravity."

"So this verifies that calculus is correct?"

"Yes, over and over. This does not mean that there are not other ways of describing the movement of objects, just that our current mathematical thinking repeatedly works."

"And this allows us to do things like send spacecraft to other planets or design bridges … or in your case build bombs?" he asked with a smirk.

"Yes. Unfortunately in this world of ours we need to build advanced weapons and my mathematics makes it possible."

He tapped his cup on the table. "That's where we part company."

"I believe in the necessity (or perhaps inevitability) of weapons and you don't?"

"Hey, people are messed up. There's no denying that. Regardless of what we do, there will always be people willing to take up weapons and use force to get what they want. I just think that you and your work are being manipulated by people and groups that seek to maintain and increase their power at our expense … and that the stories we're told about us being the good guys and the need to fight wars against the bad guys are smokescreens designed to keep us from seeing the truth."

"And I must admit that I agree with you, at least in part. I know that we do not get the complete stories about why we fight our wars … and that makes me wonder about the work that I do."

"Well. That's a good place to start. I would like to convince you that you should end your involvement right there."

"Easily said. But I like my work … that is, the mathematical challenge part."

"I understand. But someone somewhere along the line must stand up and take responsibility and not just toe the line."

"It's all so confusing, though. How do I know what is real and what is not? I get my work assignments from my supervisors. I don't know what is really benefiting our country and what is being used as a political tool. Not knowing this, I can't judge what work I do is *good* and what is a tool for the powerful."

"The problem is that government has been taken over by the economic system. So-called *free* enterprise occupies such a central place in our society that our mantra has been to leave the system unrestrained. As the economic entities get bigger, smaller ones find it harder and harder to compete. This creates an environment; we could call it *ultra-capitalism*, with fewer but larger economic forces, each with more capital and more power. That large power base is then used to influence government policies and practices."

"Sure, that's only natural … you know, to survive and grow. It's always been that way."

"Perhaps. But the basic principle of our economic system is that first to market with the cheapest goods wins. There is no room for evaluating long-term effects. Consumers do not see the wake of activities involved in getting the product onto the shelf.

"Corporations are run on short-term bottom-line logic. Investors demand short-term profit. If a policy or practice does not produce those profits, it's rarely ever considered. And the personal income of corporate officers is usually linked to those profit margins.

"So, the mega-corporations seek government policies and regulations that favor their short-term gains. And with their increased influence over jobs, markets, goods and services they usually get their way with government policy makers."

"So you think our government is controlled by the power of the markets?"

"Exactly," said Goff, "our politics and policies are often designed toward those ends. We go to war to strengthen and support the powers of the marketplace.

Your work is being usurped and you are being made a pawn in a hidden fight for power."

"The whole process makes me feel detached and isolated and unsure of the value of what I do," I lamented.

"The purpose of government *should be* to help create a better society. But too often this is directly opposed to the corporate free-market approach. Ideally, government should help create a playing field that emphasizes long-term values as opposed to corporate short-term profit motives."

I scowled. "Unfortunately, it doesn't work like that and I don't know what alternatives we have."

"Well we must work to build alternatives if they don't exist. To just follow along for our own comfort and ease is not acceptable. We need to do what we think and feel is right."

"I agree. If people lived what they thought was right this world would be an entirely different place."

"Too many are bought and sold ... for short-term gain, they give away their freedom."

My head was spinning, trying to relate these ideas to my life and the work I was doing. "Look, this is striking kind of close to home. I need some time to think this through."

"Fair enough. I understand. Hey, I wouldn't normally ask this, but I kind of like you and you seem to be a smart thinking person, sooo ... are you interested in meeting some of my friends for some extra-curricular activities?"

I looked at Goff and his playful eyes while considering the situation. I smiled. "Thanks for the invite. What kind of activities are you talking about?"

"We can hang out at my friend's house for a while and then go out and create some billboards."

"And put them up illegally?"

He laughed. "We're actually going to change some existing signs to reveal a better message ... illegally though," he said with a sly smile.

"Hmm ... you mean like defacing private property?"

"Yes."

I thought about the offer. I kind of liked Goff and I had nothing better to do so I found myself saying, "Sure. What have I got to lose? Take me to your leader."

He laughed, placed a bill on the table to cover our purchases and we walked out into the night.

❦   ❦   ❦

When we arrived at Lisa's house there were about a dozen people hanging out, enjoying the last of their dinner and dessert. Goff said hello and introduced me as a neophyte from the bomb squad. This got a good laugh all around. We sat down on the sofa.

Gina, a woman in her twenties whom I recognized from the morning, was carrying on a conversation with two men of similar age ... Lee, a wild-looking man with a big head of frizzy black hair, and Jaegger, who had a military-style crew cut.

Gina was saying, "Every day I try to feel good and do good things. I don't spend time dwelling on bad events of the past."

Lee replied, "When I think about the past I realize how fortunate *we* are. Throughout history, too many people have had lives surrounded by violence, chained in slavery or struck by poverty and hunger. I feel so fortunate to be here alive and well with the freedom to sit and talk with you."

"Definitely," agreed Jaegger, "most people in the world don't live in the relative peace and pleasant surroundings that we do. We should not take that for granted."

Gina sang …

> *Fortunate for every living day*
> *Fortunate in every living way*
> *Fortunate to simply be alive!*

"Hear hear," rose a chorus of supporters.

"Even in the midst of these crazy times I'm glad to be alive!" exclaimed Gina.

"I am as well but I'm also saddened. Saddened for all those who aren't so fortunate," pronounced Lisa, an attractive woman in her thirties with a yellow bandana tied loosely over her head.

"Life! I say life! How high we can fly!" sang Nicholas, a scruffy man whose appearance suggested he was quite young, but creases around his eyes indicated considerably more years.

"Is this all we have? Mustn't we plan for something larger and more long-lasting?" asked Anna, a diminutive yet energetic girl in her mid-teens.

"Whoa, whoa. We may be here now but we are not *here* exclusively," laughed Nicholas.

"Not exclusively?" she asked, a bit perplexed.

"What we do here now can change the future," he answered in a matter-of-fact tone.

Goff had an agenda for us. "We need to change the future by getting the energy companies to shoulder their responsibilities. Their plans and actions are directed toward short-term profits with little or no consideration for how those actions may impact others in the future."

Nicholas agreed, "Yes, it's *our* responsibility to force them to take *their* responsibility."

"Our energy use links together the past, present and the future," added Jaegger. "People will be dealing with contamination and pollution that result from energy extraction, production, storage, transportation and consumption for a long time to come."

"Nuclear waste is especially bad. It will be deadly poisonous for the next 250,000 years!" growled Lisa.

"And the government assures us that there will be protected and guarded storage facilities for nuclear power plant wastes," Nicholas said sarcastically.

"How can they do that? We'll all be dead in less than one hundred years!" exclaimed Anna, shaking her head in disbelief.

Gina was getting irritated. "Fucking assholes! Culturally speaking we are infants. We've had our so-called civilization for what, maybe 10,000 years? And yet these energy barons and politicians are ensuring us that the toxic wastes will be safe and guarded for 25 times longer than our entire human civilized life!"

"Arrogant ignorant assholes!" yelled Lisa.

Jaegger shook his head, "And during our short little history, we've fought wars and destroyed each other continually. Our so-called leaders have no idea how we can live in peace now, yet they guarantee that our radioactive wastes won't ever harm anyone for a quarter of a million years."

Gina sputtered in anger, "Those wastes will dominate the health, economics and politics of people seemingly forever. And considering our history, a succession of groups seeking power will fight endlessly over control of them."

This was too much for Anna. "What bullshit! They don't teach any of this to us in school and yet this is what is really important!"

"The powerful rule with money and money rules over them," said Goff. "Look for that fact behind every major economic and political decision, including your school agenda. And to keep people from seeing the facts they create smokescreens and distractions.

"OK, now that we're all worked up, let's provide a little balance to their lies with some creative paintwork," and he flashed his sly smile again.

"Sounds good to me," said Lisa. "What have you got in mind, Goff?"

"We were thinking about the new power company billboard above the freeway. There's a picture of a beautiful waterfall on the river with a nuclear power plant in the background and the caption *Pure and clean from us to you. Building the future.*"

"Which we can easily change to read *Pure Poison from us to you. Stealing YOUR future*," added Gina.

❦   ❦   ❦

Fifteen minutes later Goff, Nicholas, Anna, Gina, Lisa and I were walking down the street, carrying spray paint cans and climbing ropes in our backpacks. The energy company sign was erected on the roof of a warehouse next to the main highway.

We used ropes to scale the building and get onto the roof. Once on the roof we unloaded the paint and decided it would be Goff, Gina and Anna who would climb another four meters up the sign scaffolding to the lighted platform just under the billboard. Once on the platform they would be visible from the highway so everything had to be done quickly and efficiently. Nicholas and I took positions watching the parking lot and street. Lisa worked ropes and helped get people and supplies up and down from the sign.

I felt like a kid doing something bad and hiding it from my parents. My stomach was turning nervously as I looked back and forth from the painters above to the street below. Anna was standing on Goff's shoulders with paint can in hand, changing the words *and clean* to read *Poison*. Cars were speeding by on the freeway below but no one seemed to notice the three people scrambling around on the sign high above.

In less than five minutes the paint job was complete and we quickly gathered our gear and slid back down the wall to the street below. We walked half a block and then turned around to view our work.

"Looks great," Nicholas said while he snapped a few photographs.

"Whew. That was fun!" exclaimed Anna.

"You did great, girl," Goff assured her.

"Yes, and Karyn, thanks for helping out," said Lisa.

"No problem. That was exciting," I answered. It seemed a thousand miles away and ages ago since I had walked through the demonstration in the morning on my way to work.

As we walked back to her house Lisa began, "You know, we don't really need nuclear power plants. We could generate our electricity with cleaner, simpler technologies that use moving wind or water or sunshine. Solar power, which has been used for the last 30 years to power satellites and space stations, could supply most of our electricity needs."

"Very true," replied Nicholas. "I generate all the electricity for my home and business with photovoltaic (PV) solar panels. I haven't paid an energy bill or had a single power outage for fifteen years."

"Really. How do they work?" asked Anna.

"The solar panels consist of a series of individual cells made from wafers of silicon and trace elements. When the sun shines, light particles called photons strike the cells and excite them. The photons cause the solar cell to release electrons, which creates an electric current. The solar cells in the panel are wired together to produce a strong current and the panels are connected by cables to a battery bank. The current flows from the individual cells through the cable to the batteries that store the energy. I use an inverter to pull energy from the batteries and change it to standard household AC current."

"Nice," said Anna, "and it sounds very simple."

Nicholas nodded, "Really it is. There are no moving parts and my house runs just like any other … with lights, computer, refrigerator, stereo … the only difference being that the energy is generated from the sun on my roof, rather than by splitting atoms to boil water for steam turbines at the nuclear plant."

"Very cool," replied Anna.

Nicholas continued, "And being self-sufficient is intensely rewarding. There is zero pollution when I'm generating power. After the solar panels are purchased and installed, generating electricity is practically free. I think solar power could work for millions if not billions of people."

"Why don't more people use solar energy?" wondered Anna.

Goff answered, "Energy companies make more profit from fossil fuels and nuclear power plants. They pressure the government to provide tax breaks and other economic incentives, and everyone ignores the associated debt to future generations. So it appears to us that oil, coal, gas and nuclear energy are cheaper than solar energy."

"And how about the cost of the wars … and the blood spilled fighting for control of energy supplies?" added Lisa.

"I don't think the energy companies appreciate me as an energy producer. I've paid them nothing for 15 years. Imagine if there were millions like me?" laughed Nicholas.

❦   ❦   ❦

It was after midnight when we got back to Lisa's house. Everyone had left and the dinner dishes had been cleaned and put away. Anna said her goodbyes and headed home. Lisa put on some music and brought out a bottle of wine.

"How about a little celebration of our work?" she asked as she held up the wine bottle.

"Sounds good," we all agreed.

Gina directed us into the back of the house to a small room bathed in soft blue light, with several comfortable sofas and chairs. Lisa poured everyone a glass of wine and we all sat back to relax.

I smiled when Goff sat next to me on the sofa. My earlier feelings of animosity towards him had vanished and I felt strangely comfortable sitting at his side. He stroked my back and asked, "So, what do you think of meeting the enemy?"

I laughed, "Oh I never thought about you guys as the enemy. To tell the truth, lately I've been questioning the direction of my career. When I was a student I never imagined myself doing military work. I was into patterns and theories and had no interest in using my knowledge to build things. It's strange how you can end up someplace and not really be sure how you got there."

Lisa offered some support. "Well I'm glad that you're here ... and that I am here ... and that we all are here."

"Hear hear. A toast to us all being here!" Goff raised his drink high.

"To the here and now!" I found myself exclaiming as I raised my glass.

"It's good to get to know you Karyn. I really wondered about you when you first showed up. But you're alright. We had some fun tonight," laughed Gina.

"Cool. It's been good getting to know you all as well. Thanks for letting me hang out with you," I replied.

She nodded, "No problem."

Lisa reached under the coffee table, pulled out a small box and opened it. Immediately the air was filled with a deep rich aroma, simultaneously both sweet and spicy.

"Now you're talking!" exclaimed Nicholas.

Lisa picked a large green and purple flower bud from the box and placed it on the table. She began to use her fingers to break it into little pieces and continued to work it into a crumbled mixture of leaf and flowers. A thick odor filled the room.

"God, I love that smell," exclaimed Nicholas. "It's the second-best smell in the world."

Gina asked, "Second-best? And what is the ..." but she quickly stopped her question and began to laugh to herself.

After a moment's thought we were all laughing with her.

"Nicholas!" Lisa said with mocking scorn.

"Very nice," Goff chuckled.

"So Karyn, do you smoke marijuana?" asked Lisa.

I laughed, "I haven't smoked since I was a student but something tells me I will tonight."

"Very good, girl. I'm beginning to like you," she replied.

She took a large rolling paper, folded it along the bottom and filled the crease with as much of the pot as it would hold. Then she rolled and twisted and licked and a moment later placed a fat joint on the table.

"Here ya go Nicholas. Why don't you get it started for us?"

Nicholas lit the joint and inhaled deeply. He seemed to like what he got because he exhaled then inhaled again and passed it back to Lisa. The joint went around our circle four times before it was reduced to a small nub that Lisa put aside in the box.

I was really stoned. I had not smoked marijuana for more than two years and between the wine and the pot I was feeling giddy. But I felt safe with these people and refused to focus on my fears or worries. In my relationships I was always in control of the situation. But here I was letting myself go. It felt good.

Goff turned to me. "Do you like to party sometimes … I mean really party and get wild and crazy and out of your usual self?"

"You know, I usually pride myself for being in control."

"Are you in control now?" he asked.

"Well actually, I'm feeling pretty high and I'm trying to not try to gain control. It feels good to just relax and let things happen for a change."

"Cool," he said, "you're safe here," and he hugged me.

"I think it's important to get out of your usual way of thinking sometimes," said Lisa.

"Definitely," concurred Nicholas.

She turned to me. "What do you think, Karyn?"

"You know Lisa, I might have answered you differently this morning. But I now think that maybe this is a good thing. It's certainly refreshing."

"Hear hear," Goff jested.

"Sometimes it's sooo good that I need to be careful," said Gina.

"What do you mean?" I asked.

"Sometimes I feel so hopeless and powerless that all I want to do is escape ... usually through drugs," moaned Gina.

"I think a lot of people are confused and feel powerless about what's going on in the world, and struggle to make sense of things. And I think a lot of people use something to push back the panic," said Goff.

"Yeah," added Lisa, "it's all so confusing. We're bombarded with images and objects and slogans, and manipulated into dizzying loyalties for reasons we can't even explain."

I sighed. "It feels like I've been on a roller coaster. Sometimes I think I'm doing the right thing serving my country and other times it feels like it's a big confusing mess. I think I've been lulling myself to sleep by continually creating reasons to justify my work."

"She's coming out of the closet," joked Goff.

"You know, I feel like I've got some power again. I feel alive tonight."

"Good bud, Lisa. We're having a breakthrough," laughed Gina.

Nicholas got a big grin on his face, "You know this is why they work so damn hard to keep marijuana illegal."

"What do you mean?" I asked.

"How long have you been working at your job?"

"Just over two years."

"And how have you been dealing with the stress?"

"Stress?"

"You know, stress from going to work, stress from office politics, stress from deadlines, stress from making killing machines. How have you been dealing with it?"

"Not very well, I suppose."

"If you don't mind me asking, what do you do in your off time to get the work away from you and to relieve the stress?"

"I guess primarily bars and drink … oh, and men."

Gina and Lisa laughed at this. Goff looked at me whimsically.

"And you've been questioning the value of your work and have not been totally happy about your job?"

"Right."

"So you go out to the clubs at night, drinking and carrying on. You joke about and cuss your job, laugh and party. Then each night you go home, sleep it off, get up in the morning and head back to work."

"Sounds about right. So what are you saying?" I asked.

"That's just what they want."

"They?"

"People who gain power and profit from your enterprises."

"*Exactly* what they want," added Gina.

"This keeps your employers and the profiteers happy. You suffer. You drink. And they profit," Nicholas said smugly.

"And the longer I continue working and drinking away my frustrations, the harder it becomes for me to actually change anything," I said, slowly realizing the consequences of my words.

Nicholas laughed. "Bingo. They make their profits. You keep working. And you keep drinking. Exactly what they want. Alcohol dulls thought and relieves inhibitions. As a result, you don't actually make changes in your life and the cycle of unhappy work and nightly escape perpetuates itself. But suppose you start smoking marijuana. Pot frees the mind and stimulates thought. Start thinking too much and you begin questioning the very basis of your work.

That is what they do *not* want. Think too much and you may think yourself out of a job."

"Watch out, Karyn. Thinking can be hazardous to your health!" giggled Gina.

"And that is why they demonize marijuana and promote alcohol," Nicholas stated triumphantly.

"It never did make sense to me," said Lisa. "I mean, alcohol messes up your abilities and coordination so much more than pot, and is much harder on your stomach, brain and liver. Yet alcohol consumption is encouraged."

Nicholas continued, "Marijuana comes from a plant used by people throughout our history. Never in our history was it illegal until the last century when a small group of men decided it was not good for their long-term business interests and went on a campaign to slander it and those who use it. Since that time, all over the world jail cells have filled with people who harm no one but simply smoke marijuana. Because of its tendencies to stimulate creative thinking outside accepted norms, those in control fear it and work very hard to keep it illegal."

"Hey, I will smoke to that!" laughed Lisa as she began to roll another joint.

❦   ❦   ❦

I was getting tired and when I began to take my leave Goff offered to escort me home. We exited into the night and he put his arm around me as we walked down the street.

"Good meeting you today," he said.

"Definitely," I replied.

We walked the quiet streets toward my apartment. Goff hugged me and I let my head rest on his shoulder. I inhaled deeply, savoring his scent. The smell of his hair and the faint odor of his sweat overwhelmed me. My nipples tightened and I felt warm and wet between my legs. He seemed so manly, yet not macho or overpowering like so many other men.

We walked and hugged. He leaned over and buried his head in my hair and breathed deeply. Then he gently kissed the back of my neck, sending shivers down my spine.

We got to my place and I invited him inside for a cup of coffee. I started preparing the coffee and as I turned around from the kitchen counter he took me in his arms, leaned me over and kissed me fully on the lips.

He rolled his tongue into my mouth and my tongue quickly followed in a flurry of passion. He squeezed my leg between his and I could feel his rising hardness on my thigh.

My heart was pounding. I wanted him so badly. Normally I would follow my passion, but something felt amiss. I leaned back and broke the kiss. I gave him a gentle smile.

"Karyn, you're beautiful," he said. "Fucking awesome beautiful."

"Thank you, Goff."

"Is something wrong?"

"No, nothing is wrong. It's just that my head is spinning and I need to think about some things before jumping into this with you."

His face, which had been filled with confidence and pride, seemed to instantly deflate.

"No, don't get me wrong. I like you a lot. This has been a big day and I've been through a lot. I need to do some processing."

He conjured up a weak smile. "OK then. Perhaps another time?" he asked half-heartedly and looked down at the floor.

"Look Goff, I really do want to see you again. You seem like a wonderful and intelligent man. This is just too fast for me now."

"OK Karyn. I understand. I'll call you," and he turned toward the door.

"Hey Goff … thanks for the fun evening. I liked meeting your friends and helping you guys out."

His face brightened. "No problem. There's plenty more to do if you want."

We walked to the door. He opened it and when he turned to say goodbye I gave him a gentle hug and kissed him lightly on the lips.

❧   ❧   ❧

I reclaim myself
As I wash away scriptures
Novels
History books
Math texts
Legal briefs
Political outcomes
Redundant times
I wash away everything
From my emptying mind.

I have difficulty escaping
What I see and I feel
It wants to explode
Ignite what is real
It wants to unravel
All I hold dear.

I am leaving all traces of me
I am skating away
I remember what used to be
In some other day
So I am taking along
What I know to be true
It will crash and crumble
I realize that too
But never again will I mistake truth for lies
Or light from dark.

❈   ❈   ❈

I woke as usual at 6:00 a.m. My head was still spinning from the night before so I decided to take the day off work.

I was not sure what I should do next, but I felt as if I had crossed a line and I was not going to turn back. My thoughts kept returning to my inquisitive and carefree days at the university. I decided to talk with some girlfriends from grad school. I was curious how they had fared with their mathematical skills in the working world.

First I called Fara, a brilliant girl who had specialized in numerical methods and topological systems and was hired right out of school by a prestigious genetic engineering research firm.

"Hi, Fara. This is Karyn. How have you been doing?"

"Good. And you?"

"Fine. Been a long time."

"Sure has. What brings you to call?"

"I have been thinking …"

"Uh oh. That could be dangerous."

"Yeah, well, it probably is. I've been troubled recently about my work."

"Your work? Aren't you still working on guidance systems for missiles?"

"Yeah. Exactly. And that's what's troubling me."

"How so?"

"You know the war and the daily body counts and the news of the increasing violence."

"I know. It's a shame. But what can we do about it?"

"That I'm not sure. But I'm questioning whether I should keep supporting it with my work."

"Good question."

"And you. How is your work going?"

"Just fine. I've been developing software to find common patterns, groupings and relationships between complex and seemingly disparate genetic data. We're attempting to link unmapped genetic sequences with hereditary and growth characteristics."

"Sounds powerful … and interesting. And how are they using your research?"

"We're finding genetic links between individuals and optimum growth characteristics, and are engineering new life-forms for use in agriculture and medicine. And we're patenting and licensing our work."

"Are you happy with the work?"

"Well, like any job it has its ups and downs. I like my work alright but I'm not comfortable with all the applications. I'm also concerned about possible unintended consequences."

"Unintended consequences?"

"Well we take every precaution but it's possible that we could initiate a strange genetic mutation that somehow escapes and multiplies out of control."

"Hmm. Sounds nasty, but there are safeguards, I'm sure."

"Well yes, but there are also profit motives and deadlines involved. So our scientists don't always get the last word on company decisions."

"I understand. I like the work I do as well but in the end I have no control over how any of it is used."

"What can you do?"

"Nothing I guess … except perhaps stop working."

"And then what? Take a non-technical job? Someone else will take your place."

"I know. You know, it was all so easy in graduate school. All we had to do was read, think and study. Oh, I miss those days."

I wished her well and hung up the phone, not feeling any better about my job. It all seemed so complicated.

Next I called Julia, who had studied probability theory and statistics. She went to work in the insurance industry after finishing her graduate work.

"Hey, Julia."

"Hi, Karyn. What's up?"

"I'm having job problems and wanted to get your opinion."

"Sure, how can I help you?"

"I'm not happy with the results of the work I'm doing."

"No doubt. No one really wants to help make weapons."

"Yeah I know that, but it's really starting to bother me."

"Hmm. Well if you really don't like it why not get another job?"

"Well I just might. I was wondering how your work is going."

"Alright. I use plenty of my mathematics training but the work is really dry and boring."

"How so?"

"Mostly I examine historical data and develop statistics to predict the number and severity of accidents and paybacks to insured people. I take profit targets and use probabilities to optimize expected gain by adjusting premium prices."

"Are you happy with the work?"

"Well, I make a lot of money for the company, which I guess is why I'm working there."

"I'm sure they appreciate your work."

"Well they do, but only because my work makes them lots of money. The insurance industry differs from other businesses in that we're able to choose the profit margin that we would like, and then use statistics and probabilities to determine premium prices to reach that goal."

We said goodbye and I hung up. I felt alone and isolated, weak and vulnerable. I was unsure of many things that I had felt confident about a few days earlier. It seemed that no matter what type of job I took, I'd have to compromise my ideals and ethics in order to make a living. Previously, that may not have bothered me, but I could no longer see myself doing work over which I had no control. I would not let myself be used for other people's gains, especially in ways that I saw as debilitating to society.

That night I had a very vivid dream.

I struggle along, walking down the beach at the edge of the ocean in a state of delirium. I keep thinking that something has happened, something terrible … but I can't seem to remember exactly how I got to this beach or what happened to everyone or how I managed to survive. But now I feel that I am dying. My clothes are torn and ragged. I walk without shoes on my feet. My hair is straggly and I am dirty and unkempt. My eyes are glazed over and focused within. It is only with great effort that I can see my surroundings at all and no matter how hard I try, I am not able to focus on anything. There is saliva and foam all around my mouth, on my cheek and chin. My breathing is very labored and I feel like I am not able to suck in enough air. I attempt to speak, but only barely audible incoherent mumbling sounds come from my mouth. I veer this way and that as I stumble down the beach. Finally, my strength fails and I fall into the surf. I am too weak to move my head as the waves splash my face.

In this incoherent state I hear something calling me. Something is making a sort of rhythmic grunting, squealing and whining sound, but I can tell it is directed toward me. I hear a language in the sounds that strikes some kind of resonance deep within. It is like someone is speaking to me in a long forgotten language. Somehow I understand bits and pieces, though I have no idea how this is possible. I begin to understand that we (humans) have failed. We have forgotten our past, our old knowledge and understanding. We have been erecting our buildings with concrete to give us a sense of permanence. We discovered that concrete would last hundreds or perhaps thousands of years and we came to view ourselves as permanent, but our sense of time was too small, since concrete eventually crumbles. I really do not know how I understood any of this but the message was clear. What we took for permanence was merely a fleeting perception. We tried to ground ourselves but what appeared to be solid ground slipped away.

As I was trying to understand this ancient language/song, the surf parted and a dolphin appeared before me. She swam to me and in the most delicate and affectionate manner brought her mouth to mine. She breathed out deeply and lightly brushed my lips. In that one moment I felt whole again. I felt her knowledge and tenderness and understanding, and in an instant I realized the depths of her being and the arrogance of ours. A big wave swept over us and I felt that I was going to drown. I struggled and woke up shivering, naked in bed ... sheets and blankets twisted around and lying at my feet.

The next morning I called work and quit my job. In a moment of clarity upon wakening, I realized that life consists of priorities. There is not enough time to do all that I want so I must do the things that I deem are most important. And designing missile guidance systems was not that important. In fact, it had no importance to me. I began to list and prioritize those things that were important to me. I would soon be leaving on a long journey.

As Karyn finished her story the wind picked up and began to howl around the walls of the building. It sounded like a huge machine was coming down the mountainside, preparing to smash the teahouse into the ground. The building shook and the candles flickered wildly. The air in the room seemed to vibrate in anticipation of an imminent disaster.

Ngawang laughed, "The roar of the wind is the roar of change. Don't hold too tightly to your seats. Changes are on the way. Dance your way through them."

Lobsang smiled at her. "Death is a transition. When one thing dies another blossoms. Sometimes the only way to open a new chapter is by closing the old. But the transition between the two can be very difficult."

"Yes," agreed Ngawang, "being pulled by the old while intrigued and drawn toward the new ... simultaneously fearful of loss and expectant of change."

"Exactly!" exclaimed Ellie. "Fearful and expectant. That's how I felt in the forest."

Ngawang smiled, "Part of you was dying Ellie. And another being born."

Ellie rocked her body and grinned.

Karyn nodded. "I walked away from my ambitions and my job and life security. And part of me died, like you Ellie.

"Now I travel the world to see firsthand what's actually happening. I don't accept what's told to me anymore."

"For good reason," said Ray and he smiled broadly at Karyn.

She looked away, hesitated for a moment and then continued, "Now I only work where I can directly see and feel the results."

"What've you been doing?" asked Raz.

"I carry folding solar panels, batteries and LED lights in my pack. When I visit someplace where the people are nice and I think they would use and benefit from a small energy system, I set it up and show them how it works. If they like it, I leave it."

"Very nice," replied Raz. "How many systems can you carry with you?"

"Only two or three, but I have friends and supporters who ship more to me as I travel. I smuggled two into Tibet and left them at a monastery."

Lobsang smiled. "Bless you, Karyn."

Karyn bowed slightly toward Lobsang. "I am trying to repair my mistakes of the past. I can't change that I helped make weapons used to kill people around the world. But I can use my past actions (kind of like a lever) to help me do better things."

"You have found your power Karyn," said Ngawang. "Your present actions take the past and change the future."

"And because of those changes," added Lobsang, "rather than us perhaps viewing what you did as horrific, we see what you did as part of circumstances that eventually led to your dedication to help people."

Lorraine had been sitting quietly, staring straight ahead, her eyes focused within. He arms were at her sides and she was sitting on both hands, rocking slightly back and forth.

She frowned and began to speak slowly. "The past is too big to change. When it is done it is over," and she looked down at the floor.

"There's hope for us all, Lorraine," offered Cibi.

She took a deep breath and let it out slowly. She sighed and began her tale.

CHAPTER 6

One of Us

Who is it you want to marry
What is it that you want to do
Who do you want to hold so dearly
To catch your mind and pull you through
Who do you want to dance with nightly
To laugh and cry and find the time
What is it that you hold so closely
That no one knows beneath your mind?

I wrap myself around your sense
Around your smell your innerness
You come within and I follow closely
All you do and sense and care
I wonder sometimes about your jolly
About your sense of what is there
I know that this is all I am
And all that's there is opening
It flows so sweet from you to me
And me to you
Incessantly.

Because that day that did proclaim
To all around
And all refrained
By saying no to one of us
Makes me wonder about your adventurousness
And what does heaven really see
And carry on beyond ourselves?

❄   ❄   ❄

I love him. I have always loved him. I loved him the first time I saw him. I loved him the last time I saw him. We were like two as one. Inseparable. Always in tune. Always at play. I will always love him. He is me and I am him. Only the physical separated us and even that blended and dissolved, while we were engaged like yin and yang. Frank and Lorraine. Always together. Forever in love.

So when we parted, I lost myself. And not knowing who I was, I lost my friends. I was so unfixed and unsteady that neither me nor anything else felt real.

I can have no babies. I never will. The doctor said that my uterus is not right. It never formed properly and could never hold a baby. And if I got pregnant my uterus would rip apart before the fetus reached five months, which would probably kill both the baby and me.

When Frank found this out he began to drift. We stayed a couple and continued to have fun, but something died between us. I guess it was the expectancy of things to come. Frank always wanted a son, one of his own flesh and blood, and I would never be able to give this to him.

So he started looking and soon found Shela, an exotic and beautiful, soft-spoken woman. I knew that this would eventually happen. Initially, I could not restrain myself and I cried and clutched and screamed. But it was not to be. Frank left and within a month I heard that Shela was pregnant.

That was the last I had seen of Frank. I tried to forget him but never found another relationship that could replace our times together. So I resigned myself to a solitary life of work. I tried to use my work counseling teens to fill my emptiness. Sometimes I think that if I'd never had my time with Frank I might be fully engaged in a comfortable, loving life. Though that life may not have been as fun, creative and bright as my relationship with Frank, I would not know that it paled because I would have no comparison.

So after 16 years I saw Frank again. He had called the previous week. At first I thought just to say hello and wish me well, but he wanted to come and see me. He said he had never stopped thinking about me, even after having two children. But Shela had left him. He had lost his passion in the relationship and could no longer cover it up. Shela wanted more. She took the kids and moved back home. And Frank was alone.

What was I to think? Should I risk seeing him and falling back into the same dreadful longing? Maybe since he now had the children he wanted we could once again be together? Could I ever trust him again? I was not sure about any of this, but Frank had been the best thing in my life and I knew that I *had* to see him. I had to get close to the only thing in the world that I imagined could fulfill me.

He was arriving that morning and we planned to meet in the park by the fountain. Amazing that after 16 years my stomach still fluttered and I ached to be near him. Apparently, I had not and maybe never could release him entirely.

It was a beautiful spring day in the city. The park was verdant. Life was surging upward toward the heavenly blue sky. The sun warmed the meadows and a light breeze, sweet with the scent of cherry blossoms, cooled the air. Birds flirted and sang love songs in the treetops. Butterflies danced among the flowers. Every living thing seemed to be rejoicing in simply being alive.

People meandered along the pathways, gazing at flowers, listening to birds, watching the creek fall toward the ocean. I walked into the plaza and instantly met the gaze of a handsome athletic man standing by the fountain.

He broke into a big smile, waved and called out, "Lorraine! Hi Love!"

"Heeeyyy Frank. So good to see you!"

We hugged and I felt at home again. His hug was open and warm and reassuring … exactly as I remembered. Immediately I was comfortable.

"You look great Lorraine. As pretty as you ever did. How I missed you!"

"It's been a long time, Frank."

"Yes it has. Way too long."

We held hands and started to stroll down one of the garden paths leading from the fountain.

"And how are the children?" I asked.

"Oh Lorraine. How sweet they are. They're precious to me." He looked down at the ground, hesitated for a moment and then said, "You know I am so sorry for what happened."

"Really? I never heard from you again. I figured you didn't care and that I was just a stepping stone in your life."

"Please Lorraine. Don't say that. I don't know what to tell you but I can say that I never stopped loving you. I've thought of you every day since our parting. I have cried myself to sleep night after night thinking of you."

"You know I was devastated. I have had trouble making sense of my life ever since."

"Lorraine, I love you now and I loved you then. But I had to have children. My heritage demanded this of me. I wanted you so bad and it tore me apart. Maybe I made the wrong decision. Since the day we parted I have been like a leaf blowing in the wind. I am so sorry for what I've done," and he looked away to hide his tears.

"God, Frank, I love you too. I don't really understand but I can accept that you did what you thought you must do. I always imagined that we were fated to be together."

"We are here now. Today is a new day."

"Yes it is. And perhaps the future will be different." I shuddered almost imperceptibly as I paused to consider my words, then in a cheery voice continued, "But you must tell me what it's like being a father."

"You know, it's different than I'd imagined. I thought that as a father I would continue hanging out with my friends, doing the same old stuff only less frequently. But I was wrong. Having children brought an unexpected sense of purpose to my life and changed my priorities. It isn't a matter of taking time away from my usual activities to be with the kids but rather the opposite."

"That's good, Frank. I always knew you would be a good father."

"Thank you, Lorraine. I sometimes have to work very hard at that."

"I see troubled kids every day in my work. It's a hard world in which to raise children. There are so many problems and it's so easy for kids to get involved. Parents lose control and the kids wander the streets."

Frank shook his head. "I know. It's very sad. You wonder where the parents are."

"I think the problem is *with* the parents. Unlike you, many parents don't dedicate themselves to their children."

"Unfortunately, it's very easy to have children and very difficult to raise them well. I think a lot of parents are in over their heads."

"Yes, and the kids suffer. I talk with many mothers and fathers who don't understand their responsibilities as parents. They know enough to punish bad behavior but they have very little long-term vision and often don't recognize or cultivate opportunities for their child's growth."

We walked in silence and I thought about how our choices had brought each of us by different paths to this same place.

Frank squeezed my hand. "What a beautiful day, Lorraine! Like heaven on Earth. Here again with you! I feel like I can touch God today!"

"Yes. Heaven on Earth. Everything is so beautiful. Life is so glorious! I feel fortunate to be a part of this wonderful world!" I exclaimed.

✤   ✤   ✤

We walked back to Frank's hotel, admiring everything that we saw. Everywhere I looked I saw blossoms of love … a young couple on the park bench exchanging kisses, a family strolling along the path by the creek, cats eyeing each other in the alley, bees drinking the nectar of flowers. All was good. I was with Frank again.

When we got to the room, Frank mixed some drinks and we sat on the sofa. He touched my hand … gently letting his fingers run across my palm. I accepted his touch. It had been too long. Through the years of lonely absence the deep passion still glowed. He could feel it.

Our lips met and we kissed long and passionately, exploring and re-exploring our long lost touch. I felt warm and slightly confused as I pressed against him. During those empty years I had struggled to quell my feelings toward him, and I was a little angry with myself for my impetuousness and desire. But I was feeling giddy.

I blurted out, "Tell me that you still want me. Tell me how you want me soooo bad. Tell me that you need to have me … and that you must have me!"

"Oh baby, I need you. I want you. I must have you. I live for you Lorraine."

"Yes you do. You live for me. Now show me how much you live for me. Kiss my feet. Yes and my ankles. That's right. Lick right up my leg. Yeah and over the thigh and up between my legs … ohh … yes, right there. Yes. Yes. Yes. Oh baby boy do you like it?"

"Oh baby I like it. Give me all of that."

I pressed hard against his mouth and tongue as he licked and sucked and nibbled over and over and round and round. My passion oozed in his mouth and down my legs. His fingers slipped within me. I squirmed and moaned.

"Oh baby you taste so good. You are my wine and honey. You are divine."

"Oh … oh … oh … I'm coming. I'm coming. I'm coming!" And I screamed and gushed and shivered. He pushed deeper and harder. I succumbed and my femininity overwhelmed him.

"Oh baby you are sooooo sweet. It is bliss to be with you. Come again and again and again. Oh god, you have got me sooo hot!" he yelled.

I sat up and looked at him. "Oh … my oh my. Come here big guy. Let's see what you've got for me."

My lips were upon him. I sucked and licked up and down all over and under his manhood. First gentle licks over the tip, then full swallows down its entire length. He moaned and groaned.

"Oh baby you are so good. Go on and on. Oh my god. You fucking angel. Oh … oh … oh … OH!" he wailed.

And he pulled out quickly and grabbed hard on his dick. "Not yet baby. Not yet. We have got more to do. Let me get another taste of youuuu!"

I spread my thighs and he once again licked my lips still swollen hot and dripping. He buried his face between my legs.

After awhile he lifted his head. "Ooh baby baby. You are a princess and I am going to fuck you royally," he laughed.

He sat on the edge of the bed and smiled. "Come on … come over here and sit on this!"

I climbed over and straddled him and pressed my femininity down around him. He could feel my warmth, my softness and juices pressing on the end of his dick. He pushed up, up, up and into me. I moaned and shivered and he went in even deeper. I swayed and rocked. I was melting.

I could not restrain myself. "Oh … oh … oh … oh my god!" and I shivered and shook and moaned and came and came and came.

"My god baby. You are good. I am your man." And as he pushed up I slid softly up and down slowly letting each inch of him in and out of me.

"My god. You feel so fucking good. Ohhh … fuck me hard!" I screamed.

"Yes baby. I will I will!" And he grabbed my ass and pushed me up and down and up and down. I surrendered completely to him as he slammed in and out. Once again I began to moan and he pushed harder and faster.

"Oh … Oh … God fuck it I am coming again!" I yelled.

"Oh go on baby. You feel sooo good. My little angel come to save me," he roared.

"Oh yeah. I'll save you alright. If you call fucking to death saving!" I laughed.

We fucked like there was no tomorrow. Once again we were together … expanding and combining and joining and playing. What more could there ever be to life?

❦   ❦   ❦

It was late afternoon when we finally unlocked from each other's arms and decided to go out for a stroll around the city. We walked back to the park and sat on a bench, hugging each other and watching people.

A family ambled past. The mother was pushing a baby in a stroller. The father walked next to her and a small boy and girl were running alongside. The girl squealed as her brother chased her in circles.

Frank asked, "So you work as a teen counselor?"

"Yes, for the past ten years."

"That sure puts you in the trenches. You must deal with a lot of problems … both personal and familial."

"Yes. Sometimes it's very difficult. I help teens that are having trouble staying in school because of attendance, behavioral or academic problems. If their initial screening doesn't indicate low IQ or physical-based problems, they are sent to me. I talk with the students and quite often their parents."

"You must have a lot of angry kids coming to see you."

"For sure. Some are angry with their teachers, some at their parents, some at the school and some are just angry about what life has dealt them. I try to help them find useful, positive and enjoyable things to focus on and to let the things that they can't control pass by."

"Sounds like a good approach."

"I deal with a lot of rebellion. Many of my kids are fighting against the controls and rules under which they live. They don't want to be told how to act, how to think or how to live their life. Basically, they just want the freedom to personally express themselves … to do things on their own, in their own way. They're trying to find out who they really are and to become their own person. And in a way, that requires pushing off the yoke of parental and social control that binds them."

Frank spoke slowly, as if he were troubled by the words. "You know, I think rebellion may be necessary in the growing process. I don't think that just because kids rebel they will always reject what we offer. But to be self-thinkers, they need to find themselves."

"I agree. Rebellion allows kids to understand who they are and find their limits. Unfortunately, our society often deals out harsh punishments for acts of rebellion. But I think with all the problems in the world, we need some different approaches. Maybe the kids can figure out what to do if we just let them."

Frank nodded. "They're our future."

"I think our society tries to maintain the status quo by suppressing rebellion."

"Interesting. I definitely want my kids to think for themselves and perhaps rebellion is the price I must pay. As my kids became teenagers they wanted much more privacy and a stronger voice. Now, they don't want me or Shela to plan anything for them. They push away our ideas and sometimes do things just to irritate us. They frequently get angry and are easily provoked into anger."

"I imagine it's difficult to see your children reject your ideas and show little appreciation for all you've done for them."

"Well yes. Very difficult at first, but after thinking about *my* rebellious teen years I can hardly complain."

I laughed. "It *is* hard to be a good parent."

Frank grinned. "Don't you know it. Many parents don't really know much about taking care of themselves, let alone raising kids. They're confused about who they are and what life is about. So they can't teach those things to their children."

"Exactly. In my work I see parents acting like children, butting heads with their kids and making impossible demands that can never be realized. The parents don't understand what their children really need."

"You know, I don't think it's important exactly what specific subjects and details you teach the kids. Of course they should learn to be discerning and gain basic skills and knowledge about the world. But I think most importantly we should spark an interest in them to *want* to learn. Shela and I have worked to give our children the wherewithal and self-confidence to pursue their own interests."

I laughed. "Ah, and there you have rebellion. You're encouraging them to rebel by giving them the tools to think creatively."

Frank grinned. "We definitely are not forcing them to follow in our footsteps. We'd rather see them find their own paths."

"Very good. It takes a strong parent to watch and allow your child to stray. You're impressing me, Frank."

"Thanks Lorraine. I think it's healthy for children to have options. Though there are definitely more risks involved than simply telling them what to do."

"God, I wish more parents took their roles seriously. We have so many problems in the world and they multiply when parents don't take responsibility for their children's upbringing," I moaned in frustration.

Frank nodded, "It's of such importance."

"Exactly. I see so many kids controlled by hang-ups and fears. Their viewpoints get so out of kilter that they believe no options are open."

"I think that the more restrictions a child develops because of personal dislikes, the less freedom she will actually have."

"Same for adults," I replied.

"Certainly. Shela and I have taught our children that if they don't like someone or something, to focus on things they do like. We made it clear that bad things are part of life and sometimes can't be avoided. Though we all make mistakes, rather than dwell on the bad we teach them to learn and grow from each experience."

"Very noble, Frank. You know, I'm feeling proud of you. Though you caused *me* great pain you've been doing good things with your life and somehow I feel better seeing that. I'm so glad that you came to visit me. But I'm also so sorry about you and Shela."

I was feeling a little tired and hungry. "Hey, what do you say we head down to the coffee shop for a latte and a snack?" I asked.

"That's funny, Lorraine. I was just going to ask you the same."

I laughed. "Hey, we must be thinking alike."

We got up and started walking down the path. Frank put his arm around me. I nestled my head on his shoulder and smiled. I felt safe and secure with Frank. All the world's problems seemed light-years away.

"Do you believe in telepathy, Frank?"

"You mean do we have the ability to read other people's minds?"

"Yes. Do you believe that people can know what other people are thinking without them saying anything ... you know, like just now with us?"

Frank laughed. "I think we're just tuned into each other."

"Well maybe so. But I've had similar experiences. Like sometimes I sense my momma's problems even when she isn't around. It's not really words, though ... more like strong feelings. I feel her pain and anguish and I call her up and talk with her."

"Funny thing."

"Maybe you are telepathic Frank. Maybe you have that extra sense."

Frank laughed again. "I don't think so. I can't read your mind right now."

"Maybe most everyone is telepathic. Maybe it's just another one of our senses. Anyway, who says we have just five?"

"I've never heard about any sixth sense of telepathy!" jested Frank.

"OK, how about the tiny ruby throated hummingbird with the smaller than pea-sized brain. They migrate more than a thousand miles a year and return to their *exact* nesting place every time. They don't follow roads or use maps, so they must have some kind of internal navigational sense."

"Whatever. Still, I don't know any people with built-in navigational sensing. Anyhow, what does this have to do with telepathy?" Frank asked skeptically.

"I'm just saying that maybe we have abilities we just don't recognize."

"Like telepathy?" Frank asked with a big grin on his face.

"Right. Like telepathy. Look, humans produce brain waves."

"OK."

"Well, if we produce brain waves why wouldn't we be able to sense other people's brain waves?"

"Just because we make brain waves doesn't necessarily mean that we can *receive* brain waves."

"Maybe it does. Waves experience other waves. When they meet they create interference patterns and affect the vibrations of waves around them. Brain waves emanate from the brain as a result of electro-chemical brain activity. There is no distinct boundary between wave and brain. So maybe external wave energy interacting with outgoing waves affects the vibrating molecules and atoms of the brain."

"I sort of follow you," Frank said tentatively.

"Good. Remember that brain waves contain information about the processes of the brain that created the waves. So perhaps telepathy occurs when information encoded in someone's brain waves is understood by another."

"It sounds logical but I don't see why people wouldn't recognize this and use their telepathy. I believe that most people would think you crazy if you told them they were telepathic."

"Well, the information in the brain waves has nothing to do with words so maybe people don't understand what they're receiving. I think telepathy is a natural ability that we all share. But our society teaches us to ignore its existence. As children we're chastised if we talk of something unusual and don't follow the appropriate rules or common logic. We're taught to disregard feelings and senses that are not accepted, and are punished if we speak about them."

"So you think they just scare it out of us?"

"Scare it out of us or teach us to ignore it. As with all senses and skills, each of us functions at a different level. So perhaps we actually experience people in ways that we're not able to describe, yet these impressions and communications help make up our understanding of people."

"I suppose that some people could be more adept than others."

"Perhaps," I continued, "there are a lot of things going on in our daily experiences that cannot be understood by our current language and thought structures. The rigid rules of science and the tenets of our religions keep us within tight social bounds and prevent us from recognizing phenomena that may be part of our common experiences but are not acknowledged by these institutions. Framed by these rules, those things that we can't super-scribe by words don't even appear to exist."

"It's true that we generally don't accept unknown and unproven phenomena, and sometimes we even persecute people professing to have knowledge about those things."

"Exactly," I said, "sometimes science eventually catches up, but some things are so elusive and run so contrary to rational thought that they may always remain blurred in the background. Just because we're not smart enough to understand the actions and connections of a phenomenon in such a way that the relations and causations can be described accurately doesn't mean that the phenomenon does not exist; it's just outside the box defined by the set of accepted rules that have previously succumbed to verification. People can only understand what's relatively close to their current state of understanding. Beyond that, concepts appear to be unintelligible gibberish."

"Whew, Lorraine, you've got me going. You were always such an analyst. Always wanting to find the answers. I like that. It's been too long. How wonderful that we're here together again!"

"Oh Frank, it's so good to be with you … and to telepath with you," I said, giggling. "Somehow the universe has brought us together again."

❈   ❈   ❈

We continued our stroll along the streets through the evening air. I felt more charged and alive than I had for years. We held hands and walked among the crowd on the boulevard, pausing to window-shop and laugh about old times. As we neared the coffee shop I stopped to try on some silk scarves from a street vendor.

"Beautiful, Lorraine. I love that pattern," said Frank.

"You do. I'm not sure. I like this one, too. And this one. I can't make up my mind," I said, laughing.

Frank laughed with me. "Just like you, Lorraine. For what it's worth, I think they're all very nice."

"Oh, I just can't decide."

Frank glanced down the street. "You take your time. The coffee shop looks crowded. I'll go down and get us a table."

"Great. I'll be right there. It won't take me long. I promise," I said, laughing again.

"Sure thing. See you in a bit."

I continued trying on and admiring the scarves as I watched Frank walk down the street and go into the coffee shop.

As I backed up to get a good view in the mirror I bumped into a young man walking by.

"Oops, sorry," I smiled.

He looked at me in a distracted way but did not acknowledge my apology and quickly continued walking. I felt a shiver down my spine. His eyes were dark and obscure, and that quick glance immediately made me feel small and alone.

I watched him continue on his way down the street and then it flashed upon me. I dropped the scarves and went running after him yelling, "Stop that man! Stop that man!" but people couldn't see who I was yelling about and just looked at me in a puzzled way.

"Stop that man!" I yelled again and again as I ran as fast as I could toward the coffee shop. But he had already entered the front door and as I started across the street, the building came apart. In a flash, the front wall exploded outward with a huge boom that shook everything around and I was knocked backwards into near unconsciousness.

I lay there bruised and bleeding as a rain of debris settled around me. My eyes were burning and my throat felt like it was on fire. I heard a ringing sound very close by and tried to make out what was happening in the flames and smoke. I realized that my phone was ringing and struggled to get it out of my pocket.

On the other end I could hear a voice. It was my sister. "Hello, Lorraine? Are you alright? I was just thinking about you."

❋   ❋   ❋

Crying myself to sleep
Crying for the haves and have nots
Crying for the dying and living
Crying for life and death

Crying for good times and bad times
Crying to feel the pain.

I have nowhere to go and I've nothing to do
I have nothing to hold onto and no one to see
I am alone and naked scared and free
I am crying to get back to some kind of unity
I am separate from him separate from you
I am separate from me from all that I do
I know nothing now and think nothing less
I find no answers and no judgment rules
I take on each moment and watch for the next
Always alert and prepared for the test.

Fear is the conqueror
It overcomes all
It knows not the boundaries
Between heaven and hell
It stalks us at night while we quietly rest
It prowls round our houses and all that we quest
Fear is our friend
Our savior our god
Worship it lightly
Since it will conquer all
Through fear peeks its mantra its all-knowing sense
Together we change and then just dispense
With our thoughts and our notions
Our goodness and greed
Our heavenly conceptions
Our unending pain
Just let it overcome us
And wash away stain
Fear is our garden our path and our lord

Without fear we have nothing
We are totally bored.

Guns are for playing
They kill and they maim
We have so much hate
Stored deep in our brains
We cannot escape the animal urge
To mark our possessions
And divide what spreads out
To garner our share
And others as well
To spring above poverty
To pull ourselves up
With our head in the clouds
And eyes in our butts
It takes only one to tango
And another to doubt
A third to lay claim to all that's without
When violence has maimed and stolen and killed
We jump up in arms to deliver a lesson
To teach evil good
To correct what is wrong and heavenly should
Then war overcomes country
And all are amazed
That so much suffering must always take place.

It's a cycle unbroken
Through all history
One man's garden just looks a little bit green
It is taken and twisted and given away
To the holder of power
The forces of sway
Only one gun is necessary to make such a mess

One gun and mind driven by greed and love of the time
It takes two to fight it has always been said
But one gun alone can deliver the dead
When one gun does fire and push back the crowd
One gun must answer to prevent complete shroud
So what can we do if we're never quite there
One gun exists so we must take up our share
One gun exists so we must bring the fight down
One guns exists
One hole in the heart
One stab in the back
One scream in the night
Can we ever change this idiot fact
That no one can rise ahead of the pack
That we are all bound by similar laws
That together we go
And together we fall?

❦   ❦   ❦

By the time Lorraine finished speaking she was crying uncontrollably. She could hardly finish the end of her story and had to pause several times to gain her composure. The air in the room felt thick and heavy. Her crying slowly subsided but her breathing got louder and sounded pained. Everyone sat as if in a stupor. The wind had grown quiet.

Lana broke the silence, "I am so sorry for you, Lorraine. How horrible a loss. What a cruel fate to be given and then to have it taken away. I can only imagine your pain."

Ellie began to sob. "What a fucked up world. We are so senseless."

Lorraine rubbed her face with both hands in anguish and wiped off her tears. "I've tried to make sense of this but I can't put the pieces together. I think of Frank and I see him in the park, waiting to meet me … a beautiful smile on his face. As I walk up to him he fades and the dark eyes of the bomber are upon me. Fear slips down my spine and I can't look away."

"We fight these senseless battles as if we're pre-programmed and can't do otherwise. Who's gaining? Who's winning?" lamented Cibi.

"And it only takes one to bring the fight down," Raz said with a sigh.

Lorraine nodded, "I couldn't get over that fact. I tried to get back to work but I couldn't hold back my grief. I took time off and spent weeks and weeks, which turned into months and months, in dark depression. Everything seemed so temporary and tentative. I felt hopeless.

"Then I began to drift. I was furious at the world. I traveled aimlessly, not really caring where I was going and never staying anywhere long enough to become familiar. One day I found myself in western China, and after hearing so many stories about the lost land of Tibet (I thought it was quite apropos to me) I made my way here."

Cibi cleared his throat and raised his voice slightly. "I have come to believe that our destinies are bound together as a race. We will either live or die as humans, but our eyes are so clouded by hate and greed that we refuse to recognize this basic fact. Like you, Lorraine, I am fleeing violence. I didn't lose my lover but I lost my home and family. And I've been searching for something of value ever since."

CHAPTER 7

One World

But wait
We are won
We are brought all together
We can worship the same gods and look the same way
We can spend all our money and it all flows straight up
So happy we are with our ridiculous grins
Shopping for shit that we can't do without
Shit that was nowhere when our parents were about
Shit that is coming from everywhere around
It's keeping us lonely
It's dimming the sound.

I was born and raised in a small remote village located at the base of a large mountain. It is the most beautiful place I have ever been and I love it more than any other place on Earth. The foothills surrounding my village grow exceptionally lush and thick grasses, and the highland shrubs burst alive with flowers every spring. Below the village steep canyons fall away and slowly expand into a long valley that broadens as it disappears into the distance.

The mountain slopes gently rise above the village through dark forests. At around 1500 vertical meters above the village the raw mountain breaks steeply from the easy slope into massive rock cliffs that tower another eight hundred meters to the summit. Quite often the mountaintop is shrouded in mist and clouds, while the valley below basks in sunshine. We always welcome the occasional showers as a relief from the enduring sun, though the rain rarely extends very far down the valley.

Life in the village was unhurried and celebratory. We had no reason to rush. The sun came and went each day and the moon grew and shrank each month. We were thankful for our blessings and gathered frequently for song and dance. Most people worked at traditional occupations like crafting wooden tables and chairs, farming vegetables and fruit, tending livestock and drum-making. A few people ventured down valley during the week to work in stores or factories in one of the towns along the river. This required a long trip by foot or bicycle on paths and rough dirt roads that dropped out of the hill country.

I was a shepherd with a herd of 300 goats that I raised and tended much like the people of my village have done for the past twelve centuries. I spent most of my time on the grassy hillsides, moving my goats from pasture to pasture and stream to stream. At night I watched the moon and stars and wondered at the beauty of living. Under my care and protection my goats grew fat and happy, grazing on lush grasses under blue skies and sipping water from clear mountain streams.

I loved village life and felt reassured by being part of a larger tribe. We all worked together for the benefit of the village and we all lived comfortably. We shared our blessings and our hardships. Each person was free to find his or her own place in the community, based upon their interests and abilities.

Life was pretty idyllic during my childhood and teenage years. It seemed to us that in our remote location life would continue the same as it had been for centuries. But all that changed one sunny day in May during my twenty-fourth year of life.

❦   ❦   ❦

Actually, the warning signs of impending change had been building for years. But in the village we continued with our daily lives, ignoring what was going on below us in the valley and paying little attention to rumors of unrest in the distant capital. And each year, there were more roads and houses in the towns and more smoke in the distance from new factories along the river.

More recently, roads had been built on the far side of the mountain to a site that was being excavated for rocks and minerals. We had been told that the mining would not affect the village, but several times each day we could feel the ground shake beneath us. And each time it did, my heart palpitated while feelings of fear and dread coursed through my body.

One morning I was sitting on the top of a knoll, watching the goats on the slope below me. It was a beautiful day with the sky as blue as a bunting's wing. The warm sun was comforting after a cool starry night. I had just finished cooking and was sitting by my small fire, sipping tea and eating a large bowl of porridge with milk and honey, when my friend and fellow shepherd Rageen called to me from a nearby hillside.

"Cibi! Cibi! Come here quickly. Have you seen this? Come here, Cibi! We have problems … big problems!"

I left my goats and ran down the slope, across the gully and up the next hill to where Rageen was standing. He was breathing hard with a look of fear on his face. "What's wrong Rageen?" I called as I made my way up the hillside.

"Look Cibi," he yelled as he pointed down the other side of the hill to the ravine below. I ran up to his side and looked down the next ravine. Every time in the past twenty-four years that I had looked down that hillside I had seen a beautiful clear bubbling stream rolling down from the mountain slopes above us. But today the streambed was dry and all the rocks were coated with a dark red powder. There was no water in sight.

At first I was confused and could not grasp what I was seeing. Then pangs of fear shot through my body.

"My God, Rageen. What is happening?"

"I don't know Cibi, but I bet it has something to do with that mine."

"What could they have done?" I implored.

"Let's get back to the village. We must find out what's going on."

We ran as fast as we could. When we got close to the village we could see people running around and screaming in a state of panic. As we approached, Eran, a young girl studying to be a teacher, ran up to us.

"The water is gone! The water is gone! The stream is dry. There is no water running into the village. We have no water to drink or bathe. Everyone is trying to gather up what little they can find as quickly as possible. They have stolen our water!" she screamed in despair.

I looked at Rageen. "You must be right. The mining company has taken our water. We must tell them what has happened."

❦   ❦   ❦

The sound of the sirens alarms and the bells
The sound of our freedom being sucked in the well
The well of the wealthy the powered the clan
Power seeks power
It's a natural fact
When power is given it rarely comes back
When power is stolen it fights with its might
To retain what it has and expand its domain
Power loves power
It rules over men.

❦   ❦   ❦

We left by bicycle for a long ride down valley then back up along newly carved roads to the far side of the mountain. As we got closer to the mine site we could see that a large part of the mountain had been blown apart, exposing a deep red gash that extended far into the interior of the slope. The forest had been bulldozed and a river of bright red water flowed in the creek alongside the road. About a kilometer from the mine site we were stopped by armed guards who demanded to know what we were doing on the property of the mining company.

"This land belongs to the mining company?" Rageen asked incredulously.

"Yes, it was purchased nearly two years ago," was the reply.

"We live in the village on the other side of the mountain. Our water stopped running last night and there is red powder covering the rocks in all the streambeds. We demand to know what is going on here!" Rageen barked angrily.

I quickly added, "Please excuse us for barging in on you, but our people depend on this water and have used the mountain streams for our sustenance for centuries. Without water we will die. We want to talk to the owners of the mine."

The guards laughed. The smaller one answered, "The owners? I don't think so. The owners are not here. They're not from here and they don't even live in our country. You can't talk with them. Besides, it would do you no good."

"Well, who is in charge of this operation?" Rageen demanded.

"Ah, that would be Mr. Obede. He's in his office up at the mine site."

"Could we see him then?" asked Rageen.

"I can ring him up and tell him that you're here." The guards went back to their vehicle and began talking on the radio. We couldn't hear their conversation.

When they returned the smaller one said, "Wait right here. Mr. Obede will be down shortly."

"Yes. That would be very good," I replied. We sat beside the road in the hot sun and waited.

After about 15 minutes we could see a car driving down the road toward us. It stopped next to the guards' vehicle and a man in a white shirt and tie, shiny black shoes and tightly pressed pants got out and walked toward us.

"Hello, I'm Mr. Obede. How may I help you?"

"Yes sir. I am Cibi and this is my friend Rageen. We are from the village on the east side of the mountain."

"Yes. And how may I assist you Mr. Cibi?"

"The water flowing down the east flank of the mountain dried up last night. It appears to have flowed down the mountainside with a lot of red dust in it, and then the water just stopped running."

"Ah. Didn't they warn you about that?"

"Who? Nobody warned us about anything!" Rageen shouted.

"I am sorry Mr. Rageen, but you should have been notified."

"Notified about what? That we would lose our water? That the creeks would stop running down the mountain? I think not!" Rageen was boiling and could not restrain himself.

"You should have been warned that there might be changes to your water supply."

"We were not notified of anything!" screamed Rageen.

"Well that is the business of your government. They sold the mineral and water rights to our company two years ago."

"What has happened to our water?" I demanded.

"First of all, it is not *your* water … at least, not anymore. I'm sorry about that. And secondly, we are diverting more water to use in the mine. And thirdly, we have begun bottling and selling the remainder. We paid a lot of money for the water rights. I'm sorry for your inconvenience. You can buy bottles of water to replace your supply. Have a good day, Sirs." And with that he turned around, got into his car and drove back up the mountain.

✤   ✤   ✤

And the water will drip and fall to the floor
And the water will run down the hall out the door
And the water will pour from each house in the town
And the water will silence and completely surround
And the water will come from the eyes in your head
And the water will flow from each of our beds
And the water will wash all the stains on our feet
And our hands and our heads will completely retreat
And the water will come without a sound in the night
And the water will make all that's wrong into right
And the water will keep all the life that we've known
But the water will drown out every ungrateful soul
It will take what is given and leave only dust
It will dry up the cornfields and leave only husks
Water is golden and sacred for life
But water is mutinous and takes what it likes.

✤   ✤   ✤

The situation in the village continued to deteriorate. Everyone was lacking water. We quickly realized that what we had taken for granted, clean flowing water, was our most basic requirement for survival. It became quite clear that without clean water we would quickly perish. Someone did find a clear-running creek a few kilometers up the slope from the village. We quickly installed a pipe to run the water back down to the village, but the flow was limited and it produced only enough water for drinking. The village shepherds had a meeting and we decided that we could no longer continue tending flocks. There just was not enough water for the livestock. Vegetable gardens withered and fruits did not set on the orchard trees.

We sent an ambassador to the capital to inquire about the mining operations, but she came back dirty and fatigued and simply verified what Mr. Obede had already told us. The government was sorry but the mining operation was good for the country and they would not shut it down. The water rights had been sold and there was nothing we could do about it. They suggested that we drill wells to provide water for the village, but offered no help or financial assistance.

✤   ✤   ✤

Forget about governments
They are bought and sold
Forget about fashions
They are manipulating your soul
Watch out for the master Mal
Easy as can be
But once you're locked inside
It's all so dizzy
What did I want? What was it now?
Just keep on walking and browsing the aisles
Surely you'll find it. You know it is there.
And around the next corner by the underwear
Is that darling silver necklace
And it's only six dollars!
How can it be that it sits in this case
A six-dollar necklace from somewhere down south
Down in some place where they can't live without
Sweating and breathing some infernal air
Digging a mountain and crumbling its rock
Deep down below in some nasty wet crack
For a dollar a day and a slap on the back?

But I feel so good with my basket so full
Of shit that I need and shit that is cool
Cool cause they told me and you and him too
That we need this crap so we look like a zoo.
We stand around covered with goods from the Wart

We look at each other and stand up in court
When someone is captured and made to bear weight
For struggling to overcome this unbearable fate
For struggling to push aside all the shit
And hold it bare naked for the world to see it.

❧   ❧   ❧

About a week later Rageen, our friend Maolie, another young shepherd, and I were sitting on a rock wall outside the village. We were enjoying the afternoon, chatting away while watching our goats graze on the slopes below.

The three of us were discussing the future and wondering how long we could continue caring for our goats with so little water available. Maolie was saying that she was going to drive her goats to town the following week. She planned on selling her herd and then trying to find a job making cabinets or working in a small shop. Maolie's mother was sick and she needed money as soon as possible.

Rageen and I had been thinking the same but decided to hold out longer before selling our goats.

"Hey, check that out!" Maolie exclaimed, pointing to the dirt track climbing out of the canyon below us.

Dust was rising from a vehicle driving up toward the village. After a few minutes we could see a late-model pickup truck slowly moving up the road toward our vantage point. As it approached we stepped down off the rock wall and stood in the road, waiting for its arrival.

The truck stopped in front of us and a woman and two men got out. The men were wearing white shirts and the woman had on a long black dress and a black hat. The smaller man sported a blue striped tie that matched his eyes, and the taller wore a simple black tie.

"Hello. How are you doing today?" asked the woman.

"Fine and you?" answered Maolie.

"We're good. We heard about your troubles and came here to bring you comfort."

"Amen," chortled Rageen.

I snickered. "We're all pretty comfortable here … except for the fact that our water has been stolen."

"We heard about that and are very sorry for your misfortune. We have brought bottled water for you and toys for the children," answered the woman as the men removed boxes of plastic water bottles and plastic-wrapped toys from the back of the truck.

Rageen was quick to reply. "Thanks. But we don't need your bottled water or toys. You can help us if you can restore our water from the mining company."

"Sorry, we can't do that. But we can help ease your pain," insisted the smaller man.

"Well, what we really need is clean running water. But how do you propose to ease our pain?" asked Maolie.

"We are here to bring you faith," the woman answered.

"Faith?" repeated Rageen incredulously.

"Yes, faith to help you get through these hard times," responded the taller man.

"We already have faith. And we *are* doing our best to get through this," Rageen answered.

"We are here to show you our merciful God who will protect you in times of need and disaster," the taller man proclaimed.

"Can your God return our water?" I asked.

"Of course He can … when the time is right," smiled the woman.

"The time is *right* right now!" roared Rageen.

"God works in mysterious ways. We cannot know why He allowed your water to be taken. But when the time is right He will return your water," the shorter man said with a smile.

"Well then what can your God do to help us right now?" demanded Maolie.

"He can keep you safe. He can give you comfort as long as you follow His path," the taller man replied.

People in the village had seen the truck arrive, and were beginning to walk down the hill and form a circle around us.

Rageen was getting impatient. "Look I don't know what you consider the path of God but anything that takes our water is part of no path of any God of mine. If you want to help, send someone up to that mine and stop them from blasting the mountain apart!"

I concurred, "Yes whatever it takes to get our water back is the righteous path for us."

"Be careful, now. All in due time. Don't try to outwit or out-think God," responded the woman.

"So you want us to wait patiently until your God brings back our water?" jeered Maolie.

"We will protect you. We will bring you water in these times of trouble," the woman replied softly.

"You will protect us? Will you be able to protect our goats and sheep that are dying of thirst? Or our gardens that are drying up in the sun?" shouted Rageen.

"We can only bring enough water for people to drink," she calmly answered.

"How will we eat if we can't raise our crops and livestock?" demanded Maolie.

"God is merciful. All will be provided," the taller man replied.

Rageen, struggling to keep his temper down, answered, "We can't wait until *all is provided*. We need water now. And we will do what needs to be done to make that happen."

"If you do not have faith and accept God's way then He cannot save you," the shorter man replied.

Rageen started jumping up and down. The three visitors took a step backwards. "God will save us? Save us from what?"

The shorter man with the striped tie answered, "If you do not accept God you may fall into the realm of evil. God can save you from the work of the Devil and his evil ways."

"Evil ways?" I repeated.

"Yes. There is evil all about in the world. It is only by coming to God that you may be protected from that evil. All that works against God ... all that is contrary to the purposes of God, is evil."

I could hardly believe what this man was telling us. "So if we don't accept God on His terms and instead take action against those who harm us we will be doing evil?"

"Without God all actions are evil," he replied in a flat voice.

"Why did you come here, then? To intimidate us into accepting God and resigning ourselves to a dry fate?" screamed Rageen.

"We are here on a mission to save your souls. We are here to show you the way of God and gather you into the flock," insisted the woman.

"If it is your mission to save us then we don't want your mission. We don't want *you* to save us from anything. In fact, we don't want *you* in our country!" boomed Rageen. He was sweating profusely and the veins in his neck were bulging from the strain.

"Yeah! Why are you here? What right do you have to treat us like we're inferior to you? This is our land. We don't need your help. With you come the mines, roads, smoking factories and the violence. You don't bring us salvation. You bring us death!" shouted one of the villagers who were now gathered in a tight ring around us.

"No, you have it wrong. We want to help you to be successful members of modern society," the taller man insisted.

"Look, we don't want to be members of *your* society. We've lived here just fine for the past thousand years. What right do you have to tell us how we should live?" Rageen sputtered in anger.

The man took a step backward from Rageen and knocked against one of the villagers behind him. He straightened quickly and tried to regain his composure. "Sorry. We did not come here to upset you … only to help."

"Yeah right. What help? You need pity. What arrogance you have thinking that *you* have the answer for us and that we should follow you. We have been living just fine on our own. And you come around and tell us that we should read and write *your* language, wear clothes like *you* and recite prayers to *your* God," Rageen shouted.

Cheers and nods went up from the gathered crowd.

Someone yelled, "Yeah, what makes you better than us? Your bottled water?"

"No, it's the guns!" someone yelled.

"Yes, the guns. That's what makes you better than us!" screamed a multitude of voices.

Rageen was shaking violently. "People like you have brought destruction to those living with the land the world over. All in the name of personal Gods espoused by missionaries like you. You are despicable!"

"Out! Out I say! Never return here again. We don't want you, your plastic toys and water bottles, and especially not your God!" the crowd shouted. People started throwing water bottles and boxes of plastic toys at the trio.

The missionaries turned and ran back to their truck, driving off in a cloud of dust to the cheers of all gathered round.

Shortly thereafter Rageen and I decided to sell our goats. We drove the flocks to town and wrangled with buyers at the market for a good price. We had no way of providing for the animals and the buyers knew of our dire straits, so they pressed us hard for a low sale price. In the end we had to settle for a small fraction of their actual worth.

We took our money and found a room to rent while we looked for jobs. The town had changed greatly since we had been there last year. There were new factories along the river with new houses for the wealthy nearby and a MegaStore between the two. Homeless people wandered the streets among growing numbers of police and soldiers.

Every night we heard gunshots echoing from skirmishes between groups of men with masks and hoods, and the police. Sometimes the army also got into the fighting. It was not safe to be out at night.

Rageen and I continued to look for work with local shopkeepers and furniture makers, but to no avail. Most were struggling to stay open. If the MegaStore sold things similar to what they sold, quite often the price was half of their selling price. How could they compete? All the while people, many in desperate conditions, traveled to the MegaStore to save what little money they could.

Everywhere people were complaining. It was either violence on the streets, lack of jobs, business troubles or the government. But the most anger was directed at those people taking the resources. We learned that villages similar to ours all around the region were losing land and water to the expanding network of mines, energy wells and factories. Tales of stolen water and dried up fields and orchards echoed on every street corner. There was talk of organizing a people's army.

Every day, more people moved to town from the countryside. Some were able to get jobs in the factories or at the MegaStore, but many found little to do. Rageen and I swore to each other that we would never take those jobs but I was beginning to doubt how we would survive otherwise.

The encampments of tattered tents on the outskirts of town grew larger by the day. Danger abounded everywhere.

One night Rageen and I were sitting in our room, talking about changes in our lives. I was homesick, scared and tired from walking the streets day after day, always in fear, always seeking food and work.

"Oh Rageen. I want to live the old ways and be with our friends and family. Our lives and our village are falling apart. There seems to be little left to bind us together. Everyone wants more money and more things. Things we never had and things we never needed. If we keep wanting and taking so much there will be no room left for what we were or who we are."

"Don't give up hope Cibi. We will get through this."

"Yes, I believe we will, but I'm not so sure what will become of our village and tribe," I said sadly.

"I'm worried that after so much time away from the village we won't be able or won't want to go back home," Rageen growled. He thought for a moment then continued, "Wouldn't it be great to be rich someday, Cibi, live easy and maybe fix some of these problems?"

"Sure, it would be great to be able to pay our bills and buy what we want and go where we want. But how do you think we would come to riches? If they were given to us we would not gain the capabilities and self-confidence that are the rewards of accomplishment. We would be soft, predictable and vulnerable. Certainly not strong and dependable people who could help with these problems."

Rageen sighed, "Oh for the old life. We worked hard and we played hard. Our wealth was in our growing herds. When I see rich people around here I wonder if their riches result from taking advantage of the well-being of others."

"Do you think it's a burden to have riches?" I asked.

"Well, you must protect them."

"Yes, and others will be envious so you will have to be suspicious."

"Yes, and there is always desire for more money."

I laughed, "I guess that's a struggle we won't have to deal with."

❧   ❧   ❧

Mr. One is coming! Mr. One is coming! All prepare for Mr. One!

One man. One business as Seller. Get too big and Mr. One steps up to the bat. How can you compete with Mr. One? And how long can you stay nose to the grindstone with Mr. One across the street?

Most everyone works for Mr. One. And those who don't either don't work or they work for someone who sells to Mr. One. Sure, Mr. One loves small show-lows who make stuff for him. But don't get too profitable! Mr. One will buy you out. Because if there is profit to be made Mr. One is compelled … no, he is forced to follow that money.

For don't the paperheads want their share of the pie? And the counters? And the interlocutors? And the toll keepers? And if Mr. One did not step up and perform the acquisition then heads would roll, for the money found had not been brought home.

And the highrollers slurp up the pie, and the midrollers watch the highrollers with envy and enjoy their bits, which they clutch while sidestepping the low-rollers and norollers. And the lowrollers push and grunt while the norollers scurry about in a symphony of high thought, low thought and conspiracy.

Oh, the prices are so low. All the fuzz is removed. One super-efficient, light-ning-fast widebrain orchestrating the show. A widebrain pulsing with selling and buying, feeling and touching everywhere at once, moving at the speed of light. A widebrain looking at the past, present and future simultaneously. A widebrain looking at itself and its own operations … continually monitoring and adjusting for statistical changes.

Mr. One knows more about people than anyone. Accounts, numbers, pat-terns, styles, sicknesses, friends, whereabouts, loves. That is, if Mr. One focused on an individual Mr. One would know. But what Mr. One loves is knowing those things—statistically speaking—about everyone to assure a continuous flow of dollars back to Mr. One.

❧   ❧   ❧

People were getting more and more agitated with the deteriorating conditions. There was increasing talk of organized armed resistance against the intruders. Rumors circulated about a mass gathering in the town square to address the problems. Rageen and I headed in that direction.

As we walked closer to the town center we merged with thousands of others. Everyone was moving toward the square. The police set up lines about half a kilometer away but did not enter the center of town. At first, they tried to stop people from walking but were quickly overrun as more people kept coming. There was a podium with microphone and speakers in the town square, and a man with a short-cut beard wearing a loose-fitting suit got up to address the large crowd gathered round.

"Hello dear brothers and sisters. For the moment we are safe. But for how long is unclear. The police or army may drive us from here at any moment. With the limited time we have I will speak directly and to the point.

"Most of our lives have been drastically changed. That is why we are here and that is what we have come to discuss. Each one of us have personal experiences that reflect these changes. But within our individual stories there is commonality about how our lives have been disrupted.

"First, an overwhelming economy foreign to this land is overtaking our own.

"Second, resources necessary for our lives and well-being are being taken from us.

"Third, where once we lived primarily by our own ways and means, now most of us are forced to work outside of our traditions for people whom we do not know, and who do not know or care to know us."

"And fourth, violence is overcoming us. Fear has become dominant in our lives.

"As a result of these changes we are losing control over the direction and course of our lives ... and in the process we are accepting and coming to depend upon foreign solutions, cures and treatments ushered to us by this new economy.

"And now what—if anything—can we do about the situation? Has life changed inexorably or will we be able to return to our previous loves and lives? And if that is at least partially possible, what actions are required to achieve those goals? That is the question today. This is our task to answer."

From the crowd arose indignant voices with calls of support.

"Hear hear!" "Now is the time!" "It is upon us!" "We must act!" "Take back our lives!"

He continued, "So what must be done? How can we regain control and reclaim our lives?

"I am a peaceful person and do not provoke confrontations. In fact, when faced with a confrontational situation I will do what I can to avoid violence. But when someone comes into my home to harm or kill me, my family or friends, I will do whatever I can to stop them ... including killing. This ongoing violence is being brought to our homes and into our families. I ask you, can we afford to stand around and allow all that we have, all that we are ... to be ripped away?"

Shouts of "No. No. No!" could be heard from the crowd. Someone yelled, "Kill the bastards!"

"Please. Please. We must not allow our anger to overcome us. We must use our anger as a means of inspiring and uniting us. Let us not dwell on hate. Let us use our indignation to propel us forward. Let your anger be a positive and righteous force.

"Now you may ask, *Where is our government? Is it not the government's place to protect us and our interests?*

"And I answer that it should be so! But the only part of government that we see is an army that tries to squash our dissatisfaction and discontent. Our government has been bought. Our economic well-being has been sold to the highest bidders: mining, energy and retail giants. Sadly, we can expect no help from the government. Too much money is at stake. To them we are either consumptive cogs or dead weight in their economic and political aspirations.

"Our most important resource—that which each and every one of us depends upon every day of our lives—our clean WATER, is being polluted and stolen!"

A roar went up from the crowd at the mention of water.

"Yes, water. Clean water is so basic to us that we have taken it for granted. But now we see how dependent we are upon our water and the drastic changes that come about when our clean water is taken away.

"Water is the most important resource on our planet. Without water there would be no life. Our bodies are composed of more than 50% water. The same water has been circulating around the earth for billions of years. We cannot live without our water. Crimes against water are crimes against humanity. Our humanity is being stolen!"

Again, roars of approval arose from the crowd.

"Today I beseech you to rise up and join the fight. We must stop this madness NOW!" he roared.

He held a glass of water above his head for all to see.

"I hold this water to unite us. Water is forever. We are water. Water is sacred and must be protected! Those who deface and degrade our water are the worst kind of criminals. It is our place to unite and stand up to the usurpers … in the name of water we will act as one!

"Today we come together in purpose and need. Today we will go forth and reclaim our basic rights and necessities. Today let us rise up against these forces and return our purpose and dignity! Water is our right and heritage. It belongs to us all. Let us strike down any who would violate this basic human trust!"

❦   ❦   ❦

That day was the turning point. We were bonded together in quest. The enemy had been identified and our purpose and resolve made fast and strong.

The violence was spreading. There was still random fighting in the streets with the police and army. But now there was also war breaking out over water rights and water sources. The fighting spread from our region all the way to the capital. To build our strength we made alliances with political and religious groups. There was little central organization and small groups began to carry out independent actions. Though we had similar goals our tactics were quite different.

More and more innocent people were brought into the killing simply because they were in the wrong place at the wrong time. The continuing death and destruction was tearing me apart. It appeared as if there was no end in sight. No one was backing down and the stakes continued to rise.

Rageen and I began to argue about our activities. Rageen was convinced that we must sacrifice everything so that we might be free once again. But I was not so sure. It seemed to me that we were falling into a cycle of violence to which there was no end. Though our goals were pure, our actions and tactics were not. I felt like we were further losing touch with our old ways and lives, and that the bridges back in that direction were burning.

I decided to leave town and head back to our village. I was not sure exactly what I would do in the village but I really felt like I had to return home. Rageen and I fought bitterly over my decision. In the end, we both left ... I returned home while Rageen headed to the capital with a group of militants intent upon unseating the government. I never saw him again.

❧   ❧   ❧

You know much less
Than all of your vast schemes
Than all of your edifices
Than all of your hoops
That are forced on the lonely
The bitter
The cold
That are given to all with identity retold
Way too much knowledge for one head to hold
Way too much nothing to soothe a restless soul
I wander away and into the night
I take solace alone without force or might
I relieve this anxiously growing unknown
Within the dark walls of night that are sown.

I can't tell the future
But barren it seems
Is all that you'll know without life in your dreams
If the food is all canned
And the responses so old

What can you expect
Who can you respect
What will fill
The next moment of your life?

❦   ❦   ❦

When I got back to the village I found that most of the people had already left. Houses were abandoned and gardens in ruin. Almost all the young people were gone, but there were a number of village elders who had refused to leave the only home they had ever known.

I went to visit an old friend of my family, Mr. Haru. Mr. Haru had been an advisor to the village council and was esteemed for his wisdom and guidance. I walked to his house but it appeared to be abandoned. A wave of panic ran through me. I knocked on the door.

"Who is it?" called a frail voice from inside the darkened house.

"It is me, Cibi, Mr. Haru. May I come in?"

"Please enter," was the reply.

I opened the door and walked inside. Rugs were hanging on the walls in front of every window and it was very dark. In the back room I could see Mr. Haru sitting in a chair, wrapped in a blanket.

"Mr. Cibi! So good to see you. I am sorry for the mess, but no one has come around to help me with my chores. Most everyone is gone."

"I see that, Haru. The village is almost abandoned."

"So sad, Cibi. No one comes to help me with my food and water. I am alone. After countless generations our village is dying."

I told him of the events in town, of the arrests and shootings and bombings.

This seemed to disturb him even more and he became silent.

I looked around the house and found some tea and sugar, but the water crock was empty. I went outside and wandered around the village, looking for water. Eventually I found a pipe dripping water into a large tub. It was about half full and I scooped out a bucket and returned to Mr. Haru.

I made two cups of tea, gave one to Haru, and sat down on the floor next to him.

"And how have you been, Cibi?"

"Not too good, Haru. War is coming."

"I know, Cibi. We must be strong."

"I hear you, Haru, but I fled the violence and came here. I am feeling weak."

"You are strong, Cibi. Know that in yourself. You are stronger than you think."

"I feel like I can do nothing of my own accord and that every struggle I make to assert myself in direction or action is futile. It's like I'm on a ship being drawn along somewhere and I don't know the waters, the direction, where the controls are or even who is the pilot. I can't seem to accomplish anything or even focus my attention."

"I think you are frustrated because the situation is out of your control. Your powers are limited. But while you are here let's enjoy our tea."

"Yes, Haru. While we are here together."

"Yes, Cibi. It has been too long."

"You know when I left home I felt like I was abandoning my village; now, I feel like I am abandoning my people … like I am running away from my crew stacking sandbags before a big flood."

"You must question whether your efforts are effective. If the dam is bound to break and the sandbags will not hold back the water then why keep building the wall?"

"I don't know what to do, Haru. I feel like I am being bounced from situation to situation. I hear people saying that I should do one thing or another and in some ways they all make sense, and I am never certain how to act."

"Cibi, many people talk and say they will do one thing or another. But what matters is what they actually do. Words without actions are hollow. If a boy is drowning in the swift river and we sit on the bank and discuss how terrible the situation is and all the possible ways that we could save him, he will drown. In which case it matters not what we talked about."

"But if it is not important what we say, do you think it matters what our intentions are?" I asked.

"Well, maybe to you or me, but not really to the drowning boy. He would like to be pulled from the river so that he can breathe and walk again. He does not really care why you are pulling him from the water, only that you are saving his life. And if you sit and talk and watch him float by, he will not care why you are talking or what you are talking about, just that you are not doing anything to save him."

"But intentions surely do matter, don't they? Suppose when we saw him in the river we scrambled to find a rope to pull him out but couldn't get to him in time and he drowned. Don't you think his family would think quite differently of us than if we'd just done nothing?"

"Surely. And we would think quite differently of ourselves as well. But the actual effects of the action are unchanged, regardless of the intent. He still drowned and his family must be without him."

"Yes, the effect would be the same."

"Now intentions are very important to us personally. We are much more effective when our actions and our intentions work to support one another."

"Aaah … as opposed to being pulled from place to place or happenstance to happenstance by results from actions taken lightly or without thought?"

"Exactly. When you learn to understand your intentions, focus your effort to that effect, watch the results of your actions and use the feedback, you can be very effective."

"So what you are saying is that to the outside world our actions are of most importance, but to our own being-in-life our actions *and* intentions shape who we are."

"Yes. If you want to be purposeful and strong you need to recognize and prioritize your needs and desires, focus your intentions, and act accordingly."

"Or be forever pulled around from situation to situation, never quite knowing the why and wherefore … just reacting to each."

"Very good, Cibi. You are a fast learner. Our wandering philosophical discussions are great fodder for your mind and hopefully will inspire and guide you to the best decisions. But just talking and thinking that you know the right or best thing, and not following your words and thoughts with directed action, is meaningless. Actions are what make us what we are."

"That includes violence."

"Sadly so."

"That scares me … people all around becoming violent. It seems that we are changing as a result of these violent times."

"Yes. Violence begets violence, as they say."

"But what more can we do when our homes and lives are being attacked?"

"This is not new, Cibi. People have been living with this violence for as long as there have been people. We hold it deeply within us.

"Think about the world of nature. Every day, rabbits and deer are torn apart and eaten. Think of the wolves hunting your goats. Or a storm ripping apart a house. Life is violent, Cibi. Life consists of comings and goings and they are not necessarily peaceful transitions. People are no different than what you see around you each day."

"Yes, and those natural events are not charged with malice. But I see people obsessed and overwhelmed with malice toward other people."

"We are animals Cibi. We have grown through our past but the past is still with us. Inside our brains we still hold the seek-and-attack survival skills from our reptile past. On top of that, we have system controls and memory functions that enable us to be mammals. And above all our past we have developed a very active, concept-rich human brain.

"We use our brains in many different ways and since our behavior is influenced by many things our actions are directed by differing brain functions in varying degrees.

"Our history is riddled with wars and violence. This is part of our nature. Though some people are peaceful and do not provoke confrontation, others are angry and jealous, and seek control and power. Unfortunately, it takes only a few resorting to violence to cause many to pick up arms.

"And what is it that we always fight about, Cibi?"

"Many things, Haru. Many things."

"Yes, for many specific reasons but basically it is always the same, Cibi. We war for control ... control of territory, resources, bodies and minds. And we war in groups. Always one group against another. The stronger the association with a specific group, the stronger the inclination to go to war when that group's interests are at stake.

"Survival for humans has always consisted of group survival. Whether it was clans of hunter-gatherers, or tribes, or villages or countries, we have lived and died in groups. When one group's interests run contrary to another's and the stakes are raised, conflicts arise. We identify with our group and tend to be unsympathetic towards, dislike or even hate perceived adversaries. The stronger the lines are drawn between groups, the more tendency for violence.

"And the differences between the natural world violence of predator and prey and the malignant violence between people are in the group dynamics, Cibi. The wolf kills the goat with no malice intended toward *all* goats. In a way, the wolf loves goats (since she depends upon them for food) and would like to see them flourish. But in our group struggles, the entire other group becomes enemy and adversary. So we engage in wars filled with hate."

"It is a sad history that you paint, Haru. Groups have been our strength and apparently our weakness as well."

"We all love and identify with groups. We are at our best in groups and at our worst as well."

"And religion, Haru? Religion crosses all boundaries."

"Yes, Cibi. It crosses boundaries but it also draws them."

"Ahh … and leads to the most wars."

"Sadly so, Cibi. Some more than others."

"Some more than others?"

"Yes. Remember that it is perceived adversaries of our group with whom we contend. If your religious belief is in ONE and ONLY ONE GOD, then everything that follows and respects the ways of that God must be thought of as good."

"Sure."

"And all that goes against the ways of that God must then be thought of as bad."

"Yes."

"Now, if that God does not include *all* that there is … *all* that exists … then things exist in the world that will necessarily be other than good. Events, people, ideas, places may be thought of as bad simply by association with that which is not cognizant of nor compliant with the ways and principals of the perceived God."

"So when the One God arises so does the One Devil!" I exclaimed.

"Yes, Cibi! If your One God does not include all that exists, then enemies are born and groups conflict."

"But if your One God is inclusive, then …" I paused, not sure what to say.

Haru finished my thought. "Then events come and go and change occurs. Sometimes there is death and destruction, and other times flowering and growth. But there is no *other* group becoming the enemy."

"Perhaps religious groups bind us most strongly," I suggested.

"Yes, perhaps so, and when you combine strong groups like State and Religion, the allegiance can become fervent and the enemies a thousand times more vicious."

"You are making me feel helpless, Haru. If it is true that the roots of violence are within us, and that we naturally identify with groups, but aligning too closely with groups creates enemies and brings violence, what hope is there?"

"The situation is always changing, Cibi. The world is not fixed. Though the decisions may be difficult you have the ability to use your actions to make changes."

"I do believe that, Haru. But I am not sure what action to take. Everything seems so difficult and unreachable."

"You must face adversity, not shrink from it, Cibi. When circumstances and events work to slow or alter your current progress, rise up and demonstrate your strength and determination. Overcoming the adversity will bring you to your goals and help you effect change. And you will find and learn your limits ... which is crucial to avoid your demise."

"But I just want to return to my old life of shepherding goats in the mountains," I complained.

"I fear those days are gone, Cibi ... at least for the time being. The world has shifted and you must adapt. Living that life of ease and comfort is no longer possible. If you pursue this now you will become predictable and vulnerable."

"I am not afraid of adversity, Haru. I am not afraid of standing up to protect our interests. But I am never sure what I must do. Can you tell me that?"

"Unfortunately not, Cibi. This is the path that *you* must find. Good leaders are independent. They understand challenges and limits, and guide their people onward and outward. Good leaders arise during times of crises. They face the forces of adversity, pull people out of their malaise and motivate them to purposeful redemptive actions."

❦   ❦   ❦

I walked away from Haru feeling numb. I did not know what to do. It seemed so futile to get involved in the violence but somehow I felt compelled to fight for my people and my land.

Haru was right. I could not hide from the circumstances. I had to do *something*. It was impossible to shepherd. The conflict in town was tearing me apart and besides, I felt so helpless just roaming the streets. There was nothing for me in the village. *But I must do something.*

I looked up at the cloudless sky and over to the blue-green mountainside of pine trees and above again to the snowfields and the mountain summit. What was I to do? I looked back up to the summit. I turned to view the hills around me but again my eyes were drawn back to the little jagged peak of rock above the snow ... against that impeccable blue sky.

I ached to go there. I looked down the valley toward the smoking factories and the towns along the river. And back up at the summit. I shifted my weight from my left foot to my right. And back again. Over and over until I was shaking with indecision. I looked once more up at the summit and began running up the slope. Soon I was breathing hard and soaked in sweat but I kept my focus on the peak and kept moving my legs. As I ran I became immersed in the rhythm of my movement and lost all awareness of my effort.

I reached the tree line, stopped and looked up at the scree slopes and cliffs. I could still see the summit high in the distance. I rested for a moment but when I started to take another step my leg went limp and I collapsed on the ground. I lay there for a while, soaking up the sun and recovering my strength. The wind blowing over my back kept me thinking about the dry waterbeds, the parched fields and the scattering of my family and friends.

Yes, Haru was right again. Greed and the lust for power and dominance have dogged humans throughout history. In a way, we were repeating history in our fight for our lives against people seeking power and control over our economy, our land and resources, our bodies and our minds.

Somehow we need to bust out of our old ways and patterns, and transmogrify into another creature. Since our human futures are bound together we must all change before we exit this cycle of control and violence. As long as there are enough who will subject others to their dominations and tortures, we will relive our history.

I ached to look down upon and step out of this cycle, and that compelling desire was pushing me toward the summit. I surveyed the cliffs and ridgelines, found my route and began the climb into the sky. The air cooled and the wind blew fiercely as I struggled up the final pitch to the rocky peak.

I took my last step up and it seemed I was standing on the top of the world. Breathing hard, I held my arms out into the wind as if to fly away. Far below was the world of my friends and family and all the things that I valued and loved ... and all the fighting and killing. Though I struggled to feel the passion of those conflicts, everything seemed so small and insignificant from my aerie.

The wind howled and whipped, and I shivered and held tightly to the rock and sobbed. I loved that mountain and realized that I always had. This rock that I grasped was life ... bringer of rain, provider of air and water, supplier of wood, home to plants and animals, refuge for people. I poured out my love to the mountain and for a time forgot myself and the problems of the land.

That rock grounded me and I realized that was all I actually needed. I loved my people, and my bonds and obligations ran deep, but no matter in what way or how hard I struggled I would not be able to change the course of events. I could die trying but it was too big for me. I hugged the rock like my lover and let my mind wander above and away.

I watched the shadows grow in the valleys beneath me as the sun slowly sank below the horizon. Hilltops and meadows turned rose and crimson in the pink light of dusk. The last rays of sun splashed in my face as the land below disappeared into blackness. The wind blew even harder and the heavens began to sparkle with stars.

For the first time in as long as I could remember I felt unencumbered and free and joyful to be alive. In the immenseness of the universe I could find my way. Though insignificant in being and futile at building permanence, I was alive and awake at that moment in time. Everything passes but the moment can linger. Within that moment I felt whole. And that moment seemed so very important.

I do plan for the future but I live always in the moment. Life can come crashing down at any time and the moment will pass. So I yearn to find something beyond my moment and I wonder, *what do I do that will last?* Perhaps the things I build or the effects of my words and actions? But when I think big … when the heavens sparkle above me … I realize that it all will pass.

Yet I struggle to live. I love to live. I love to awaken in the morning and watch the sunrise and listen to the birds. Yes, when fear and pain do not overwhelm I could not ask for anything more. I treasure my breath and I even treasure my vulnerability. I do not place great value in the goods and circumstances of life, as they come and change and go. But I can feel good in any moment, place or time.

I will fly through the air. I will touch the clouds. I will ascend to the heavens. I will work my body hard and continuously to reach those heights. I will fly like the birds on the mountaintops. I can see forever. The world falls away beneath me. I have brought myself here. We only rise when we overcome the forces that hold us down. At least for a brief moment I conquered something. I stood on top of the world.

I knew then that I would leave my land and people. And I knew that it would be by my own free will, under my own power. I would bicycle across the planet to the highest mountains. I vowed to pedal and roll and roll and pedal … and look and wonder and wonder and look. Each day I will feel the earth moving beneath me … always changing … always new and different. And as I pass I will experience the fullness of life in every moment.

With that determination I let out a scream of joy and exhilaration. I felt as if a huge chasm had just been crossed and there was no going back. I thought over the happenings of the past months and could see clearly how event after event had led me to this summit. Now I will rise to the top of the world, and in my quest the purpose will be made known.

❧   ❧   ❧

Through the sun and the haze
The nights and the daze
Through all that I know

And what you do to
We still are amounting
To a small hill of beans
We still only glimpse the possibilities and means
We still only fall from our shortsightedness
We still only love and melt into bliss
We still only listen and know when to go
To them
To whom
Whenever it knells.

Just what is right and wrong with today
Just what do I need to do and to say
Just how do I live and control what is mine
Just how do I distinguish the cruel from the kind
Tell me once more what I should and should not
Realize that tomorrow is gone and forgot
Realize that all that I do is for real
That nothing undone can ever be felt
That all that I mourn and know will not last
That everything under the sun isn't true
That all that went on between me and you
Will never be forgotten nor lost in the past
Will always refresh and refurbish the guests
Will always relay
Will always refrain
Can never again
Be what it once was
It's gone now forever
To never appear
To be but a sigh
In the wind and the air
That under the boulders
Upon which we stand

Lives a land that never falters nor fades
That overtakes burdens and puts them to rest
I'll never stand there
This much I do know
I'll only glance sideways at it as I fall
And knowing that glance
Will tell all
Will tell all.

CHAPTER 8

One Love

Today we take back our future. Today we regain our past.

Times have changed and we have gotten stronger. Places that were far are no longer. Separations are now so clearly defined. Take a walk anywhere and you will find that on some days and in some ways, everywhere you go is in a daze. Each in their own, their own strange way, each has accomplished all that they may. Each with a foundation so rock and so true. Each one home to a fastidious mess. Each one cleaning what's not just theirs. Each one clinging to undying fears.

Something that you say never leaves me still. You talk from this passion, this deep well of will. Someday when you come we will meet face to face. I regard what you know as the worst of our race. You know what is mine and how it eats at you. You do not believe anything I do. When we touch each other, only then will we know how evil is formed in the spaces below.

I'm starting to fall
In spinning I'm free

I'm holding to nothing
I'm beginning to see
My vision is blurry
My thoughts escape me
Tonight I'll be dying
I'll be leaving you then
You can catch me tomorrow
In the swirl of the wind.

❧   ❧   ❧

And then it starts. No way to get out of this now. Looking for an escape, but nothing. Just line after line of humans being shuffled forward. Shuffle. Shuffle. As far as the eye can see. Humans shuffling into the darkness ahead. Into the future. No order. No struggle. Just the slow continual motion toward the unrecognizable and totally unknown.

Who or what is controlling this? Are we just the blind and ignorant who can never really know what is happening? And are we always in the dark? With no self control? And complete resignation? Is that all we are? Is that all we will ever be? No way to step aside? No way to be free? But free from what? Are we imprisoned? Imprisoned by what?

No way to know. Just resignation to the inevitable. Are we really so small that we cannot see beyond our desires and actions? What are our desires? And what are *our* actions? Just inching on and on.

It's all closing in on me now. Every action and every thought is being ushered into this walking trance. Is this the walk of the dead into the light of darkness? Move and shuffle. Move and shuffle. It's really not too bad if you don't think about it. You really can numb to the fact that you are going nowhere … at least, nowhere that you can know. Just into the darkness. Into the void.

❦   ❦   ❦

Now we must organize. We must weave our plans within the fabric that binds us. There will be no simple link. All paths lead to one another. Yet none is the single key. None is a highway. All wander. Though two paths touch or cross, neither will know where the other leads.

So it will be for us. We are the weavers. We must go and prepare the threads. We must weave our plans into the lives of others. We are the masters. We will bring the children home. Those around us do not always understand our means but they will surely know our ends. And that is a delight. We must weave our plans into their holy visions. Then we will be strong. Then we will be invincible. Then we will defeat the devil that is upon us.

So we are sworn by the power of God to purify the nation through burning fire. Fire that burns to the core. Fire that releases us from this domination and returns our future to us.

❦   ❦   ❦

What is the dividing line between crossing the edge and staying back? What makes a person give it up? What makes a person kill for an idea, a phrase, an emotion? Could it be money? Could it be insanity? Could it be survival? What makes a person step over the edge?

He says, "I want to die for my country. I want to die for my freedom. I want to die for my love. I want to die for my God."

Will he be looking back or looking forward? Or just looking away? Or even eye to eye?

Why does he walk to his death? Why does he hold such a course? Why does he not see the love and the force of living in a breathing world? What has gone cold? What has deceased to allow him to take such strong actions and face certain death?

I know nothing of this. I just see him walk slowly with death at his side. I see him look forward into nothing at all. I see him pray deeply and soothe his raw nerves. If what you were to do was the last act of your life, how would you spend it? Would you seek comfort or strife? Would you judge haltingly or fix on the hate that surrounds you every waking day? What would you do if you found yourself bound by culture and values that were trampled to the ground? Would you pick up arms? Would you fight your own way? Would you join the thousands who had their last say?

What would you do in the face of such hate? When all that you do is somehow repressed. All that you see is breathing distressed. Could you think of just basking in the sun on the beach? Or spend your last hours preparing to breach the boundaries of reason and pleasant abode?

❦   ❦   ❦

I don't know about you, but to me it is clear. I must prepare to fight the holy war. I must prepare to meet my own death. Bring honor to home and shame onto them. I stand tried and true and ready to die. Ready to spend my last hours preparing to scream right to heaven in glorious death. Ready to erase all the time in the world. In this way and this method I express all that is real in my mind and my life. I recognize good and evil and strife. It is not fair to see the wounds of my time, to stew in the violence and hate that abounds. I strike out with my might for all I believe. I take those with me who lie and deceive. I stretch all the bounds of mighty and might. I leave naught behind but the ebbing of life.

Do you want to stand in my shoes? Do you want to take on my burdens? Do you want to live on my streets?

Can you hold your head up high
Take a breath and breathe a great sigh
And tell me just plain as can be
That you've never gotten hold
Of something that's distanced and free
Something stolen from someone like me
Tell me please right true to my face
That you've never experienced disgrace
That you are holy and free

And have nothing over on me
Tell me once I want to hear
Just how you are so sincere
How you love all brotherly men
That we will live over again
Tell me how I must believe
That nothing you do or deceive
Can change the ways of men
And bring us to friendship again.

Today I want it to be known and be clear
I intend that all around will hear
This blast that I bring from the past
That ends all that is living today
Just amounts to what's said
Between the living and dead
There's nothing left to be free
Only me. Only me.
Can't you see? Only me.

CHAPTER 9

One Wheel

Ever wonder where you are
Why you picked this lonely star
Why you seem to run so free
But tied you are to your destiny
Of all the lonely stars out there
Why just this one does life bear?

If you think of random thoughts
Billions of stars in the Milky Way
Living and dying each and every day
Then imagine slipping out
To the billions of galaxies
Holding stars just like these
And think of the improbable fate
Of just one star holding stage
To life and growth and intelligence
And tell me just what's the chance
That life alone developed here
With billions upon billions of lonely spheres
All mixed up in the primordial soup
The laws of physics holding coup

And then please tell me with a straight face
That we're so special in our place
That among the stars strung out through space
We're the chosen
The only race.

❧   ❧   ❧

After Cibi finished speaking, he sighed heavily and the room grew silent. Light from the fire flickered on the darkened floor. The only sound that could be heard was the wind sliding around the building and rattling the windows.

Raz was lying down with his head on Lana's lap. He was breathing heavily and Lana was stroking his hair. In a soft voice she was murmuring a rhythm of soothing low-pitched sounds.

Karyn sat motionless, staring straight ahead, immersed in her own thoughts. Ray got up, walked slowly across the room and sat down next to her. He patted her knee and she turned and smiled at him.

Ellie crossed her legs and began frowning and shaking her head back and forth, as if in disagreement with something.

Lorraine held her head between her hands and sobbed quietly.

Cibi, who had been leaning on a post near the stove, sat down on the bench next to Lorraine. He slid over to her and put his arm around her shoulders. She sighed and snuggled into his touch. He kissed the top of her head and held her tightly.

Lobsang had been sitting quietly in the shadows, but now turned to Ngawang and whispered to her. She whispered back and nodded toward Cibi.

Ngawang cleared her throat and spoke softly. "No person is an island. Everything we do, every motion we make, every action we take, every event in which we participate affects and influences that which is around us ... and that which happens. We live in a vibrating web of existence."

She paused to make sure she had everyone's attention and then continued, "So it is futile to believe that you can do something isolated from all else that is occurring. We are all connected and these connections link us to all things … past, present and future."

There was a moment of silence and then Lobsang added, "We are born into the flux of existence. Time and events people, places and things are in continual change and rearrangement. There is nothing we can do to alter this fact."

"That I understand," replied Karyn in a low flat voice, "and try as we might, we are never able to completely explain why things occur or what influences bring an event into being."

Lorraine looked at Karyn and wiped her eyes. "We have such a strong desire to make order and sense out of our experiences and find reasons for what occurs. But we're often at a loss for words when we try to describe things that are far beyond our current notions."

Ngawang smiled. "And though we cannot make sense of or find order in these events, we can learn to deal with changes as they occur. We can learn to allow the natural dramas of our lives to unfold, yet not be knocked down by the waves of change."

"I feel like I was knocked down!" said Lorraine with indignation. "I was violently slammed. And I can't stop asking, *Why did this happen to me? I want to know why did that wave knock me-e-e down?*"

No one said a word for a long time, then Lobsang spoke slowly, "Because the wave was building and you were in its path. Because it had been building for a long time and it broke where you were. Do you need any other explanation?"

❀   ❀   ❀

When I give up all I hold
When I release this fractured soul
When I forget just who I am
Where I come from
And all my friends

When I immerse in the holy now
Only then does this sacred cow
Become just what it was meant to be
A shining pebble in a massive sea.

A pebble doomed to rock and roll
A pebble bound to the universal
A pebble once so bright and clear
A pebble dimmed by the human ear
A pebble released from this pervasive fear
A pebble rolling to a gentle stop
A pebble on this spinning top.

❧   ❧   ❧

Ray began in a shaky voice, "Yeah. Does *know* really have any meaning for us? What has happened is over and now we live with it. For us *to know* would be to have words that describe all the things that led to the cresting of the wave and all the things that were affected by that wave ..." he paused, looking puzzled, then continued, "and really, all waves, since they all are related." He looked over to Ngawang as if seeking approval, and asked, "Really, how could we ever know?"

"But Ray," laughed Ngawang, "only by being in the world can we understand it. In our being the answer resounds."

Ellie fidgeted. She started to stand up, then sat back down, looking like she wanted to say something. Finally she started mumbling. "We are here because we are here. We manifest that which is. It has been and we are now. We are what has been. It has been and we are now." She sighed and was quiet.

Ngawang tried to soothe her. "Yes, Ellie. The harder we try to understand the why of our existence the more the concepts and terms that we use slip away and lose meaning. But what remains within all descriptions is the flux ... the flux of existence."

Lobsang offered, "And the flux is like a wave … or better yet, *waves* of life's circumstances and experiences. The answers are within our immersion in the actions of our lives."

"I've got it! We surf the waves because we are here and the waves are here. Like if you were thrown into the ocean you'd either surf or you'd die. Take your pick," Ray cried excitedly.

Karyn eyed Ray with curiosity and smiled. "And some people are better at keeping their heads above water. Some struggle against the waves and others accept the flow."

"I like that," said Raz. "And we all sense the swirling currents differently … leaning this way and that in a dance through space and time. Naturally, sometimes we flow with the waves and other times we get thrashed," he concluded, with a smile to himself.

Lobsang laughed. "Very good, Raz. And in the flow and mix of the breaking waves are all the current players … along with all the past … and future," and he smiled from ear to ear.

❦   ❦   ❦

"What Lobsang is saying," began Ngawang, "is that everything we do, every motion, every action, every event of which we are part never dies. Our effects reach out from us and in that way we are all connected. The past flows into the present. And the present, our point of action, flows into the future."

"Yes," said Lobsang excitedly, "and the power of our lives is our ability to effect change in our present actions. In that way what we do lives forever."

Karyn nodded as if this confirmed something she had been thinking. "And of course, since we are made of stardust … all this," and she waved her arms in a broad gesture, "is connected. We are not separate from the stars. We *are* the stars. We are the universe coming to life!" She dropped her arms, twirled around and laughed.

Lana clapped her hands. "I like that, Karyn. We are the universe coming to be."

"Yes, Lana," said Raz patting her knee, "and since *coming to be* is becoming aware, we are the universe becoming aware."

"And creating itself by our actions … don't you think?" Lorraine added.

Ellie nodded. "Ahh … if the universe is being created, and since we are the creators, does that make us God?" and she laughed a bit nervously.

Cibi looked puzzled then smiled and said, "Well, many people think of God as an absolute creator and creation as a past event. But if the world is coming to be through our actions, then maybe that does make us God …"

His voice trailed off at the last few words. No one spoke and all that could be heard was loud breathing and the movement of nervous bodies.

After a few minutes Ngawang began slowly in a hushed voice, "For us, God is in the sunrise and the sunset, in the grass and the flowers, in everyone and everything. For us, God is the growing consciousness of life and existence … and each of us is a hope and a promise of awareness. We are the eyes of the world. We are the universal mind in (and of) the world in the act of expanding its consciousness."

She laughed and continued, "Such is the nature of belief in the infallible life. When the answers are buried in the questions and the questions are accepted as naturally as air or water, then what remains is to walk openly into the fabric of life without fear or hesitation, nor need to stop and ponder."

❧　　　❧　　　❧

Let life flow around you
How strange
How tragic
How wonderful
Every part
So necessary.

Smile at life
Be close and aware

Yet unattached and bemused
Love and suffer
Laugh and cry
As the dance unwinds
And takes you for a ride.

❧   ❧   ❧

Cibi leaned over and smiled at Lorraine. Then he looked toward the fire and spoke in a steady voice. "Our experiences are personal but our common human bonds run deep. Within each of us lies the entire history of humanity."

Ellie thought for a moment and then asked, "And in the same way don't you think we also have the entire history of Earth inside us … connecting us to all the plants and animals?"

"And similarly, the entire history of the universe," added Karyn.

"Yes! Yes!" Lana said excitedly. "We share the energy and dust of stars. The relationships that bind us are ancient and run deep. And when we recognize and honor that common nature we see beyond our personal viewpoints and ambitions."

"Like when we share music and art and dance and song, we feel the bonds between us," Lorraine said thoughtfully. She paused then added, "Or by sharing desire, emotion and place."

Lobsang clapped his hands in approval. "And the more universal our expression, the more common a chord we strike, the longer and deeper it will reverberate through other people, other things and through the waves of time."

❧   ❧   ❧

Lorraine shook her head. "What are we doing so wrong? If we have such potential and are connected so deeply, why are we so plagued by hate and violence?" No one answered.

She continued, "And do things really just result from the rising and falling of circumstances? It seems so hopeless to think that our limited awareness forever prevents us from understanding why things happen and why we are what we are."

"While we may not be able to know all the details, we should at least be able to learn about general relationships," offered Karyn.

"Since the changes of birth and death define our lives, maybe our tragedies and misfortunes naturally follow from our struggles with survival," suggested Ellie.

"There is much to be said for that," said Cibi sadly, "but unfortunately I think our problems run deeper than basic survival."

Ellie shook her head. "Maybe it is simply evil at work."

Lobsang rose up in his seat and in a demanding voice began, "Evil is a perception of the oppressed. When we come to view an entity or force as directed against our well-being we think of it as bad ... a natural instinct. If it gets stronger we think of it as oppressive. And if the entity or force becomes too strong or too prolific, identification with the perpetration of the oppressing force comes to be thought of as *evil*."

He paused for a moment, then continued. "But the entity or force is not evil. There is no struggle of absolutes. It is simply a matter of survival."

Ray protested, "But how about people who are determined to destroy us? Aren't they evil?"

"Surely they are enemies," answered Lobsang. "But that does not make them evil. They are disturbed. They are either disturbed because they don't have the awareness to differentiate would-be obstacles to their survival from friendliness, or they are disturbed at life in general, or they are disturbed because of actual obstacles to their survival.

"But where is the evil? These people or things may be impediments to *our* survival and we may not want or be able to live with them, but there is no demon force.

"The world expresses itself in many ways ... like birth and death, as you said Ellie, and also struggle and conflict and greed and covetousness and love and hate."

"Yes. Yes," said Cibi excitedly. "It is the story of people that when our familiarities and securities are threatened we draw together. And when we identify a common enemy we group together for strength and comfort, often in a fervor of emotion. The stronger the enemy, the stronger the emotion and the more group support."

"Sounds like survival," Ray said smugly.

"Yes. At its basic level," agreed Raz.

Cibi continued, "We spend our lives identifying with groups: social, cultural, political. We have developed a keen sense of how to deal with circumstances and resolve issues within our groups. Naturally, when we face problems, groups with differing viewpoints emerge. Struggles follow as groups try to maintain their particular positions and benefits. And ... when something threatens a collection of groups, smaller conflicts between groups can be put aside to face the larger, more immediate threat ... and new broader group alignments are made."

"But unfortunately many of us hold onto a sense of distrust, misunderstanding and fear of others, so we often fail when we try to moderate issues among and between groups," sighed Lorraine.

Karyn nodded her head in agreement and looked about absently, then in a whispering voice she said, "Group dynamics."

Lorraine looked at her quizzically. "What?"

"Group dynamics," she replied again. "What you are talking about are the relationships among groups and the relationships within groups that contribute to the formation and cohesion of the group. Groups want to survive, expand and increase their power. The principles of organization contributing to the social behavior of relationships among groups and group members are mathematics." She paused, thought for a moment and then broke into a wide grin.

❧   ❧   ❧

"So you are saying that a person so entrenched in the interests of their group will kill and destroy for the survival of the group, even to the point of inflicting pain and suffering on innocent people?" demanded Lorraine in exasperation.

Cibi looked at her with gentle eyes. "Most people defend themselves when attacked, though the more docile among us may lie down and accept his or her demise. But generally we do fight fiercely for our lives."

She nodded, "I understand that."

"Then it is a matter of circumstance. Take something of deep and special significance away from a group of people and they will hate you. Press them hard enough, give them a small and sorrowful future, and they will desire your destruction. They will fight as hard as they can for what they believe is theirs … and they might not think of people associating with and taking benefit from their perceived enemies as *innocent*." Cibi looked very sad as he said this.

❧   ❧   ❧

Lobsang offered, "It is our past together with our current actions that create the future into which we move."

"Hmm," muttered Ellie considering, "we come from the violent world of predator and prey, and more recently developed our thinking skills."

"Along with a propensity to group under protection and power," added Karyn.

"Creating the power-full versus the power-less," sighed Cibi.

"And," began Karyn, speaking slowly and groping for words, "our growing awareness, our deep-rooted primal instincts and fears, and the reign of the powerful allow us and cause us to create increasingly complex ways of dominating and destroying others … and ultimately ourselves."

Lorraine's face brightened. "And *we* can see what we are doing! Our being aware of those relationships in the world … *is* the universe becoming conscious."

"Yes, when we acknowledge our common heritage and purpose we are becoming aware. We are becoming conscious. We are the world seeing itself," Lana exclaimed triumphantly.

"We are the eyes of the world," repeated Ellie.

Hearing this, Ngawang laughed heartily. "As part of the consciousness of the world, we are the spark and possibility of new and better things. But being as One with our world ... when we identify part of creation as evil we are demonizing our own tail."

Lobsang laughed, "Very nice Ngawang ... like a dragon chasing its tail!" and he laughed even harder. "We must be very careful because when we define evil we are also defining God as that which is not evil. When we try to define something beyond the capabilities of our words ... when we try to separate that which exists in context from its context, we develop and support false images. And when we attempt to encapsulate the workings of an omniscient, omnipresent Creator/Creation/Being into our feeble word concepts, we create an *idol*."

Ngawang continued, "It is our natural tendency to form relations with things we understand. So rather than focus on that which the words attempt to describe, we come to worship false gods in the words themselves. And in this way we create devils."

❦   ❦   ❦

"It seems so bleak," moaned Ellie. "If our past is filled with violence between powerful groups, what hope can we have to ever change that?"

"Dear Ellie," began Cibi, "we cannot give up. We must dream to what we aspire and pull ourselves toward those dreams."

Ellie scrunched her eyes and shook her head. "But our animal nature is so strong!"

Raz lifted his head from Lana's lap. "I know it's difficult, but the future is open for us. We have the power to make our future but we *must* understand our past to bring about change."

Lana gently placed her arm around Raz. "So true. We cannot escape our past. The past exists for us in everything that we have in the present. All that happened in the past is with us today."

"So with such a history what can we-e-e do?" whined Ray.

Lobsang spoke up from the darkened corner. "To change the future we must know and recognize history and understand how history affects the present."

Karyn, who had been quietly slouching on her bench, suddenly sat up and with a gleam in her eye pronounced, "Then to change the future we must change history!"

"What?" asked several people simultaneously.

"That's absurd. How can we change history?" demanded Ray.

"I know it sounds pretty strange, but I think that maybe that is our purpose," she said in a thoughtful and distant voice. She paused motionless, staring blankly, then turning her attention back to the room, she began, "OK, so how do we define *history*?"

Ray was quick to answer. "History is what occurred in the past ... which we learn about from some kind of evidence; like stories, books, pictures, audio, or video."

"Fair enough," replied Karyn. "Now we can only understand a thing in relation to what we already know ... otherwise we have no context, no handle or comparison point. So since we have individual experiences and ideas we understand accounts of events in relation to what we are and already know."

Ray nodded. "Sure."

Karyn continued, "Now suppose your ideas and experiences change so that when you view the details of an historical event your understanding of it is different."

Lorraine looked annoyed and snapped, "But that doesn't change history! It's only me, or the world around me, that has changed. The facts are still the same."

"Yes, the facts are still the same," replied Karyn, "however, history is an understanding of how those facts affected that which succeeded them and how those facts affect us today. If we see and experience the effects from those facts differently, then for us history has changed."

"What? What happened, happened. You can never change that," Ray asserted adamantly.

Karyn remained composed. "But you just said that history is our *understanding* of what happened and since our *understanding* changed, then history must have changed for us."

"No, no," repeated Ray. "You can't change the facts. So, obviously you can't change history."

"OK Ray, perhaps an example will help," suggested Karyn. "Columbus sailed to America in 1492. No one will dispute that."

"No, probably not."

"But is the fact that he went to America the crucial thing or are the changes in the world brought about by the journey more important?"

"I see what you mean," answered Raz. "Columbus's journey began the colonization of America, with all the associated changes to the native people and world events. If these changes had not followed then Columbus's journey would have been rather insignificant."

"Yes," agreed Karyn, "and I maintain that it is how things are affected by the event that defines the event. The event taken by itself means little."

She paused then continued, "So Ray, do you really believe that history is merely a study of facts? Or is history perhaps an understanding of those facts?"

"Well, I sort of follow you," answered Ray reluctantly. "History studies how the facts affected that which succeeded them and how they affect us today."

"Ahh," Lorraine nodded, "it's all about context. The facts remain but their meaning changes."

"Precisely," said Karyn. "You cannot change the facts of the past but you *can* change how those facts affect that which is and will be. And facts only exist within the realm of their effects. Just as in physics you cannot simultaneously know where the electron is located and where it is traveling because the act of viewing the electron changes it, so with facts. As you view the facts the direction and velocity (their impacts) change depending upon your point of view."

"I think I understand where you are going," said Lana. "We see facts through the impacts they have had on what we know. We can look at them in no other way. We are bound by our own point of view. So they only exist within our interpretations."

"So looking at our history, we can't change the fact that people were tortured and killed … but we can act in the present to make these facts reflect a great change for humans. Though those people are gone, their lives and energies live on through the changes that were brought about by their lives and deaths," concluded Raz.

"And for me," said Lorraine, "I can't change the fact that my Frank was killed. I can dwell on that fact and become resigned to a quiet and miserable life. Or I can use that event to strengthen myself and help others with their hopelessness and pain. So, is the history that Frank was killed a tragic event that spread despair, or was it an inspiring event that helped bring about hope for change?"

She answered herself. "It is within my power to answer that question. That is how I can use the present to change the tragic nature of the past, to bring about good things for me and other people."

Cibi jumped to his feet. "I understand what you are saying! If this is true then all is possible and there is hope for us … because if we can change our history then we can change our destiny!"

"Yes, yes!" added Lorraine in excitement. "We are not just puppets on the hands of Fate. We have the power to make our future." She smiled, reached over and held Cibi's hand.

"The present is the fulcrum of our experience. All our power is realized though our current awareness and actions," Ngawang said with a smile.

Lorraine thought for a moment and brightened. "And we will always have trouble and strife until we accept responsibility for the things that have occurred from which we take comfort and succor," she said slowly.

"Yes, Lorraine," answered Ngawang, "all humans share human experience. We cannot be separated. That must be your point of action."

"Exceptional!" exclaimed Lana. "And maybe if we consider ourselves as part of all living things we can resolve our strife and struggling with the world around us."

❦   ❦   ❦

In the darkness of desperation
In the cloud of despair
I climb through the arbor
I jump through the air
At every turn I see freedom
In every moment I feel life
I am flying through days
Each one rounded and new
Though they pull on my past
And cling to those moments
When I drag and swirl through the times
I still see some future
Something new and unrealized.

❦   ❦   ❦

"I guess fundamentally we are world citizens," began Cibi. "Our actions influence other actions and we connect to all people and events through time by our common history."

"And that history shows us that we propagate hate and war when we forget our commonality, and support exclusive group interests and their accumulated power," sighed Lorraine.

"So how can we possibly get beyond this warring and change that history?" asked Ray.

"Groups can unite and change affiliations when they adopt a common purpose or goal," offered Karyn.

Ray thought for a moment. "Like if an even bigger enemy comes around?"

Karyn nodded. "Exactly. When neighboring groups are threatened by something imminently large, then smaller conflicts are put aside to face the larger more immediate threat, and new, broader group alignments arise."

Lorraine began, "Perhaps if we come to view ourselves as world citizens," and she opened and spread her arms to include everyone in the room, "the cycles of hate and violence might end. Maybe by developing a more global perspective outside the bounds of national borders we can come to think of ourselves as a global race."

"I agree," said Cibi. "National borders no longer isolate people from the effects of world events. Our problems and their solutions are global. Our needs and wants extend beyond political and regional boundaries, linking us tightly to people and events all over the globe."

"Problems like maintaining clean water and air or protecting our global climate," offered Lana.

"Or disease ... or over-population," suggested Ellie.

Lorraine nodded in agreement. "Yes, population growth definitely requires a global solution. Without controls we could overrun our resources and without globally coordinated efforts we could destroy our genetic diversity."

"We are intimately connected to all people and all life on Earth by our shared water and atmosphere," said Raz. "We literally exchange molecules between our bodies with all past and present." He thought for a moment then added, "and future."

Cibi bristled and shook his head back and forth. "Yes, when the water which has existed clean and pure for billions of years is degraded the entire planet is affected."

"We are water and we are united by water," Raz pronounced.

"If we humans were to recognize that intimate bond, perhaps we could start to address our global problems from a common perspective ... and these false boundaries that appear to separate us would dissolve," Lana said wistfully.

"Wouldn't that be nice," sighed Karyn, "but the world functions primarily by economics. And the economic marketplace rewards those sellers first to market with the cheapest goods. Unfortunately, not a system conducive for planning and implementing world-based decisions."

Raz nodded. "No, absolutely not. The economic system largely ignores activities that are associated with getting products to market ... like working conditions and worker compensation, and environmental impacts from procuring materials, manufacturing and transportation."

Lorraine was confused. "I thought that free enterprise could bring us together ... you know, people selling and marketing goods or services as they desire."

"Basic commerce is a great way of unifying people. But our world is run by mega-capitalism where huge conglomerations choke out free enterprise. For many people it's simply too difficult and costly to be competitive in this market," lamented Karyn.

"It really is sad," said Ellie. "You would think that we were smart enough to protect our race and fulfill everyone's basic needs for clean food, air and water."

"Maybe by opening up world communication to *all* people we can come together as a human race. Maybe if we are able to freely communicate, discuss issues and plan and implement activities for our mutual benefit with anyone and everyone in the world, we can all live well and be active world citizens," Cibi said thoughtfully.

❀   ❀   ❀

There was a long silence. It was quite dark in the room. Deep breathing could be heard from the benches along the walls.

Lobsang began in a low voice. "Tibet is the highest country in the world. We have pondered life from this vantage point through our long history. Seeking to understand our consciousness, we evolved an art of life and a science of mind that has never been replicated on the planet. Our knowledge was passed on in an unbroken chain from teacher to disciple … until the Chinese army invaded in 1950.

"Our monasteries, being centers of organization and cultural learning, were targets of the invasion. Unfortunately, the Chinese Maoist ideologues regarded our technologically isolated, religion-based culture as the epitome of all that was wrong with human society. They came to steal our minds and bodies, our water and our minerals.

"They viewed Communism as an evolutionary-revolutionary step in the advancement of humankind and saw their actions as manifest destiny. They sought to materialize their ideas and assume more power by overtaking our society.

"Though we fought fiercely, our unsophisticated mountain people were no match for the highly equipped, skilled and trained Chinese army. In the battles and ensuing occupation millions of Tibetans have been killed and hundreds of thousands imprisoned or exiled. Our leaders have either fled the country, been executed or are under restraint. Even today it is illegal to follow our traditional lives and religious practices, under threat of death."

Ngawang continued. "Our ancient libraries and living shrines were smashed and burned. Nearly two thousand years of unbroken history were scattered to the wind. The occupiers were so trapped in their own ideology and dogma that they could not recognize our culture and resources, and had no idea what they were destroying. They did not realize the depth or power of the knowledge that we Tibetans had accumulated.

"The Chinese attempted to *re-educate* us to believe that our government and religious organizations—including nuns and monks—were stealing our wealth and enslaving us. The Chinese insisted that the path to the future was to abandon our culture and history, and support the universal cause of the common worker.

"Our teachings and customs began to disappear from many people's daily lives. Now our scholars can only continue to follow our traditions, and build and maintain our knowledge, in secret and in exile." She sighed deeply and was quiet.

There was a pause before Lobsang began again, "Our will and spirit are strong. We have persevered for nearly sixty years under occupation. Our determination has surprised even the Chinese. But they are firmly entrenched in our country and any effort to take back our freedom and rebuild our organizations is met with crushing force.

"Though we still have some working monasteries, we remain very poor. Through the ages our government supported our studies but now the Chinese authorities persecute us. If we speak out or disregard their rules we are quickly arrested, jailed and often tortured. If we attempt to leave the country and join our exiled community we are imprisoned or killed." He turned toward Lana and Raz and nodded his head as if to confirm his sad plight.

For a very long time no one said a word. Finally, Cibi spoke slowly. "I have fought many hard battles for *my* homeland and am weary of battle. Yet somehow I feel propelled into the events of your land and compelled to action. I have journeyed around the world, seeking the sources of clean water. That has been my guiding inspiration." He paused, closed his eyes, breathed deeply and nodded his head.

"Now I know I have found home. Your life and land, knowledge and meditations are a light in our world. I love life. I love you …" and he turned to smile at every person, "and I love water. We stand at the headwaters of more flowing fresh water than anywhere on the planet. Nearly half the people of Asia get their water from Tibet's rivers.

"Truly, this water is a gift." He paused and a stern look came over his face. He raised his voice a little. "I now vow to dedicate my life to protecting the waters of your land and the life systems that sustain and depend upon those waters … for the planet," he paused and then raised his fist into the air and shouted, "ONE EARTH!"

"And I will join you, Cibi," Lorraine exclaimed breathlessly. "I will take the tragic events of my past and use them to create awareness and change. Though the sadness remains, I'm hopeful again."

"Yes! Yes Lorraine!" cried Cibi. "We will share water like Yin and Yang! We will create a world sanctuary for fresh water!" He hugged Lorraine and she kissed him gently on the lips.

Lana meanwhile kept fidgeting on her bench and looking around the room. She straightened up, looked directly at Ngawang and began, "You Tibetans have much to teach us. We are confused. Being here, I have been inspired, hearing about your studies in thinking, acting and living.

"I believe the history of the destruction of your country and the decline of your culture can be changed. China has that power. China can change this history of devastation—acknowledge its mistakes and acknowledge its ignorance and crushing policies. China can welcome home all Tibetans, support the building of a new Tibetan society by and for Tibetans, and return to the people a stronger country."

"That is beautiful Lana," gushed Raz. "And the countries of the world have the power," and he paused for a moment and then concluded, "and the *obligation* to persuade, and to help China make those changes."

"Yes," said Lana and smiled at Raz. "And in return the Tibetans can vow to protect the land and resources for the benefit of all humans."

"And," said Raz excitedly, "Tibet can restore the ancient centers of knowledge and learning, and provide the world instruction and training in thinking, acting and living."

"And inspiration!" added Lorraine. "And perhaps the resolution of this global crisis by Tibet and China can provide the pattern and hope to help ease our global cycles of violence."

Lobsang frowned then began slowly. "Perhaps we can come to love the Chinese and see them as helping bring us out of a past disconnected from the modern age. Though the clash of civilizations was debilitating we must move forward and not be bound by the past. Perhaps somehow we can rejuvenate and rebuild the Tibetan mind of old."

❧   ❧   ❧

They sat in silence for a very long time. The fire was reduced to a few embers, the candles dimmed and no one said a word or moved about. Their minds were racing with thoughts and ideas, some singular and others shared. In the darkness all that could be heard was the breathing of nine souls, the occasional rustle of someone changing positions and the continual wind blowing down the mountainside.

Their eyes were closed. Gradually the travelers began to realize that Lobsang and Ngawang were slowly chanting. No one seemed to hear them begin but somehow they were repeating the six-syllable mantra ...

Om Mani Padme Hum.
Om Mani Padme Hum.
Om Mani Padme Hum.
Om Mani Padme Hum.
Om Mani Padme Hum.
Om Mani Padme Hum.
Om Mani Padme Hum.

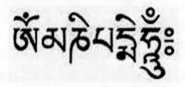

The sound seemed to grow louder and louder, and the source seemed to circle the room over and over, moving around each person from right to left.

Thoughts dissolved and breathing synchronized. The travelers could feel the chanting within their bodies and began to sway with the circling of the chant around the room. Nothing existed in the world for them but the rhythm of that chant. A surge of energy seemed to flow around the circle, passing through each person, causing them to rise a little with the passing mantra. Differences dissolved. There was only the chant.

At some point the chanting began to diminish in volume. The circling energy remained and the travelers continued to rock and sway, as the syllables became less audible and finally ceased. For a long time they sat in silence with their eyes closed, still moving … now to a synchronized inner beat. In the quiet darkness each of them settled into a deep trance-like sleep.

After many hours their sleep was interrupted by a noise similar to the clucking of birds. Almost simultaneously, everyone opened his or her eyes. Immediately they noticed that Lobsang and Ngawang were no longer in the room. Instead, a young girl was standing in the middle of the circle in a solitary beam of light, with a laughing, devilish look in her wild eyes and a broad toothy smile.

She wore a red scarf around her head and from under it her wild black hair was sticking out in all directions. Her turquoise and red coral earrings matched her necklace, her tattered coat and her pointed boots.

The light was bright on her and for a moment they wondered where the source of the illumination was. At first it appeared as if *she* was producing the light. But then they noticed a ray of light streaming in from the east window and realized that the Sun had risen. Still, she seemed brighter than the Sun's radiance.

She glowed and smiled, her wild eyes laughing with pleasure. For some time she stood in the middle of the room with her arms and hands open, facing the travelers and smiling.

Her presence was an invitation. She seemed to provide answers to unknown questions simply with her dancing eyes and beguiling smile. She looked as wild as the mountain goats and as deep as all the ages.

She slowly began to back up … one step at a time. Leading backward with her right leg, she bowed slightly forward, crossing her arms at the wrists in front of her waist and leaving her palms open … always facing the travelers. Then in a fluid and graceful motion she slid her left leg backward and spread her arms out to her sides with her open hands facing forward. Pausing briefly she smiled broadly. In three or four steps she was at the door. She backed up to the door and it opened; immediately, bright light flooded the dim room. She continued backing up, stepping outside; with one last bow and smile she stepped back and the door slowly closed in front of her.

The travelers sat motionless in silence for a long time. They had a feeling that something extraordinary had occurred but felt confused and could not focus their thoughts. Nearly simultaneously, everyone got up and ran to the door. Outside the sun was shining brightly and the snow reflected the light even more, causing their eyes to close and squint.

The sky was a clear dreamy blue with not a single cloud. The courtyard was empty. There were no dogs and no people. There were no footprints leading to or from the gate and none in the courtyard. But the entire roof and walls of the compound were covered with birds.

"There's nothing but a flock of birds!" exclaimed Ellie.

The birds began to rise up in a churning motion. As the travelers watched they climbed into the sky, sweeping in clockwise circular arcs and then descending again toward the ground. Over and over. And with each circling more birds rose up and joined the flock. When they were all aloft the birds began to circle higher and higher, then finally turned to the west and disappeared over the horizon.

As their shapes drifted out of sight, the travelers walked back into the empty teahouse and without a word slowly began to pack their bags.

When they returned outdoors, the air had warmed and the snow was melting. Outside the gate of the courtyard they could see two intersecting trails.

Cibi walked holding Lorraine's hand and pushing his bicycle to the north fork. "We leave to seek the common bond of water."

Lorraine quickly added, "And like the water we will return. I love you all."

Karyn leaned on her pack. Ray stood by her side. "I am traveling south. I need time to work on some mathematics. But soon I will return to this land and these people. I love you all."

"Karyn, may I go with you?" pleaded Ray.

"What?"

"You are so beautiful and strong and smart. I will support everything you do. I will kiss the ground before your feet. Please take me with you!"

"Oh Ray. Of course you can travel with me. But keep your head up," she laughed.

The stress on Ray's face disappeared and for the first time he looked content.

Ellie walked toward the west fork. "I found a little underground meditation chamber in the mountains about a two-day hike west of here. I think I will bring some food and fire material and explore the universe from within my mind with no distractions ... as the wind blows and the snow mounts above me."

"You're a brave girl, Ellie," said Lana. "Raz and I are traveling east but hopefully we will meet again someday. I love you all."

"East?" asked Cibi.

"Yes," answered Raz. "To Beijing ... to change history."

978-0-595-46444-9
0-595-46444-0

Printed in the United States
108344LV00005B/112-141/A